The Snatching of Susan Bauford

Also By A.J. Kepitis-Andrews

Mostly Behind The "8" Ball (2014)
Take It Easy (2015)
Dollars From Heaven (2015)
Easy Does It (2015)
The Seeing Eye Crocodile (2016)
Jeb's Legacy (2017)
77 And Still Behind The 8-Ball (2018)

The Snatching of Susan Bauford

A soda thriller with a whisky punch

A.J. Kepitis-Andrews

Kepitis-Andrews, A.J. 1940 –

Fiction

ISBN: 978-0-6452389-0-7

Dedicated to Eva.
My thanks for her help and devotion with completing this book.

Contents

CH 1. THE WEDDING WITHOUT A BRIDE

Through the thin veil of her wedding ensemble, Susan Bauford looked at herself in the mirror. She was quite pleased with what she saw, a twenty-four-year-old bride about to become Mrs Ashley Barton. She never thought of herself as particularly beautiful, but other people kept insisting she was, and she never argued the point. She was happy to be a natural blonde with a good figure but now, through the veil, she conceded that perhaps the others were right, she was beautiful but then, through a veil, who isn't? The important thing was that she was happy.

A few months ago, she graduated from law school, and after the honeymoon she was to take up a post with Huntingdale & Partners. While still studying, she indulged in only one pastime, hang gliding, introduced to the sport in a roundabout way.

A fellow foreign student, Akim, reportedly the son of an Arabian Sultan, became quite smitten with her forever seeking her graces, he was becoming a pest. The more Susan rejected his advances, the more passionate he became. He could not fathom how a common Australian girl could reject the advances of an Arabian prince. Susan was quite friendly towards Akim but drew a line at the thought of going out with him.

"Is it because I'm an Arab?" he once asked her angrily.

"That's got nothing to do with it, Akim. I don't care if you're Arab or Chinese or even Irish for that matter. I'm here to finish my law degree before I start any serious socialising."

"Does this mean you are rejecting me as a friend?"

"Of course not, we can be friends, we are friends, so why not leave it at that?"

Susan did, but not so Akim. He kept on looking for outlets which could attract Susan's attention. Not long after, he spotted Susan sitting on a bench in the university quadrangle eating a sandwich.

"Susan," he addressed her, sitting down beside her, "have you ever had the feeling or wished to be free?"

"What? No. I am free, what do you mean?"

"I mean to be really free, physically free. To be able to rise above the sea, the trees and mountain tops, to be free above this planet."

"I don't know what you are talking about!"

"I am talking about gliding through the air over mountain top to mountain top."

"I still don't know what you mean?"

"I mean like flying and you in control of that flight."

"You mean just like a bird. Sure, who hasn't, but what's that got to do with anything?"

"I could teach you that."

"What! Teach me to fly, like a bird? With wings?"

"Yes, exactly that! With wings, your own wings."

"You're joking, aren't you? Flying with wings?"

"Yes, it's called hang gliding. I do it almost every weekend and I find it exhilarating. I could teach you very quickly."

"Now that you mention it, I have heard something about it, but isn't it very dangerous?"

"Only if you let go of your wings or you get hit by an aeroplane, but there's more chance of a bus hitting you on your way home."

"That sounds really interesting. Is it expensive?"

"No, I have many wings at home, my father sent me the best money can buy. What colour do you like, red, yellow, white but not blue.

***

Susan found hang gliding frightening at first, but after her first leap from a cliff face, she found it exciting and spent most of her Saturday afternoons south of Stanwell Park with a group of other enthusiasts, soaring, diving and rising with the thermals. Akim was amongst the enthusiasts, but other than a friendly word he got no further in the quest for Susan's affections. This left him smouldering and looking for other opportunities.

It was during one such sporting afternoon when she literally bumped into Ashley. Floating in the sky, both of them took the advantage of an up-draft. Ashley rose from below her and bumped Susan's glider wing. Fortunately, it was just a token bump which had no serious consequences, but then again it did. She got to talk with Ashley once on the ground, more like apologising with each of them taking the blame.

Since that slight sky malfunction, they became virtually inseparable, culminating in this, their wedding day. Susan lifted, then dropped the veil several times, each time studying the reflection.

"If Ashley says I look better with the veil down, I'll kill him," Susan mused in good natured humour.

"No, you won't," Anne, one of the two bridesmaids in the room with her, corrected Susan, "if he says that I'll kill him first."

"You're both being silly," Lucy, the other bridesmaid interjected, "Ashley will say no such thing. With or without the veil, you look beautiful Susie, and Ashley of all people knows this."

"Come on ladies," Susan's father's voice could be heard through the door, "the cars are here. It's time to get this show on the road."

***

Jim Bauford parted the curtains in his living room just enough to better observe the two white Rolls-Royce with white ribbons streaming from the cars' radiators to their windshields, letting one and all know that they were in the wedding business. This was a proud and yet sad day for him. His only child was about to leave the family home forever, but then there would be grandchildren, and she wasn't leaving the country, just moving to Sydney's Newport, not all that far away.

It seemed almost like yesterday, when he announced to his pregnant wife Norma that he was no longer a bookmaker's clerk but now a fully accredited bookmaker with his own stand at Randwick Racecourse and good prospects to have a stand at other Sydney venues. From that day on he had never looked back. Shortly after Susan was born, he had purchased the substantial residence at Putney, the only home Susan had ever had. And now she was leaving. Jim was determined to give her the best send-off money could buy. Then a thought went through his mind. This was probably the first Saturday in over twenty years when he was not at the racecourse exchanging money and banter with the punters.

"Come on, ladies," Jim urged, "let's get a move on and not keep the groom waiting at the altar."

A rustle of wedding skirts was all that was heard as the bridal party walked down the drive and entered the wedding cars.

Jim and Susan made their way into the lead car with the chauffeur fussing about the car door, making sure no part of the wedding gown was caught in the door and obvious to observing passers-by. Norma, the two bridesmaids and the Matron of Honour entered the second car and at the sound of a horn blip from the lead car. Both vehicles eased down Waterview Street heading east towards Gladesville and the church on Victoria Road.

"I've never been in a Rolls-Royce before, Dad," Susan uttered excitedly, "it really is quite something, isn't it?"

"You bet, darling. Maybe your husband, shortly to be, will buy one for you if you play your cards right."

"Oh, come on, Dad, Ashley's far too practical for something like that."

"That may be so, but I'll tell you what, if you present me with a grandson, I'll buy you one."

"What! You're kidding right?"

"No Susie, it's a promise. You give me a grandson and I will give you a Rolls-Royce."

"You're really serious?"

"I promised and I am serious."

"Dad, these things cost a small fortune!"

"Of course, they do, but they're cheap when compared to a grandson."

"How do you work that out?"

"Susie, cars are just cars. Eventually they all wear out, but for me a grandson will never wear out, well, not during my lifetime anyway."

"In that case, shouldn't you give your grandson a Rolls-Royce?"

"What's the point? He can't drive it for at least sixteen years."

"Maybe then you should throw in a chauffeur!"

"I am."

"You're kidding, really?"

"No, I'm serious. The chauffeur is you."

"Stop it Dad, let's talk about something a little more serious. Why don't you buy one for yourself?"

"No way, Susie. Imagine what the punters would say if I arrived at the racetrack in a Roller?"

***

The wedding cars moved at a ceremonious pace down Waterview Street and the lead car containing father and bride made a left hand turn into Charles St. It had just made the turn when a utility vehicle, parked on the opposite side of the road, sprang to life and crossed the road right in the path of the lead Rolls-Royce. The driver of the wedding car applied his brakes urgently and was able to stop without colliding with the utility. The second wedding car also had to take evasive action and with brakes screaming, came to a halt only centimetres from the rear of the lead car.

The moment the utility traversed Charles Street a large blue van, which had been parked near the junction of Waterview and Charles Streets, accelerated from its spot, and turned into Charles Street, stopping next to the wedding cars.

Two men wearing white surgical face masks jumped out of the utility and approached the lead car. One of them, forcibly opening the driver's door, placed a cloth over the surprised driver's face. The other man opened the left rear passenger door, and grabbing Jim in a headlock, placed a cloth over his mouth and nose. The unexpected lightning speed of the assault so totally surprised Susan that all she could do for the moment was scream but not for long. The man, having anesthetised the driver, now overpowered her, and she too was quickly dispatched.

Simultaneous as this was happening, two men leapt out of the blue van. One of them overpowered the driver while the other one threw a small package in the rear of the car which burst into an ether smelling white cloud.

The blue van then moved parallel to the lead car, and Susan was pulled through the open side door and bundled into the van. All of the assault team then crammed into the van as it took off in a hurry, leaving the utility remaining where it was.

This abduction was handled with such precision that the two witnesses who were nearby had no idea what was happening until they approached the wedding cars, and even then, they weren't exactly sure what had occurred. However, they were astute enough to call the police.

***

The Church of Christ on Victoria Road Gladesville was fully stocked with well-dressed people chosen to honour two families at the nuptials of their offspring. Some were already inside seated while others lingered outside waiting to greet the wedding party as they arrived. At first their conversations were brisk but sedate, and then one or two started to look at their wrist watches, soon to be joined by others following the same activity.

A church usher also consulted his watch and then addressed the outside guests.

"Would you all like to move inside, ladies and gentlemen. The bride should be here any minute now and you can watch her walk down the aisle. Would you please!"

Most of the guests took little or no notice except for the very few who obeyed the directive.

"She's already fifteen minutes late," someone called out.

"She's probably caught up in traffic," the usher volunteered.

"That's bullshit," the same voice replied, "she's coming from Putney and it doesn't take fifteen minutes to get here. Besides it's Saturday afternoon so there's not much traffic."

"I'm sure she'll be here any minute now," the usher replied.

***

Inside the church Ashley and his best man Hugh sat on a pew nearest the altar. Both of them were attired in black dinner jackets with a flower spray in the lapel. Ashley had been adamant at only having a best man and no other male attendants. The only reason he gave when challenged was that it was his wish. Hugh had been his best friend since childhood, and while he had many other friends, he did not want to create a bad feeling amongst them.

"She's already twenty minutes late," Hugh looked at his watch and stood up, "what the hell can be holding her up?"

"I don't know, maybe there's been an accident or something."

"Sure, but you'd think, seeing it's a wedding, someone would have contacted the church. If it involved the coppers, surely they would have sent a car or something?"

"Hugh, I don't know and neither do you so why don't you just shut up and wait. We'll all find out sooner or later," Ashley snapped back.

"All right but it's your funera … your wedding. I'm surprised you're not pacing up and down, tearing your hair out. I would be."

"Then why don't you do that for me? Isn't that what being the best man's all about?"

"OK, I'm happy to do a bit of pacing for you, but the hair thing, is almost history so I'll do the up and down pacing and you do the hair thing."

"Just shut up and sit down."

"For Christ's sake, Ashley, aren't you just a bit nervous?"

"What's there to be nervous about? We'll all find out soon enough."

***

Instead of moving into the church, a number of people already inside had come out, all of them gazing at their watches from time to time.

The parking spots for the wedding cars outside the church had been reserved, but by now they became conspicuous by their vacancy. A few people ventured out on them, craning their necks in the direction from which the cars should be approaching, but apart from general traffic, no wedding cars.

Then someone shouted, "Look, here they are!"

Sure enough, in the distance one could see two cars amongst the other traffic bearing the unmistakable wedding ribbons. A sigh of relief could be sensed amongst the waiting guests but instead of pulling in at their reserved parking places, the two cars drove on.

"The stupid bastards," a man yelled out, "they've missed the church, they're off to some other church."

"No, they're not," another man put in, "Jim told me he hired white Rolls-Royces, and those were grey Jaguars. It must be another wedding."

The watchers resumed their former 'edge of the seat' vigilant stance.

More than forty-five minutes had passed and still no sign of the bridal party. Many of the guests were now of the opinion that something quite serious had occurred, but what? Even the minister was becoming concerned. Especially when no telephone call had been received as was usual if some unexpected delay had taken place.

Then after nearly an hour of worry, a car pulled into the wedding car spot. It was a marked police car. Two uniformed policemen got out of the car and entered the church grounds amongst outbursts of 'what's happened?'

"We'd like to see the minister please," one of the policemen asked a bystander, "and we believe the groom's parents are here?"

"The minister is inside the church and he's with the groom and his parents," said the usher, who had witnessed the police arrive. "If you follow me, I'll take you to them."

They entered the church and proceeded to the vestry. The minister was seated at his desk with Ashley's parents sitting opposite him. Ashley was standing by a bookcase, supposedly studying its contents. Hugh, who had volunteered to act as a lookout from the church door, followed the two policemen into the vestry.

"You must be the groom's parents?" The policeman wearing a sergeants stripes addressed the sitting couple.

"Yes, I'm Ken Barton and this is my wife, Penelope."

"Something's happened!" the minister interjected. "What's happened, is it an accident?"

The policeman ignored the minister and continued, "I'm sergeant McWilliams and this is constable Ryan, we're from the Gladesville Police Station, and you must be the groom." the sergeant centred his attention on Ashley standing by the bookcase.

"Yes, I am, what's happened? Has there been an accident?"

"Worse than that, sir. It's my duty to inform you that your bride has been abducted."

"What?" was the one word which echoed throughout the vestry.

"How do you mean, 'abducted'?" Ken Barton rose to his feet.

"The wedding cars were ambushed in Charles Street by two other vehicles and at least four men used some sort of anaesthetic to knock out the bridal party, and the bride was forcibly bundled into a blue van and abducted."

"You mean kidnapped?" the minister asked.

"If you like, sir, although when someone is kidnapped, there is generally a ransom demand, and we don't know about that yet."

"Oh my God, this is horrible," Ashley's mother Penelope whimpered, "and the rest of the bridal party, what's happened to them?"

"They were all taken to Gladesville Hospital to be checked out, the same as the two drivers. The doctors have to identify the substance used to see if there are any aftereffects."

"Who would do such a thing and why?" Ken broke in, "The Baufords are doing all right, but they are hardly millionaires. What if they ask for more than Jim can pay? I shudder to think. Naturally I'll help out as much as I can, but I've got limitations as well."

"That's very decent of you, sir, but as I said, it's early days at the moment and we don't really know what we're dealing with yet. Once the forensic team complete their investigation and we have thoroughly talked to the two witnesses, we'll have a much better idea."

"You have witnesses! That's good news. Did they get the rego numbers of the utility and the van?"

"The utility, yes, they abandoned it. It turns out to be a stolen vehicle anyway, and my guess is that the same goes for the van. We should know in a couple of days."

"So, what happens now? To us I mean."

"You can go about your business as normal. I'll need all your names and addresses, and you can expect a visit from someone from the detective squad very soon."

"And what about the wedding guests, what shall we tell them?"

"That's up to you, sir. I suggest you tell them what you know so far, which isn't very much but it's better than nothing. Just stick to the facts."

"I've got an idea, Dad." Ashley joined the discourse.

"Why don't we ask the guests to go to the reception place and we can explain it when they're all gathered there."

"After what's happened, Ashley? You want the guests to go to the reception when there isn't going to be one?"

"No, not quite like that, Dad. Look, the reception is all paid for and to cancel now. At such short notice, I don't think Susan's dad will get his money back so why waste it?"

"In a cock-eyed way that makes some sort of sense, I suppose," Ken conceded, "but instead of a celebration this could turn out to be a wake."

"I agree, but let's face it, the guests have a right to know what's happened and on top of that they'll be hungry, so why waste the food?"

"All right, let's do that, but somehow I don't feel very hungry."

***

At the Rose Garden Retreat Reception Centre, most of the guests assembled and found their places. Some had obviously gone home but not too many. When the guests were seated and looked towards the bridal table, they witnessed a seldom seen sight.

One half of the bridal table presented the groom, his best man and his parents. The other half was vacant. Ashley rose to his feet, tapping an empty wine glass with a fork for silence.

"Ladies and gentlemen, first I want to thank you for your patience and support for what should have been a happy occasion. Sadly, it is not. While we all were at the church waiting for the bride to appear, other forces were at work to see that this did not happen. On her way to be with you all, Susan's wedding cars were ambushed, and she was abducted. For what reason, I don't know except that we soon expect a call asking for a ransom to be paid for her release. To those responsible, I say make your call and make it quick, and I will do my level best to meet that demand, but please don't harm her in any way. As to the rest of the bridal party who should have been seated at this table, they are, as far as I have been told, well, and in Gladesville hospital undergoing observation and examination to see that they are in no danger of any aftereffects and for that reason, cannot be with us.

"The future of my bride is uncertain, but the police have assured me they will be doing all that is in their power to ensure her safe return.

"I knew that on this day I was going to have to make a speech. What I didn't know that it was going to be this one and not the one I prepared a week ago. Sadly, I must ask one thing of you, and that is to fill your glasses and drink to Susan's safe return while silently offering up a prayer for this to take place."

At this point a waiter filled Ashley's glass, and the guests attended to their own.

"To Susan's safe return!" Ashley stretched out his arm and then lowered the glass to his lips as the guests did likewise. "To Susan's safe return," was echoed throughout the dining room.

"And now, please enjoy your meal, I am sure that I speak for both Susan and myself."

"Amazing fellow that Ashley," one guest quietly announced to the people at his table, "to hold himself so well together after what's happened. That's quite remarkable. I would have turned to jelly hours ago."

A murmur of agreement circumnavigated the table. Having finished the meal, the guests were nervously looking for a reason to leave. There was no point in continuing with levity and general wedding banter. Those who chose to leave first were mobbed by a crowd of media reporters. Cameras of all descriptions were pointed at them, and questions came from all sides. Clearly, the cat was out of the bag.

***

At the hospital, the bride's side of the party were thoroughly checked and examined for any aftereffects following their ordeal. All were pronounced ready for discharge late in the afternoon except for Norma Bauford who was still in shock. As the others left, Jim asked if he could remain by his wife's side. The hospital readily agreed.

Holding Norma's hand, he reflected for the umpteenth time the afternoon's events.

"Why Susan?" Jim asked himself in self-recrimination, "I don't think she has an enemy in the world. Then why her? Surely not for ransom but what else, it's gotta be ransom. But then they must know I'm a bookie and while bookies make a good living, they're not up there in the millionaire class. I suppose I could scrape up twenty or maybe fifty thousand in cash but surely this would be a paltry sum to ask for. Their planning and upfront costs would probably be more than that. What if they ask for a million? There is no way I can come up with this sort of money, not even if I sold the house. That's a stupid thought, as if they would hold Susan captive for the months it would take to sell the house. Maybe they made a mistake and kidnapped the wrong person. Yeah, that could be it. Crooks are crooks because they're not very smart. But they would have had to do some research before they grabbed anybody and the whole thing was done like it had been precisely planned. They got the timing spot on, and they knew exactly where we'd be. I'm buggered if I know, but why Susan? I wonder where she is right now? If they phone and ask for money, there's no way I'll do anything unless I hear her voice on the phone. Maybe she's dead already. No, they must expect me to want talk to her before I'd do anything."

This thought comforted him a little but not enough.

***

Norma was discharged from hospital at nine the following morning. Jim had been with her all that time, and although he had little or almost no sleep, he felt a lot happier as he drove her home.

Once back in his Putney home, Jim thought it best if Norma spent the day in bed.

"Why don't you just relax for the rest of the day. I'll make us some tea and toast, and you can have it in bed."

"Relax, Jim!

"How can you possibly say relax when Susan's still missing?"

"I know dear it's difficult, but you have to try, you can't be much help to Susan if you're a nervous wreck."

"Well, I am a nervous wreck and there's nothing I can do about it. It's the not knowing that makes it worse. All sorts of stupid, horrible things keep going through my mind. I know it's stupid, but I can't help it."

Just as Jim was putting on the kettle, the front doorbell rang.

He took off his apron and went to answer it.

Two men were at the door looking a bit odd as both were wearing suits and ties.

"Yes, gentlemen, how can I help you?"

"I take it you are Mr Jim Bauford?"

"Yes, that's right."

"Mr Bauford, I am Detective Henderson, and this is Detective Pike from Central Police.

"How do you do?" Jim replied, "I take it you are here about the business in Gladesville yesterday?"

"That's correct, sir. May we come in?"

"Certainly, please do," Jim opened the door wider and admitted the detectives, escorting them to the lounge room.

"I was just making some tea, would you gentlemen like some?"

"Thank you, sir, that won't be necessary. We just want a few details from you and then I'll be on my way."

"You won't mind if I have some then," Ken asked, "I've just gotten home from the hospital."

"No, no, you go right ahead, sir. We just have some questions we'd like to ask you about the abduction yesterday."

"The police already have. Yesterday at the hospital when I came to."

"We know that, sir, but we're not the Gladesville Police, we're from City Central. You see, sir, the Police Force as a whole and the

14

State Government take abduction or kidnapping very seriously, so if we do go over some used ground, please bear with us."

"Certainly, by all means."

"Thank you. Now, your daughter's name is Susan Bauford?"

"Yes, that's correct."

"And this is her residential address?"

"Yes."

"Now, sir, would you have any recent photographs of her."

"I'm sure we do, lots of them, I'm sure. I'll ask my wife to have a look for you. How many would you like?"

"If we could have a bit of selection that would be great. We'll pick a few, have our lab copy them and then you can have them back."

Jim excused himself as he left the room to talk to Norma and on returning asked,

"Have you any news about my daughter?"

"Not really, sir," Detective Pike replied. "That's why we are here. We need all the information we can get.

"Fine, go ahead and ask."

"Is there anyone your daughter had a problem with or anyone who didn't like her, for whatever reason?"

"I don't think so, Susan's a very open person and gets on with everybody."

"What about boyfriends, I mean old ones, anyone she'd stopped seeing?"

"Not really, as a matter of fact she didn't have any boyfriends while she was studying. Ashley was virtually her first but that was after she graduated."

"I see. What about financial worries?"

"I'm the one who has those. While she was studying, I gave her an allowance, but she was always very good in managing it and never asked for a penny more."

"I have to ask this, but what about drugs? Did she ever use any illegal substances? You can answer that openly, as it will not go on record. It's just between us."

"Definitely not. She hated them and was a campaigner against their use. Why are we talking about her in the past tense? She's not dead, is she?" Jim became suddenly alarmed.

"No of course not. She wouldn't be much use to those who kidnapped her if she was dead."

"So, it is kidnapped then, not abducted."

"It looks very much that way, sir."

"Then I could expect a phone call any moment."

"Yes, that's one of the reasons we're here."

"I see, I expect you'll be tapping my phone then?"

"We've already done that, sir."

"What? When?"

"Last night, sir, as soon as we got the call."

"What if they use a mobile phone? What then?"

"A little trickier, but we can trace them."

"I see. Well, so far there's been no phone call, and last night I came up with a theory. Susan does not have an enemy in the world, and whoever kidnapped her must know that I am a bookie and therefore not a millionaire. Suppose this kidnapping was a case of mistaken identity and they simply kidnapped the wrong person?"

"I'm sorry Mr Bauford, but there is no way in the world this could be a case of mistaken identity. It was too well planned and planned by professionals. They had been watching your daughter for some time to learn her routine and the clincher is the route the wedding cars took. The kidnappers knew the exact route. They had to know, otherwise they could not have set up the ambush with such precision. How they got to know the route is another question. Personally, I think one of the drivers was duped into talking about it when he thought he was having lots of freebie drinks amongst newfound friends."

"You're probably right," Jim conceded.

"I certainly hope I'm right Mr Bauford because if it is a case of mistaken identity then you'll never see your daughter again. Believe me, I know that from sad experience."

16

"So, what happens now?"

"Now Mr Bauford, Detective Pike will remain here, in your house and will wait with you for the phone call. He will shortly instruct you in what to do before it comes. Please follow his instructions to the letter."

Detective Pike then went out to the police car and returned carrying a small suitcase.

"We've no idea exactly how long this is going to take," Pike told Jim. "So, I've brought a change of underwear and a toothbrush."

Sunday ended and Monday began, then Tuesday and Wednesday.

No ransom call materialised. Wednesday leapfrogged to Sunday. Detective Pike was relieved by another policeman and Sunday came round again but the ransom call didn't.

CH 2. THE WAITING GAME

Detective Pike shook his head in disbelief, surely the kidnappers would have attempted some form of communication by now? If not by telephone, then by some note delivered or posted or even shoved into the letterbox during the night, clumsy as that would be, but nothing! It looked like he would be resident at the Bauford's home for another week, if not longer. Not that he minded, Ken had so far been a very generous host and Norma, an excellent cook. He could have 'take-away' meals delivered to him, but Norma wouldn't hear of this. Now he had to arrange for some more fresh clothing. The Department cooperated by sending over a relief detective while Pike was at his small flat in Darlinghurst selecting clean clothing.

On his return to Putney, Norma insisted he change immediately as she was about to do a wash and his current apparel was to be part of it. Reluctantly, Pike agreed, and, having changed he once more resumed his vigil. The hours turned into days and then more days and it was becoming apparent that no ransom demand was going to materialise.

"You don't suppose they've killed her?" Ken asked in trepidation."

"I don't think so," Pike replied, "In kidnap cases where the victim had been murdered, the kidnappers still asked for a ransom. The Thorne case immediately springs to mind. The little boy was killed almost immediately, but the kidnapper still held out and got the ransom."

"That's cold comfort I must say."

"I know but there it is. Until we receive other information, we have to hang in there for as long as it takes."

"Exactly what does, 'as long as it takes,' mean?"

"I wish I could answer that. Look, Mr Bauford, it could be another week or so, but I don't think it will go into months."

"But you just said, 'as long as it takes?' So why not months?"

Pike knew that he was in a bit of a bind. He was aware of the trauma which the Baufords were undergoing and wished he could come up with a straight answer but there was no straight answer.

"I'm aware of what I said but there is no way of qualifying that. I said, 'not months' purely from past experience. The kidnappers know that I am here monitoring the situation. They also know that after a period The Department will recall me. When? I don't know, but they will not leave me here forever. My personal theory is that those responsible are monitoring your house, waiting for me to leave. Susan's abduction was not carried out by some amateurs looking for a quick buck. This was done by professionals who took great care in planning the whole thing. All they are doing now is waiting to contact you without a police presence."

"I understand all that," Jim interrupted, "but you'll still have my phone tapped, won't you, and if they're pros they must know that too?"

"Of course, they do but without a policeman there to monitor the call and guide you, it gives them an edge."

"How?"

"It will give them the chance to bully you and frighten the crap out of you by giving you descriptions of what they will do to your daughter if you don't cooperate."

"I see that, but all that will be on the tape of your phone tap."

"Yes, it will but your answers will not be the same without me listening in and guiding you."

"I see what you mean, so where does that leave us?"

"Still very much behind the eight ball, I'm afraid. Look, by now the one thing I'm pretty sure of is that when they contact you, they will not want a policeman to be within a mile of you. They mightn't even use the phone. A bloke or a kid may bump into you on the street and slip a note in your pocket, or a passing car in the early hours of the morning will drop a letter in your post box, or they'll send you an untraceable letter by post. These are just a few of the possibilities. Like I said, these guys are professionals and right now they are keeping you guessing and softening you up, right up to the point where you'll agree to anything they ask, just to get your daughter back."

"It paints a rather morbid picture, doesn't it?" Jim sat down in an armchair, cradling his head in his hands.

"I'm afraid it does," Pike agreed.

***

Kenneth Benjamin Barton regretted selling the 'Valley View Horse Stud' he established in the Hunter Valley near Singleton, only days after having sold it. Had it not been for the urging of his wife, Penelope, he would have been happy to live out his life on the Stud. Penelope, however, had other ideas. Most of her social set were based in Sydney as were her other cultural pursuits. At first, dinner parties at the Stud were a novelty for her friends in Sydney, but the long four-to-five-hour drives from Sydney to The Stud and back were taking their toll on their social lives, and both Penelope and Ken found themselves driving to Sydney at every given opportunity to promote and enjoy their social life.

When their only son, Ashley, came of high school age, he was enrolled in a private boarding school in Sydney, thus making commuting between Sydney and The Stud even more frequent. Ashley really loved The Stud, during school holidays and often on weekends, he would travel home bringing one or more of his friends with him. Ken often wondered whether Ashley was a popular student or was The Stud the main attraction?

Penelope, who was christened Doreen after her grandmother, never took to the name. She considered it too bourgeois, and when she reached the age where she could do something about it, she changed her name to Penelope Doreen. She retained Doreen as a middle name simply to stay in the good books with her grandmother but otherwise never used it.

Penelope's social world mostly revolved around Sydney's Eastern Suburbs, and it became the area of interest when searching to purchase a new property. Valley View Horse Stud sold very quickly for what Ken thought was an excellent price. He had set a high price on the property, leaving himself a good margin for negotiation. He was therefore surprised at the early sale and the lack of haggling on the part of the buyer. He admonished the real estate agent for not asking more, but the agent managed to convince him that he was just lucky that the buyer was determined to have the stud. There had been other parties who had viewed the property, but their offer was lower.

In the meantime, Penelope was staying with a friend in Randwick utilising her time to search the Eastern Suburbs real estate market, finally settling on a house in Clovelly, which apart from being quite rambling also offered a glimpse of the Pacific Ocean.

At first Ken was lukewarm with Penelope's choice. The house seemed too large and the garden too small, but he knew that arguing the matter with Penelope would only result in weeks of frustration and icy dissent, making marital relationships out of the question. His main concern was more about his own comforts. By profession Ken was a civil engineer, but since inheriting the horse stud from his family, his only engineering skills were vested in the stud.

The transition from Valley View Stud to Clovelly kept him busy for some weeks but now he found himself in early retirement. Following the rounds of social 'housewarming' parties arranged by Penelope, Ken felt the seeds of boredom germinating. Ashley had left the family cocoon and bought his own house in Newport, much of it with the financial help of the family. Ken spent a great deal of time helping his son refurbish his house to his son's liking but that too had come to an end. Ken looked at his financial situation, which at this point was quite healthy. The difference between selling the stud and purchasing the house in Clovelly was quite substantial, but Ken knew it would not maintain their present lifestyle, even if interest rates increased.

After dinner one non-social night at home, Ken thought it best to take the matter up with Penelope.

"Penny my dear, I think it's high time we discussed a little matter that's been worrying me."

"You worrying? That's something new! What's on your mind?"

"It's our lifestyle, dear, that's the worry."

"What? What's wrong with our lifestyle?"

"It's not the lifestyle so much. It's the cost."

"Nonsense, we've got plenty of money!"

"At the moment, yes, but at the rate we're spending it, it won't last forever. The money is going out, but apart from a little interest there is nothing coming in."

Penelope remained silent for a while but not for long. "If that's what's worrying you, why don't you look for employment somewhere?"

"I could ask you the same question."

"Don't be silly, Ken! I've got a job. Looking after this house, that's my job. If I were working somewhere else, what do you think would happen to the house? Who would clean it, do the cooking, do the shopping and everything else that goes with it? Then there's arranging our social life. Besides that, what would I do? Take up waitressing? That would go down well in our community standing, wouldn't it?"

"I don't mean waitressing as such, but we do have to do something. We can't go on too long just wasting money."

"Is that what you call it? Wasting money?"

"I'm sorry, I didn't mean it like that. It's just that I've looked at our financial situation, and it's clear we have to look for some extra income."

"Then look for it! You started out your career as an engineer, so why not look for something along those lines. I understand engineers make pretty good money."

"Actually, they do."

"Fine, then why don't you look for something there? You're the one crying poor."

"As a matter of fact, I've been thinking about just that."

"Good, then why don't you go ahead. In a way it might be good for you. Give you something to do instead of moping round the house like a lost weekend."

"What do you mean, lost weekend?" Ken responded a little hurt.

"I'm sorry, darling, I didn't mean it like that, but you have been a bit listless lately. No, I mean another interest is probably just the thing you need to put a little sparkle back in your life."

"I know what will put a bit of sparkle in my life."

"Really, and what's that?"

"You. Why don't we go to bed now, I mean right now?"

"What about the washing up? Who's going to do that?"

"You are, in the morning."

***

Over the next few days Ken looked up old acquaintances and other contacts, discreetly probing for information about employment possibilities but with little success. He scoured newspaper advertisements and managed to get a few appointments for interviews but all of them ended up with the same bottom line, "Mr Barton, I'm afraid you've been out of Civil Engineering for far too long. Things have changed tremendously since you last worked. I'm sorry, but we are after someone who is up to today's technology." This was almost a standard reply.

***

At one interview with an engineering firm in Randwick, the interviewer was a little more sympathetic, "Look, Mr Barton, I understand your situation, but at the same time you must understand ours."

"Oh, I understand it all right. Today it's the young Turks taking over the jobs, years of experience count for nothing these days, we just get thrown on the scrap heap," Ken replied rather acidly.

"That's not quite correct, Mr Barton, your hands-on experience is only some eight or so years and then, according to your application form, you went into the horse breeding business where your engineering skills were of little use. In the meantime, construction methods have undergone a tremendous change. That's the problem."

"Sure, I'll grant you that, but with a little brushing up I'm positive I can get back into the swing of things."

"I'm sure you can, but our situation is that we need engineers who can be productive from day one. You can appreciate that, can't you?"

"Yes, I suppose I can. Well, thank you for seeing me anyway," Ken replied and rose to leave.

"I'm sorry, Mr Barton, I'd like to help you, but I have bosses too."

"Yes, there's that too, I quite understand."

"Look, I've just had a thought, it's not quit the same thing, but you might consider it."

"Really, what?"

"Would you consider doing some draughting work for us, on a part time basis? I know the money's not quite the same but it's something!"

"Blimey, that is going back to the basics. How would that work on a part time basis? Do I come here for a couple of days a week, and how would I get paid? On an hourly basis?" Ken brightened up a little.

"No, we'd pay you for every completed project at an agreed price or the going rate if you like. You could even work from home if you like and in your own time. Once you finish an assignment you bring the drawings back to our office and hopefully pick up another one."

"That could be interesting. I'd have to get a proper desk and easel and other bits and pieces."

"We could even help you there. We have stacks of equipment laying around here, not being used. We could ship it to your place on an 'on loan' basis and you're all set up."

"That's a very good of you, I like the sound of it. OK, how and when do we get started?"

"Good. Let's see, it's Tuesday now, so what say you come back here on Thursday afternoon, say three o'clock, and we'll sit down and work out the details."

"Thursday at three it is then, and thank you very much Mr Worthington, I really appreciate this."

"Not at all, besides, you'll be doing us a service as well and call me Bill."

***

Penelope was more than pleased when Ken broke the news to her.

"That's wonderful, darling, and really that's not like working for somebody else, it's more like you're self-employed."

"Yes, I suppose I am if you look at it that way. I'm still my own boss."

"Of course, you are. You should get a sign made up, and we'll put it up at the front gate. Something simple but dignified. What about a brass plate saying, 'K.G. Barton ... Draughtsman etc,' what do you think?

"No Penny, no sign or plate. For Christ's sake, I'm not a draughtsman, I'm an engineer and should anyone ask what I'm doing, you tell them I'm working on an engineering project, and that's all you tell them."

"All right but why?"

"The why does not matter. What matters is, is that's how I want it."

"Fine, if that's what you want. There's no need to snap."

***

Ken had been working for a few months making drawings for

J.J. Engineering in Randwick. He enjoyed the occupation and the solitude as well as the rewards which, whilst not a fortune, were still quite substantial.

Ashley phoned one evening to announce that he had met and been going out with a young lady for some time and wanted to bring her over for dinner so that his parents could meet her. Talking to his mother, he lauded her attributes as well as that she was the daughter of a prominent Sydney bookmaker. Thinking about her social status, Penelope wasn't overjoyed by this development, but Ken assured her that bookmakers were socially very acceptable and reminded her that without them their former business as a stud farm would not have been as viable as it had been.

Early on a Wednesday evening Ashley and Susan arrived at the Barton's Clovelly home for dinner. Ken took to Susan immediately and Penelope warmed to her once Susan announced that in only a few months now she would be receiving her law degree. That established, during dinner Ashley further announced that he and Susan were to become engaged and thereafter plan their wedding. The announcement took Ken and Penelope completely by surprise, and after a short gasping silence it was Penelope who broke the ice. "Darling, that's wonderful news, I've always wanted a daughter, well daughter-in-law," she left her chair and went over to Susan and embraced her.

Ken turned to his son and, shaking his son's hand, clapped him round the shoulder.

"Congratulation's son, well done, she's a beauty. You sure know how to pick them."

When Penelope and Susan both went to the kitchen to organise the desserts, Ken leaned over to Ashley and asked, "What about Susan's parents? Have you told them yet?"

"Not yet, dad. We're going to Susan's place on Friday night to break the news."

"That's wonderful, son, I'm really pleased for you and don't take this the wrong way son, but I must ask, is she still a virgin?"

"What! Come on dad, this is the 1990s not the 1890s."

***

The Bauford's were eagerly looking forward to meeting Ashley. Unlike Ashley's parents, they had already been briefed on him from the very first date Susan had had with him.

Both Jim and Norma liked Ashley and were more than impressed that in his early years Ashley ran his own small but profitable finance company.

"Quite the opposite to my business," Jim observed during their first dinner meeting.

"How do you mean, 'opposite?' Ashley asked.

"Well, in your business you have to worry if your customers will pay you back what they have borrowed, and in mine I have to worry how to pay my customers out if all the favourites romp home."

"Does that ever happen?"

"Not often, thank God, but now and then it does."

"What do you do then?"

"Pay up and look happy."

"What would happen if you ran out of money?"

"That rarely happens. Every bookie has an emergency fund set aside just for such an event and you dip into that, but that evening you dine on a toasted cheese sandwich."

Although they had never met, Jim Bauford was familiar with Ken's former horse stud, and thus the breeder and the bookie had a lot in common.

Instead of a dinner party at home, Jim had suggested meeting at a restaurant where he would be the host, thus saving Norma the trouble of preparing dinner and worrying about its acceptance and the cleaning up afterwards.

When the wedding plans came up for discussion, both parents were allowed very little input. Susan took the lead and informed both parties that the wedding would take place soon after she obtained her

Law Degree and started her working career.

"Actually, that's very sensible," Ken observed, "you will both have your feet on the ground, and you'll be able to plan your lives from a pretty solid base."

"What about a family?" Norma asked. "Have you any plans when you intend to start that?"

"Yes, we do," Ashley answered, "but not for the first year or so. We plan to let our hair down a little, you know have a bit of fun, travel maybe and then make you grandparents."

"Good idea," Ken intervened, "enjoy life while you can and then put your nose to the grindstone."

"That's not very nice, Ken," Penelope admonished him, "Raising children is not exactly like having your nose to the grindstone."

"I didn't mean it like that, dear. What I'm saying is that there is nothing wrong with having a bit of a fling while you're still young. Stock up with a few good memories, then you'll have something to fall back on once you're tied down to childcare. You can't exactly enjoy the wonders of the Niagara Falls nursing a one-year-old."

"I think that those matters are for the young couple to decide, wouldn't you agree?" Jim entered the discussion, "Besides, I don't think Norma's not quite ready yet to be referred to as grandma."

"Ready or not, I'll be happy whenever that event takes place, but in the meantime, enjoy what life has to offer," Norma concluded.

***

A routine had been established at J.J. Engineering that Ken would drop off his drawings on a Friday afternoon, and Bill Worthington would pay the fees there and then. At the same time, Bill would brief Ken on any project he had for him for the following week. Sometimes there was nothing, but this particular week Worthington had a great pile of drawing he required by Monday morning.

"Wow!" Ken exclaimed as he sorted through the pile, "I don't think I can get through all of these by Thursday night. I'll need at least another day."

"Hmm, I really need them by Monday morning." Bill looked worried, "Do you think you can get them done by Friday night?

Ken examined the pile again, "Probably, but how do I get them to you? The office is closed for the weekend."

"I'll be in the office on Saturday, till about lunchtime. Do you think you could do it by then?"

"That should be OK. I'll work on them through Friday night if I have to and get them to you on Saturday."

"I appreciate that, Ken, I really do. OK, I'll wait to see you here on Saturday morning, and we'll fix up your money as well, and see if I can find a bit of a bonus."

"No need for that, Bill. I'll be happy just to get them done for you."

***

On Saturday morning Ken phoned the office around midday. "Hi Bill, I'm all finished and am leaving for Randwick now."

"That's terrific, Ken, thank you. I'll be waiting."

From Clovelly, Randwick is only a short drive but, on the way, the traffic was very slow.

"You'd think on a Saturday the traffic would be pretty thin," Ken mused while he was waiting for a green light. As he neared Randwick the penny dropped, "Ah, of course. Saturday, horse races at Randwick. Ah well, Bill will have to wait a little longer, there's nothing I can do about it."

With an armful of tubes containing drawings, Ken entered the office.

"Thank God!" Bill exclaimed when he saw Ken entering, "For a moment there I thought you may have had a prang."

"Naw, nothing like that, just racecourse traffic."

"Of course, I didn't think of that. Anyway, you're here and believe you me, that's a lifesaver."

Bill inspected some of the drawings and nodded in satisfaction, "Great stuff and thank you. Now we'd better fix you up and both of us can get out of here." He rose from his desk and went to the office safe, "I'm sorry, Ken, but I can't give you a cheque, I need two signatures for that so I'm afraid it's gonna be cash only. Hope you don't have a problem with that?"

"The only problem I'll have with that is that I'll probably spend it a lot quicker."

"Yeah, tell me about it," Bill chuckled as he opened up the safe. Taking out the cashbox, he counted out the contracted sum and then peeled off some extra $50 notes. "Here's an extra $400 for your trouble. A small bonus shall we say."

"I told you, you didn't have to do that," Ken protested.

"I know but the company can well afford it, and look at it this way, if we didn't have the plans for Monday, it would have cost the company a hell of a lot more."

"Yes, I suppose there is that. Thank you very much anyway."

***

Driving back the traffic had thinned out quite a bit. Ken was feeling quite good about things. His pockets were stuffed with cash, it was a beautiful day, and passing Randwick racecourse a wild thought struck him.

"Why not spend the rest of the afternoon at the races? Penny won't be home until round about six and I haven't smelt horse shit for a hell of a long time." The idea appealed to him, and, spotting a place to park, he pulled over. Extracting his wallet from his back pocket, he examined its contents.

"There it is, my Members Car Park Pass." He turned the card over, "yep and it's still valid." He exited his parking spot and did a 'U' turn, heading back towards the main entrance of the racecourse.

Throughout all the years Ken operated the horse stud he was never much of a punter. He was often on a racetrack, but this was nearly always for self-promotional reasons. He did place bets but for small amounts and then only on the horses coming from his stud. He put it down to public relations.

He soon spotted Jim Bauford's bookmakers' stand and headed for that. He knew well enough that this could not be a social visit and was happy with the exchange of a few words while a race was in progress.

"Ken, good to see you! What are you doing here?" Jim almost shouted over the heads of other punters.

"I thought I might come and make some money for you," Ken shouted back as he looked at the race form.

"That's the spirit, always happy to take your money."

When the placing of bets was declared open on the next race, Ken approached Jim with two $50 notes.

"I'll have 100 bucks on number 7, Red Julie, thanks Ken."

"Red Julie! She's running at 125 to 1, Are you sure you know what you're doing?"

"I told you, I'm making money for you."

"Fair enough." Jim took the $100 in exchange for the betting slip.

Red Julie started out somewhat mediocre but then put on a burst of speed, leading the rest of the pack by two furlongs as she passed the winning post.

"Whatever made you pick on Red Julie?" Ken asked as he counted out Ken's substantial winnings.

"Nothing really in particular. The long odds, I guess, plus I knew that horse when she was called, 'Princess Penelope'."

"Strewth! Keep your voice down, don't want the stewards hearing that!"

"Sorry."

"Are you sticking around or is this just a casual visit?"

"I might stay for the rest of the afternoon. I just love the smell of horses."

"Yeah," Jim thought, "that and the smell of my money." Ken stayed on and placed bets on four more races, three of them winners.

Back home in Clovelly, Ken emptied his pockets. He had started out from home with barely $50 in his wallet and returned with $4,810 now laying on top of his desk plus some coins he didn't bother to count.

Still in a bit of a daze, Ken rolled numbers through his mind. His sizeable win led his brain setting up a number of scenarios of what ifs, how much, what are the options and why nots? He had never envisaged gambling as a career before but now the poof was spread all over his desk. Beginner's luck, lucky break, one-off thoughts cropped up during his deliberations.

"Was it really beginner's luck?" The thought repeated itself time and time again, "I'm not so sure about that. I know horses, I can spot their strengths and weaknesses a mile off. What if I put this knowledge to obtain financial gain? It can't be illegal to benefit from what one has learnt. Look at doctors, they spend a few years learning and then go out and get on the gravy train. So, what's the difference? I've spent more years studying horses, than doctors have studying medicine. So why can't I capitalise on my hard work and earning?"

These and similar thoughts whirled through Ken's mind, changing many of his earlier convictions as he gathered up his winnings, looking for a place to store them. He decided to tell Penelope nothing about his win. Past experience had taught him that whenever there was a bit of a windfall, there was always something of great urgency that she had to have, and the windfall was converted to shoes or a crocodile-skin handbag even though her wardrobe was near bursting with shoes and handbags.

***

Without a word to Penelope, Ken became a punter. As a sort of cover he still kept his part time job with J.J. Engineering and he discovered when he opened a betting account with Jim Bauford, his presence at the racetrack was not required. He could place his bets by telephone. However, he did go to the racetrack whenever he could, without arousing Penelope's suspicions. Ken was not very interested in form-guides published by the press. He wanted to get as close to the horses as he could, unlike his son, who preferred illegal casinos.

***

Ken's 'beginners' luck' held. He kept a meticulous record of all his bets and horse's performances. He noted, with some satisfaction that he was doing much better when he could see the horses before the race as opposed to when he had to rely on the form-guide. This meant more visits to the racetrack which also meant finding excuses with which to placate Penelope. This proved to be easier than he first thought it would be. He made much of his newfound friendship with Jim Bauford and told Penelope he was off to have a beer with his friend at the Member's Bar at the racetrack. This suited Penelope very well, as she too was more than often absent from home attending a garden party or a game of Bridge with some other ladies. Thus, they became almost like a Swiss cuckoo clock. When the little man with the rain umbrella came out, the milkmaid with her sun parasol stayed in and vice versa.

***

A few months before his son's wedding, Ken's luck turned. No matter what he did, his selections refused to be first past the winning post. Jim consoled him by saying that that's the racing game and his run of bad luck was bound to change but at the same time keeping a worried eye on Ken's credit limits on his account.

The time soon came when Jim had to call in Ken's account and refuse any more credit until this was settled. It was an embarrassing moment for both of them, but irrespective of their relationship, Jim had no alternative.

Ken was not blind to the situation and dipped into his holdings, settling Jim's bill but at the same time opening up two other accounts with different bookmakers and hoping this would not reach Jim's ears. It was a vague hope as it is in any closed-shop industry. Bad news quickly penetrates any social barriers.

When the news first reached Jim's ears, Jim was quite philosophical.

"A man's got the right to spend his money where and with whom he wants to," Jim reasoned. "As long as he pays my account, he's free to do as he wishes." This was Jim's reaction. It was fair, but it did not encourage Jim to like it.

***

By now Ken was hooked on gambling. Not only on horses but included now were visits to gambling casinos and dens where his favourite game was Blackjack. Again, he started off well but soon established a win/lose pattern with the accent being on lose. His cash holdings now dwindling at a steady rate, it planted the loser seed in Ken that the next session would restore his holdings. It didn't.

***

The Bauford house was in a state, close to mourning. Weeks had passed and still no news of Susan's fate. Detective Pike arrived and informed Jim that the current policeman on watch was to be removed and was not going to be replaced.

"OK!" Jim exclaimed, "but what happens if tomorrow they phone or call or whatever?"

"That is very unlikely. It's been too long for that to happen now," Pike replied.

"Does that mean she's … dead?" Jim could hardly get the last word out.

"We simply do not know. It is a possibility, and you must brace yourselves and prepare to face that. But to be honest, we don't know."

"It does not make any sense. It makes no sense at all. They wouldn't have kidnapped her just to kill her. Why? Susan's done no harm to anyone to warrant this. Why kidnap her if they wanted to kill her? They could have shot her on the spot. Why go to all the elaborate way of abducting her if all they wanted to do was to kill her? They could have done it through the window of a passing car. I simply cannot understand this. It makes no sense, no sense at all," Jim almost sobbed, and Norma could not hold back the tears.

"I totally agree with you, Mr Bauford, we are in the same boat. We have hardly anything to go on with. What we have is your daughter's DNA, and should a body turn up with the slightest description of her, we will get a match."

"That means she's dead," Norma wailed. "You think she's dead, don't you?"

"I didn't say that Mrs Bauford. We've considered the possibility, but we don't know, and unless we come up with a body, we may never know. I'm sorry to have to say it so bluntly, but that is the reality."

"You are quite right, detective, and thank you for being honest with us. You have all been very good and supportive, but now we must face the awful truth that we may never see our daughter again and commence our grieving," Jim let out long-held-back sigh as the two policemen prepared to leave.

CH 3. THE VICTIM

The twin engine Cessna touched down in Darwin Airport and taxied to its designated spot. As it was a local flight, Bankstown, Mt. Isa, Darwin, there were few formalities. Neither Customs or Immigration were involved, only a few landing times and other flight details which the pilot completed over the radio.

A white hearse approached the Cessna and was guided to align itself with the cargo hold of the plane. Four men gently transferred a wooden coffin from the plane into the hearse. A tall thin man from the Cessna joined the hearse driver. The vehicle then headed for the International Air Freight section of the airport.

A custom's officer in his early thirties examined the documents accompanying the coffin, and then walked round it with papers in hand, inspecting it.

"Svetlana Lubina, 24, from Slovenia. Awfully young to come to Australia just to die?"

"I agree," the thin man replied. "Apparently she went for a swim in an unprotected beach, got caught in a rip and drowned."

"I'm not surprised, these bloody tourists, they never learn. They seem to think that every other waterway in the world is a millpond, like the Mediterranean. Well, all the papers are in order, so she can go to her rest in Slovenia. Just one thing that puzzles me?"

"Oh! What's that?" The thin man asked, a little alerted.

"Why on earth would her family have her shipped back from Sydney via Darwin? Why didn't they just put the body on a plane in Sydney?"

"Yeah, we wondered about that too," the thin man was quick to respond. "Apparently, her family have some good connections with air freighters in the Eastern Bloc, and they gave them a good deal. I noticed that the plane she is flying back in is some Balkan airfreight company I've never heard off."

"You're probably quite right. The plane she's booked on only flies Zagreb to Darwin, unloads, loads up and is off again. It's got no landing rights anywhere else in Australia. She's probably flying back gratis, if as you say, the family has connections."

"Don't know about that. We got paid up front and for us that's all that matters."

"Too right," the custom's officer laughed, "well, we'd better get her ladyship on board, and by this time tomorrow she'll be probably lowered into some hole in the ground in Slovenia, wherever the hell that is."

***

"Everything OK, Leo?" the thin man's apparent boss asked as he rejoined the party aboard the Cessna.

"All OK, Ari, She's on her way. Just as well we had a cover story for using Darwin. The custom's guy got a little suspicious, but he bought it."

"Did he poke around the coffin or ask any questions?"

"Not really. He did walk around it for a bit of a look, and I got a little worried he might spot the air holes."

"No chance of that, he'd have to take the lid off to spot those.

Bloody clever the way our bloke carved those in."

"Yeah, now I just hope she doesn't wake up during the flight and start creating merry hell. The air holes let the air in, but they will also let any sound out."

"I wouldn't worry about that. I gave her enough sleeping juice to put her out for up to thirty-six hours. That should hold her until it's dinner time in Slovenia."

***

Slowly Susan drifted from unconsciousness to a semiconscious, muddled state of mind. She tried to rationalise her situation but as she did so, her train of thought stopped, and sleep took over but not for long. Ten or fifteen minutes longer, and again she struggled to regain full control. To her surprise, it took an effort to try and open her eyes, but she persisted and when successful, a strong headache was her reward. She shut her eyes quickly, and this seemed to help ease the headache but not her sense of curiosity.

From her prone position, the first thing she saw was the grey cement ceiling which at one time had been painted white as the white strands of peeled paint hanging down suggested. The walls too suffered from the same dilemma. Looking about her, she first saw that she was wearing her white wedding dress and lying on a grey, striped kapok mattress stretched over an ancient iron bedframe. There were no windows in her place of confinement, and illumination was supplied from a single electric light bulb, centrally hanging from the ceiling.

"This must be some sort of a cellar," Susan thought, "Perhaps once a wine cellar. What am I doing here? How did I get here? I'm supposed to be getting married in half an hour!" She sat up in the bed and swung her legs over one side. A slight feeling of vertigo overtook her but cleared soon. In the far corner of the cellar Susan spotted an old woman sitting at a small table knitting. Surprised by this, she automatically let out a stifled cry.

"Oh! Who are you and what are you doing here?

"Ah ha, sleeping beauty is awake," the old woman observed in a very heavily accented voice, put down her knitting, and rose from her chair.

"Who are you and where am I?" Susan almost shouted.

"I am here to look after you and let boss man know when you are awake. My name is Rosa."

"Sure, but where am I and what am I doing here, I'm supposed to be in the church by now, getting married?"

"No, no, you don't get married, you in Ljubljana now, in Slovenia.

Soon you go into mountains."

"What! What are you talking about? I'm somewhere in Sydney about to get married. That's why I'm wearing this dress, see? My wedding gown."

"Sure, I see but you still in Ljubljana, in Slovenia and you no get married. Not today."

"This is some sort of a joke, right? I don't even know where Liu … lib … or Slovenia is!"

"No matter, you here."

"All right, why am I here?"

"Boss man will tell you. Now that you are awake, I go get him and oh!" the old woman reached for a carton under her table, "before I go, you take off wedding dress and put on these clothes. They should fit you good. I measured you while you still sleep."

Susan approached the table, removed the lid from the carton as well as the thin wrapping paper inside, and took out a neatly folded black acrylic skirt. She shook the skirt loose and held it by her side. It looked like it was made to fit just above her knee and was her exact size. Next to the skirt was a folded, pink chiffon blouse, almost see-through but not quite. Under the blouse lay a pair of black, slipper like shoes featuring a half high heel and by the look of them, brand new. Susan removed her right, white satin wedding shoe and tried on the slipper. It fitted perfectly. It was obvious the old woman knew what she was doing with a tape measure.

Susan looked at the wedding gown she was still wearing. By now it was a little crumpled and not at all practical for everyday activities, plus it was uncomfortable to wear when moving about. She decided to do as she was told and discarded the wedding outfit for her newly supplied wardrobe.

The old woman gathered up the wedding dress and proceeded to the cellar door. From a pocket in her long and loose woollen skirt she fished out a large, almost ancient looking key, and, unlocking the door, she left the cellar, locking the door behind her.

"Not too bad at all," Susan thought as she inspected herself, "it's certainly the right fit. I wish there was a mirror." Tucking her chin in, she tried to see as much of her bosom as she could. She noted the faint outline of her white bra. "Not too bad, I've been more daring before."

Having completed the wardrobe change, Susan began to inspect her surroundings. Not that there was much to see. A large cement hole, presumably underground. No window, just a steel air-vent in the ceiling. No sink or water tap and no toilet.

"What if I have to go to the toilet? What do I do then? Perhaps there is a chamber pot under the bed, let's see."

There was no chamber pot under the bed but there was a substantial bucket there with what looked like a splash of water in the bottom.

"What now? This can't be some sort of a joke. If it is, it's gone too far," Susan sat down on the bed pondering, "I can't be in Slov … Slovenia. I don't even know where that is? How did I get here and why? What the hell is going on? What did the old crone mean when she said, 'soon you go into mountains?' What mountains? Why would I want to go into the mountains? Just what have the mountains to do with anything? Hang on, maybe Ashley's in the mountains? Maybe Ashley concocted this whole thing up as a wedding of the year story. He does have a flair for the dramatic."

For a few short moments Susan let her imagination run away with her. A white wedding on a white, snow-capped mountain somewhere in Thredbo. The guests all rugged up and awestruck. Television news helicopter crews filming the wedding ceremony from above and reporters doing much the same thing at ground level. That would be quite a pageant. Suddenly, a thought flashed through her mind, 'The wedding dress, they've taken away my wedding dress!' she just realised but moments later let out a sigh of relief, 'of course, the dress was a bit crumpled. They are probably giving it a press now, so it looks good at the reception.' Satisfied with the explanation, Susan resumed her reverie.

The reception would be held in a ski lodge, the guests toasting the bride and groom, but instead of champagne they would be holding glasses of gluvine or hot rum toddies. Susan was warming to the thought. She took stock and examined herself. She was unhurt. There were no bruise marks on her, and she had no pain or any other major discomfort. Obviously, whoever was responsible for her abduction had made sure she was not injured in any other way.

"It's got to be something like that," Susan rationalised, "I'm not really in Slovenia, more than likely somewhere in The Snowy Mountains. I wish there was a window in this place so I could see outside!" These thoughts brought Susan some comfort but with that she also felt anger welling up inside her, "but why would Ashley do such a thing? Surely if he had wanted a wedding in the snow, he would have brought the subject up or at least hinted at it. But then again, Ashley loved flirting with danger, that's how we first met, hang gliding. Come to think of it, we didn't really bump into each other in the air by accident. I think Ashley engineered it, just to get to know me." Susan started to reconstruct that slight mid-air collision when she heard a key turn in the cellar door.

The old woman returned, holding the door open to let an elegantly dressed middle-aged man enter the cellar.

"Like I told you, sir, she awake and as you can see, all changed into the clothes you picked for her."

"Yes, thank you, Rosa," the man replied in almost a vintage Oxford, English accent. He was of average height, curly brown hair and an athletic build, "I see, Miss Susan, you have already learned how to obey orders by shedding that wedding gown. Good, hopefully this gets us off to a good start. My name is Mathew and from here on you will be my responsibility, taking orders from me and obeying them accordingly. I hope I'm making myself clear?"

"I don't know what you are talking about, and I don't much care," Susan lashed back, "and I'm not in the habit of taking orders from anybody let alone a stranger. Now, tell me just what the hell is going on here before I start ..." Susan didn't get to finish her retort. Mathew walked up to her and with an open hand slapped her in the face with a force so hard it sent her reeling to the floor.

"Obviously, I didn't make myself clear enough," Mathew said quietly and then bent down and slapped Susan again on the other side of her face, "Perhaps this will convince you and if not, I can keep this up for hours. Now get up and sit down and remember what I said. Here, I can be your best friend or worst enemy, the choice is yours."

Surprised and dumbfounded, Susan struggled to her feet and sat down on the chair next to the table.

"Who are you and why are you doing this? I don't know you from Adam."

"You soon will, my dear, it may take a little discipline but I'm sure we'll get there."

"What are you talking about? Discipline for what? And where is 'there? Where is Ashley and where is my dad? And just what the bloody hell is going on here? You have no right to …"

Again, Susan did not complete the sentence. Mathew moved quickly to the table and delivered another slap to Susan's face but this time with a little less ferocity.

"Keep this up, young lady, and you will soon become damaged goods, and I would hate to see that happen. Now, you may ask me questions but only one at a time. That is good discipline for beginners. I will decide if I want to answer it or not and I will decide as to whether to punish you or reward you. Let me stress that a quick slap on the face is the rock bottom mildest of punishments. Is this getting through to you? Are you clear on the rules so far?" Mathew shot an angry glare at Susan.

Susan did not reply, but, covering her cheek with one hand, nodded twice.

"Splendid! That answers your first question covering discipline as you've just had a mild taste of it. Now," Mathew went on, "I have no idea who Ashley is nor do I much care, but I assume your dad is still in Sydney wondering why you ran off."

Susan couldn't help interrupting Mathew, "What do you mean

'ran off?' I didn't run anywhere. I was drugged and forced to be here. You have no right to hold me ..." Susan let the sentence trail off as she noticed an angry look form in Mathew's dark brown eyes, "Sorry," she murmured, expecting another blow.

"Wonderful, you are a quick learner, and no doubt will settle down to our discipline very nicely. Now as to 'what the bloody hell is going on here?' Quite a lot actually, quite a lot. In about an hour or so a helicopter will call for you and you will be transferred to an Alpine spa in the mountains. This is actually an old monastery purchased by our syndicate and refitted to cater to every whim gentlemen of disposable means may desire. It is a little remote, and thus a helicopter is really our only mode of transportation."

"What has that got to do with me? I've never been in a spa or had any wish to visit one."

"You were not paying attention, my dear. I just explained to you that this is an exclusive spa for gentlemen of independent means who enjoy the better things in life and can and are willing to pay for them."

"I see," Susan replied, as she eagerly started to piece together the small strands of information passed on to her, "So I really am in Slovenia?"

"Of course, you are my dear. Where did you think you were, your Bondi Beach?"

"I still don't understand. What does Slovenia have to do with me or a spa for that matter?"

Mathew let out a small chuckle as he looked at Susan. "You can tell this one's from Australia," he thought to himself and then out loudly he continued, "a great deal, a very great deal actually. You and others like you are the cornerstone of our enterprise. Without you, we may as well pack up and go home. In a spa like this one, our clientele need, no, have to have, hostesses to service their needs. This is where you come in, you will hold the position of hostess."

"That's ridiculous. Surely you can find enough girls to work as hostesses locally. You don't have to abduct females for that?"

"If only that were so. Unfortunately, our clientele are very particular and demand variety. Variety in hair colour, in figure, in race and even nationality. Australian ladies are currently the flavour of the month. You are so far away and difficult to obtain, that's what makes it so interesting and desirable for them."

"I still don't understand, what's the difference between an Indian hostess and, well, an Australian one?"

"Since you ask? About $4000 US dollars an hour."

"You're kidding, $4000 and hour?" Suddenly Susan stopped. The whole thing was now becoming clear to her. The more she reflected on what had been said the clearer it became. She felt the blood drain from her face and became weak at the knees and ankles. "You mean forced prostitution, sex slaves, that's what this is all about?

"We prefer to use the term, 'hostess'. It has a much better ring to it and really, it's not such a bad deal, you will live in luxury, have access to a multitude of designer clothing and almost every mod con available. Regular and free medical check-ups and so on, plus stunning alpine scenery."

"Oh, how wonderful, all this just no freedom, no friends, no family and no future. What more could a girl desire."

"Look, I'm starting to get a little tired of this conversation. The chopper is due any minute, so we had better get you ready for the next stage of the trip."

"What do you mean, get me ready? The only trip I wish to undertake is the one home. I insist you release me and arrange for my return to Australia. My family and the Australian police will be looking for me and they're pretty good at finding people. Once home I promise I won't press any charges. Just let me go."

Mathew smiled as he replied, "Even if I were to release you, the Slovenian police would arrest you."

"Arrest me for what?" Susan interjected, "I've done nothing wrong here."

"You are an alien my dear. You don't have a passport. You can't travel anywhere."

"Then how did I get here without a passport?"

"In a coffin, my dear. Corpses don't need passports. Now let's get ready. Rosa, the needle!"

Rosa had been waiting for the order and had a hypodermic needle already in the palm of her hand. For an old woman she moved quickly and plunged the needle in Susan's shoulder. Susan hardly felt the prick.

***

The helicopter landed close to the cellar's outer door. Two men jumped out and entered the cellar, returning almost immediately carrying a stretcher with a blanket draped over it. Mathew was right behind them, and, as soon as the stretcher was aboard, he entered the chopper and signalled the pilot to take off. The whole operation took less than five minutes.

***

Detective Edward, or Eddy Pike as he was mostly called by his colleagues, stood at his office window on the fourth floor of the Police building, staring at the building across the street, but he wasn't looking at the edifice, more like staring through it. Too much time had passed since the Bauford abduction without a word from the abductors. The whole saga made no sense. What was the purpose of the kidnapping if no ransom or other demands were made? Possibly it could be a case of straight-out murder but why Susan? She had no known criminal connections, absolutely no love triangle complications as the 'wedding day snatching' would suggest, and even if this was the case, why abduct her when she could more easily be dispatched in the wedding car?

Then another thought entered Pike's mind. Perhaps contact was somehow made with her father, but he feared to tell the police and made his own arrangements to hand over whatever ransom was demanded. But then where was the victim? Killed as soon as the ransom was paid or if not, stashed away in some relative's place waiting for the hue and cry to die down? Possible but improbable. From what Pike had learned about Susan, she did not strike him as a person to agree to such a proposal and besides that, surely, she would want to be with her husband to be? On top of that Susan's father would have to be a very fine and skilled actor for Pike to fail to notice a change in Jim Bauford's attitude.

Two sharp knocks on the office door and detectives Phil Morrison and Annie Goodall entered the office without waiting for an invitation. They were the team selected to work with Pike in solving the 'Bauford Case.' Morrison because he was a bright young detective, and Goodall because it was felt by upstairs she could contribute by looking at things from a female perspective.

"You did say three o'clock, didn't you?" Morrison reminded Pike who was still staring out of the window.

"Yes, I did and thank you for being so prompt. I've been hounded ad-nauseam by upstairs for progress in the Bauford case, and I've run out of rabbits I can pull from a hat. I thought it best if we sit down and go over again all the details we have and look for something, anything we may have missed or anything we could investigate further."

"We've done this a dozen times already, Eddy," Morrison protested, "I for one, can't think of a single thing."

"I know, but let's go through it again. The vehicles used by the kidnappers, have they provided any more information? Soil samples, grass seeds, anything, anything at all?"

"Apart from them being stolen vehicles, very little and close to being nothing. Before they were dumped, they were very thoroughly cleaned. Two partial prints we found in the van turned out to be the owner's. I'd say that whoever nicked them wore gloves and kept them on all the time."

"OK," Pike continued, "Now I have a theory which I know will sound stupid, but I want you to listen to it and tell me honestly what you think. If you think it is crap, then just say so but listen anyway."

Pike then laid out his thoughts that Jim Bauford had paid the ransom and said nothing more to anyone.

"You know, Eddy," Morrison quietly said, "there just might be something in what you say. Let's face it, it is a possibility and from all the theories put forward, it's the only one that makes any sense. Why would the kidnappers wait so long before they even hint at wanting a ransom?"

"Well, I think it's a lot of crap," Anne Goodall joined in, "I saw Jim Bauford only yesterday, or rather he saw me and from the look of him, I'd say there's no way he knows his daughter is safe and sound. In more ways than one, he's getting worse as this thing drags on."

"Thank you, Anne, that was my immediate second thought, but something did happen to Susan and seeing there's no sign of a motive it could be that she is already dead, maybe due to overdosing on the knockout drug and thus depriving the kidnappers of their bargaining chip."

"I don't think so," Anne let out a sigh. "What makes you say that?"

"Look, this was no ordinary kidnapping. This was planned like a military operation. Planned and executed by professionals."

"OK but for what reason? Susan's no duchess or rich widow, she's just an ordinary, attractive Aussie girl, so why would anyone want to snatch her? What do they hope to get out of it?"

"I think you have just supplied a motive," Anne brightened up.
"Really! How?" Pike queried.

"You just said it, 'she's an ordinary, attractive Aussie girl,' you just said that."

"Sure, I said it, so what?"

"Just think for a moment. What would you do if you kidnapped a beautiful girl? I mean what would you do if you wanted to make a few bucks out of a young attractive girl?"

"You mean like become her pimp or sell her off to a brothel?"

"Something like that."

"You're crazy, there isn't a brothel in the country who would dare even to think of buying a sex slave."

"I agree with you there, sure, not in this country, but you've heard of the sex slave industry operating overseas."

"You're kidding, how would they get her out of the country, even if they managed to somehow sedate or hypnotise her and say they are taking her to Europe for specialist treatment. She didn't have her passport on her on the way to her wedding."

"Come off it, Eddy. People have been coming into this country without passports for decades. Where there's a dollar, there's a deal."

"I'm rather warming to Anne's suggestion," Morrison chipped in. "That would explain the lack of a ransom note or demand or contact of any kind."

"Sure, but all this professional activity for one girl?" Pike queried.

"Who said there's only one?" Anne asked. "Currently, there's seven missing young women from Perth, five from Adelaide, five from Darwin and if I recall correctly about eight from Sydney. None of them had such dramatic abductions as Susan and most are assumed to be girls who simply wanted to lose themselves and disappeared of their own free will."

"OK," Pike said somewhat resigned, "All of these are possibilities but then why select Susan and abduct her in such a public way? They could have more easily snatched a girl off the street or someone leaving a pub. Why go to the expense and risk of publicity, and let's face it, the snatching of Susan had to be a very expensive exercise?"

"I agree, Eddy, but Susan was who they had on their shopping list."

"Shopping list!" Pike retorted, "shopping list! What do you mean by that? What shopping list?"

"Just that and I believe this often happens. Look, let's for a moment imagine some super rich voyeur suddenly develops a lust for a young Nigerian woman with boobs the size of watermelons. By spreading a little money around, he would soon find a willing supplier. The supplier then hunts around for a suitable candidate, maybe ever two or three. He may even take a few discreet photographs and present them to his client and all things being equal, a contract is drawn up. The victim is then stalked and at the appropriate moment, snatched and before anyone can say, 'Jack Robinson', the girl is raped in the palace of some Sheikh or Emir or Wall St magnate and when no longer a novelty, she is sold off in a clandestine flesh market. These people have fetishes and enough money to feed them. To some of them, raping and enslaving a girl from Australia is a novelty, like another feather in their cap."

"I understand all that," Pike agreed somewhat reluctantly, "but Susan is hardly a big boobed Nigerian woman. Why would anyone select her? She's an Australian lass, living in Australia and thus shielded from the eyes of super cashed up voyeurs."

"Granted," Anne went on the defensive, "but she did attend university in Sydney."

"So what? She and a few thousand other girls."

"Correct again, but our universities are filled with the sons of many foreign magnates. Suppose one of these sons bumped into Susan and tried to hit on her but was rejected. Humiliated, he complains to daddy of his shabby treatment. Daddy considers this a gross insult and lets his son know that he will have his heart's desire and family honour will be salvaged."

"A bit far fetched," Pike commented, "but feasible I suppose. Stranger things have happened before. The next step then should be to contact Interpol and see if they can come up with more information."

"I already have," Anne quietly replied. "What! You have? Who authorised this?"

"No one officially. I have a friend who works for Interpol in Berlin. I was chatting on the phone to him the other night and the subject of Susan came up. The scenario I gave you was actually his, not mine."

"You do get around. How did you get to be hobnobbing with Interpol?"

"Quite easy and hardly hobnobbing. He's my brother-in-law. He married my sister Thelma three years ago, who now also works for

Interpol as a secretary."

"I see and I suppose, now, we'd better now contact Interpol on a more official basis."

CH 4 SPA SHANGRILA

The helicopter dropped altitude and began a lazy circle round the rugged crest of a mountain which was the base for a former monastery built by Italian monks during the early 1400's when their order for spiritual solitude was first established. From the air it almost resembled a castle with a solid wall erected around the perimeter. In the centre a large, two storey, stone building took pride of place with four single storey annexes running from the centre, blending in with the outer wall, forming a cross. At the wall archways were constructed in the annexes so that one could circumnavigate the mountain top freely. The courtyards between the annexes were cobble-stoned and one had a large, white circle painted on the stones. The helicopter pilot reached for his radio microphone and after making contact reported, "one large stretcher full of merchandise on board coming in. Have two men standing by."

"Already here and waiting. Come down at your leisure," was the only reply.

Pepe watched the helicopter bank and almost slide down until it was immediately above the buildings and then sink down almost vertically and land in the middle of the painted white circle below.

"Mario, Gaitano, let's go!" Pepe ordered in Italian. The three men left the building and walked quickly over the cobble stones, reaching the helicopter just as the main rotor shut down. The sliding side door opened, and, standing at the open door, Mathew called out to Pepe.

"Pepe, you jump in here and help me, and you two stand by and get ready to receive the stretcher."

Susan was still unconscious as she was manhandled out of the helicopter into the care of Mario and Gaitano.

"Is she all right boss?" Pepe asked Mathew. "She looks quite pale and tight round the eyes?"

"Yeah, she'll be all right in another half hour or so. The old crone in Ljubljana pumped the whole barrel of sleeping juice into her. I told her about half, but these monkeys don't listen, do they?" Mathew replied, "give her another half hour or so and she'll be all right. Oh, and when she comes to, make sure she eats something, anything she wants. She starts earning her keep tonight and I don't want her retching or passing out or whatever, understand?"

"Yes, boss, no problemo." Pepe acknowledged the directive and hopped out of the helicopter, ordering his two subordinates to bear the stretcher to its destination. They carried the stretcher to one of the two annex buildings and set it down on the bed in one of the eleven rooms in the annex.

"Now, let's just push her off the stretcher and onto the bed but be careful. No bruising, we don't want to damage the merchandise, eh?" Pepe ordered.

"This one's a real good looker," Gaitano observed as he took hold of Susan's feet, manoeuvring them from the stretcher, "nice legs too."

"Yeah, and just look at the tits. Nothing wrong with them," Mario agreed as he held Susan by the armpits and transferred her to the bed where he cupped his hands over Susan's pink blouse and fondled her breasts.

On seeing this, Pepe burst out, "Hey, Mario! What the hell do you think you are doing?"

"Just checking out the merchandise, she don't know from nothing, she's out cold."

"Knock it off compadre! She's valuable merchandise. For what you've just had our clients would shell out over 200 bucks. Want I should take it out of your pay?"

"Jesus, Pepe, just having a bit of fun.

"Fun nothing, with mitts like yours you'll bruise the merchandise and then we got damaged goods so just stop it."

"You know, Pepe, that's what shits me about this job. We're up here in the clouds and we aren't getting any and the stupid thing is that this is what this joint's all about. Do you ever think about that?"

"What if I do? Mr Mathew is quite democratic about it. Just save up some money and you can have as much nookie as it will buy. Now throw a blanket over her and we can get out of here. I still have to talk to the cook."

***

It was mid-afternoon when Susan opened her eyes. She first noticed the soft blanket covering her, and for the second time in a short space of time she went through the process of wondering where she was and what she was doing there. Slowly it started coming back, and it made her almost nauseous. She sat up in bed clutching the blanket to her chin and commenced to look around. At least this was better than her last awakening in the cellar. The room was large with a very high ceiling. What she presumed was the outer wall was solid rock with two glazed slits serving as a window. The other walls were rendered and hung with huge tapestries depicting hunting and garden party scenes. Sitting on the bed, she noted it was a mahogany, four-poster with a lace edged canopy, and a doorway almost next to it suggested an en suite bathroom. Near the left-hand corner of the outer wall was a very large and ornately carved timber wardrobe and a matching chest of drawers next to it. Turning her head more to the left she saw a display cabinet but could not see what it contained. Facing the entrance door was a leather lounge suite consisting of two leather armchairs and two settees encircling a large timber coffee table. Against the wall at the back of the suite was what unmistakably was a bar with four bar stools in front of it.

Susan dropped the blanket she was clutching, and, swinging her legs round to the edge of the bed, she let her bare feet touch the floor where a warm shag pile carpet greeted them. She sat on the edge of the bed for a short while somewhat bemused. Somehow, she expected this to be another concrete cellar, but this was something else. "Wow," she thought, "this must be where they keep royalty before cutting their heads off." Suddenly, the thought ceased to amuse her. She stood up, feeling a little giddy but only for a moment. Looking down on herself, she saw that she was still wearing the black skirt and pink blouse she was forced to don earlier and calculated that she could not have been unconscious for too long. She looked around the room again, this time making sure there was no one else present. Curiosity overcoming fear, Susan started exploring her surroundings. As the wardrobe was nearest to her, she started with that. Opening its wooden door, she expected it to be empty, but to her surprise it displayed a row of elegant female garments neatly hanging from the cross bar. There must have been at least twenty to thirty different outfits ranging from formal wear to street clothes. She took out a dress and held it against her. It looked as if it was tailored for her. Taking out a few more items convinced her that all were her size. Surprised, she turned to the dresser next to the wardrobe. Opening a top drawer, she found it was filled with female underwear, and on closer inspection she found that all the items were the same size, hers. The drawers displayed a selection of shoes, she tried a few, and to her surprise they fitted her almost perfectly.

"It looks like I've been expected," Susan mused as she turned round, and the bar at the other end of the room made its presence known. She walked over to it and entered the barman's capsule confronting a display of liquor any nightclub bar in Sydney would be proud to show off.

The display cabinet facing the bar was just that, a few statuettes and vases, but when opening the lower wooden doors, a large television set revealed itself as well as a cassette player and shelves containing a collection of cassettes. Susan shut the cabinet doors when something caught her eye in the corner of room nearest the cabinet. Approximately 180 cm from the floor two sturdy iron rings were cemented into the wall about 250 cm apart. Centred between the rings, from the ceiling, hung a swivelling, large iron hook. Looking at that hook, a shiver ran down Susan's spine, but she did not know why. The floor immediately below the hook was no longer carpeted but was covered in approximately two square metres of carpet-colour-matching, ceramic tiles.

"No doubt about it," Susan mused as she sat down in one of the leather lounge chairs, "not exactly Spartan is it? I wonder if that door is locked?" She got out of the chair and tried the door. It was not locked. Susan opened it slightly and peered out. All she could see was a dark, empty corridor either side of her. Her first impulse was to run either left or right and find her way out. She was about to do this when she stopped.

"Where am I running to?" the thought flashed through her mind. "I don't even know where I am, and I'll bet there is no police station just around the next corner." Reluctantly, she returned to the room and sat down in the same chair, tears welling in her eyes.

"I've got to get out of here. When I find out more about where I am, I'll find a way out." The thought renewed her spirits and she wiped away a tear, "there has got to be a way, there just has to be, there always is, I just have to find it."

***

Without a knock or warning the door opened and in came an elderly woman carrying an arm-full of white fluffy towels. Somewhere in her fifties and with greying hair, she had an aristocratic aura about her. She wore a grey dress which could have been taken for a uniform. In her younger days she would have been considered a great beauty, and even now she could win a heart or two.

"Good afternoon," she began in English, "my name is Patra, and I am your house mother."

"Oh! Hello, you mean my housekeeper?"

"No, I mean house mother, if I am housekeeper, I do as you say but I am house mother, so you do as I say."

"I see," Susan retorted slightly guardedly, "and what is it that you want me to do?

"Listen to and obey orders. Do that and we get on fine. First thing, in a few minutes you have food coming. You eat, you need strength. Anything you want to know you ask me, not the others. You want to talk to bosses like Mr Mathew, you ask me first. Understand?"

"Yes, I understand but can I ask you a question?"

"Ask!"

"Where am I?"

"You don't know? You're at the 'Spa Shangrila', a place for gentlemen of means to relax and recover their energies."

"Yes, but where exactly is Spa Shangrila?"

"You don't know? You didn't see when you fly here?"

"No, I didn't see anything! I was zonked out by some drug they pumped into me."

"Ha so, of course you were, I forget sometimes. You are in the Julien Alps in Slovenia."

"And this room! Why am I in this room?"

"This is your room for as long as you are here."

"Am I a prisoner here?"

"There are no prisoners here, only hostesses and staff."

"Then I can leave whenever I want to?"

"You can leave only when Mr Mathew say you can."

"So, I am a prisoner here!"

"No, I told you. Prisoners are criminal people who are put in jail. This is no jail. You can move about the place free. No one stops you."

"Yes, I noticed the door was unlocked," Susan probed, "so how do you know I won't run away?"

"Can you fly a helicopter?"

"No."

"So, where you going to go? The only way in or out of here is by helicopter. There used to be a road but that's been washed out many years ago. Ljubljana is hundred kilometres away. The first night out in the mountains the animals probably eat you, so you see, you're free to go."

Susan shuddered a little at the thought and quickly changed the topic of the conversation.

"If you say this is my room, then what are all those clothes doing in the wardrobe, they're not mine?"

"They are for you to wear when you are looking after our guests. Mr Mathew select them personally."

"How did he know my size?"

"That was easy, you got measured up good while you were sleeping, you know." Patra gestured, imitating a drugged person. "Then he select what he wanted from our general stock wardrobe."

"You have a stock wardrobe here, full of all different sizes?"

"Of course, we're not in city now. There are no shops to buy a dress from when you need one."

"No, I don't suppose there are. So, what happens now?" Susan asked.

"Now, very soon Pepe will bring you something to eat. Pepe is your man boss. You want to know or need anything you ask him or me. Only he's not allowed to touch you, you know what I mean? He try anything, you tell me right away, but I don't think he will. Pepe's a nice man, but with men you never know." Patra rose to her feet, indicating the chit chat was over and left the room.

***

Alone once more, Susan studied the room and then nervously walked over to the television cabinet. She tried to figure it out and succeeded but received only two channels, both of them broadcasting in a language totally foreign from her. She then investigated the cassette player and found it came complete with a radio. Twiddling with the station selector, she heard a lot of static at first but then the clear sound of music which she recognised was Mozart. Walking back to the four-poster bed, she sat down on it and surveyed it again.

The bed was solid, with the sides and ends timber clad to the two pull out drawers on each side. Susan pulled out one of the drawers to find it contained a number of nightgowns of different shades, all of them sheer, almost see through. The second drawer was empty.

On the other side of the bed the first drawer was empty. The second was full of surprises. There was a selection of leather straps and two short-handled whips with multiple short leather thongs attached to the handle. Next to them were four shiny metal handcuffs. A small shiver ran down Susan's spine as she lifted out a set of handcuffs. She had no doubt in her mind as to their usage. Another shiver followed as she replaced them and shut the drawer. Now more than curious, she inspected the headboard of the bed and found what she hoped she wouldn't. Two large U bolts were driven into the headboard equidistant from the centre and secured with lock nuts on the other side. The foot of the bed revealed nothing out of the ordinary.

Susan sat down on the edge of the bed thinking. Tears welled in her eyes as she thought about her immediate future. The door to her room was unlocked. Another thought entered her mind; she could go through that door, find the nearest spot and fling herself over the wall. The thought didn't last for long.

"What's the point," she rationalised, "they get a dead body and what do I get? I get to be dead and lose any chance of seeing these bastards get just punishment … no, that's not the way. I will survive this … no matter what … I will track these bastards down and I will kill them myself! Prison is far too good for them."

***

The door opened again, and a small trolley emerged with Pepe pushing it.

"Here some food for you, you eat, and when you finish you pull twice and I come and take it away."

"Thank you, but what do you mean, pull twice?"

"Oh! You don't know? OK I show you." Pepe went to the display cabinet and next to it showed Susan a long yellow sash cord which disappeared into the ceiling. "This one here, you pull down one times, and kitchen will know you are finished, OK?"

"Thank you, I will remember that."

"Good but remember, one times. If you pull only two time and no more, security will think there is trouble in room and come quickly. OK, you remember?"

"OK, I'll remember."

"Good, now you eat," Pepe ordered and left the room.

Susan inspected what the trolley had to offer. She lifted the warming covers and found that she had a small serving of what looked like eggplant, probably the entrée, she thought, and then a dish of lamb cutlets with some vegetables and a sauce. A small container of some sort of pudding sprinkled with grated chocolate. Covered in a tea cosy, a small kettle was also on the trolley plus the cutlery and condiments needed for a meal.

"Not bad," Susan thought, "much better than I expected. She wheeled the trolley over to the one and only timber upright chair in the room and sat down to eat. After the first mouthful, Susan realised just how hungry she was. On reflection, she tried to remember her last meal. Breakfast, she suddenly recalled. Breakfast on her wedding day.

"What day is it now?" she wondered as she voraciously devoured her meal. "What time is it now?" was the next question. She looked at her left wrist only to discover her watch was no longer there. Looking up at the window-slits she could see it was still daylight, which didn't tell her much. She sipped her tea, and to her surprise it tasted much the same as the tea back home. Again, the thought came to her that she really was home, and all this was some sort of fantasy, an illusion, but recalling the slapping Mathew had given her earlier and her present surroundings soon dispelled that thought.

Finishing her tea, Susan felt much revived. Remembering Pepe's words, she walked over to the hanging sash and gave it an angry yank.

***

In less than ten minutes the door opened once more, and Mathew entered the room followed by Patra and Pepe.

"Ah, the lady has a preference for Mozart," Mathew remarked, referring to the music coming from the radio, "Very commendable."

Pepe went straight to the trolley and, after a quick tidy up, pushed it out of the room. Mathew went to one of the reclining chairs and sat down, beckoning Susan to do the same. Patra remained standing.

"So how was your dinner? Satisfying I hope!" Mathew asked.

"It was fine, thank you," Susan muttered a reply.

"Good, now we can get you prepared for the rest of the evening."

"Prepared? What do you mean, prepared? Prepared for what?"

"You'll see soon enough. Patra! Get the lady's wardrobe ready please. You know the requirements."

Without answering, Patra went to the wardrobe and started rummaging through the hanging garments.

"This evening you will be hostess to one of our guests right here in your room, and I am here to instruct you on the rules of your behaviour. Do you understand me so far?"

Susan felt a lump of revulsion at the back of her throat. She gritted her teeth but said nothing.

"Like that is it then?" Mathew sounded a little miffed. "Never mind, they all do at first, but they all succumb to the reality and believe me. Given a bit of time it's not so bad and can be quite pleasant. So, Susan, look at me as I explain your duties. Susan, I said look at me!"

Susan sat there with her head lowered and said nothing. "Susan, look at me or would you rather enjoy some pain I'm ready to inflict on you?"

Susan was quite rigid, but she did look up at Mathew.

"That's better, now that wasn't so hard, was it? Now listen carefully. Our guest, your guest, is your master and your boss and at all times you will obey his wishes. You are his slave and concubine, and you will do as he tells you no matter how much it upsets you. If he wants to fart in your face, you will let him. If he wants you to lick his balls, you will do so. If he wants you to drink you will drink. You will sing, dance, do a strip, whatever. You will do this, and you will have a smile on your face. Do you understand that?"

Susan did not answer but nodded ever so slightly.

"Good, our guests, too, have rules. Thy are not allowed to physically hurt you or draw blood. They must never leave bruise marks anywhere on your body. If they do, you must report this straight away to Patra. Now is that clear?"

Susan sat there as if in a trance but nodded slightly.

"Good," Mathew said quietly, "Petra, have you got Susan's outfit ready?"

Patra came over and laid out some clothes on the coffee table. A flesh coloured, almost see-through blouse, a pair of long, purple, silk pantaloons which billowed out at the ankles and a pair off-white, silk slippers with toes that curled upwards almost into a question mark.

"Now you take these and put them on," Mathew ordered, "just these and no underwear, and put a comb through your hair and leave it long."

"I don't have a comb."

"Go into the bathroom, you'll find everything you need in there. A touch of makeup won't go astray either nor will a bit of jewellery. Patra will give you a hand."

Patra gathered up the clothing and, taking Susan by the elbow, steered her towards the bathroom. Mathew got up and went to the bar where he poured himself a neat cognac and sipped it as he waited. A few minutes later Susan and Patra emerged from the bathroom.

Mathew studied Susan for a moment, "My but don't you look like an Arabian princess," he commented, sipping his brandy, "Your host will be pleased."

Susan felt embarrassed standing there on display in a virtually see-through costume, but as there was nothing she could do about it, she resigned herself for the worst.

"Your host will be here shortly," Mathew informed her, "So, remember, behave yourself well and there will be rewards, but play up and be uncooperative and there will be repercussions like, well, you don't even want to know right now. I suggest you have a stiff brandy or two while you wait. It will settle the nerves."

***

Susan sat on the side of the bed watching the door, dreading to see it open once more and contemplating at what was to follow. She wasn't a virgin, having had two sexual encounters during her university days but these were by choice, not what was virtually by force. The thought of a stranger coldly fondling her body and then entering her would take some getting used to. Maybe a brandy or two might be of help.

She went to the bar and found herself a brandy balloon. Filling the glass to almost the half level, she resumed her spot on the bed. She sipped and waited. The glass was nearly empty, but the door remained closed. The brandy seemed to do its work and she poured herself another one, equally as full. Still the door remained closed. Maybe no one would come. Maybe this was just a ruse to prepare her for later. Maybe, maybe. Then the door opened, and a tall Arabic young man entered the room. Susan looked at him in disbelief.

"Good evening, Susan, nice to see you again," the young man said as he entered the room.

Hearing him speak, Susan's jaw dropped, and she stammered, "Akim," she managed to blurt out, "Akim? Is that really you? Have you come to get me out of here?"

"Of course, it's me, the same Arab boy who taught you how to hang-glide. The same Arab boy you didn't want to know. I was the one who had you brought here. I'm hardly the one to get you out of here although I can if I want to."

"What! What are you saying? You brought me here? How? I don't understand!"

"I know you don't, so I will explain. I taught you how to hang glide, am I right?"

"Yes, but what has that got to with anything?"

"A lot. I taught you, and under my teaching you became quite good at it and what did I get for it? You didn't even say thank you."

The words stung Susan like a wasp's barb. She quietly moved over to the living area of the room and sat down on a recliner chair. "Of course, I did, I remember very well and not only once, I thanked you several times."

"Yes, in words, but I did not teach you in words, I taught you in deeds, in action."

"So, I don't understand. What do you mean?"

"I mean this; I taught you and even gave you a glider, one of my best, but when I asked you to go out with me, you refused."

"Yes, I remember that but that was never a part of the deal. I never said, teach me how to hang glide and I will go out with you. Had you made that one of the conditions I would have said no. Thank you for the offer but no."

"Because I'm an Arab in your all-white, snooty land."

"Akim, you know that had nothing to do with it. I don't care if you were a German or an Aztec Indian. You were just not my type, that's all."

"Ah, but that Ashley, he was your type, but don't forget it was through me that you met him."

"In a way, I suppose so but so what? Things simply happen this way. It's not like it was planned or anything."

"I'm not suggesting that. What I'm saying is that I did you a favour, and in my country when you do someone a favour that favour must be returned by another favour as soon as possible."

"Then why did you not explain that in the beginning?"

"There was nothing to explain. Everybody knows that."

"This is getting us nowhere," Susan surmised, "You said before you had me brought here. Why?"

"To teach you a lesson."

"What lesson and what have you to do with this place?"

"The lesson of humility, and my father is a shareholder in this place."

"All right, you have brought me to this place, and believe me I have been humbled. You also mentioned you could get me out of here. Please, get me out of here. I promise I won't say anything to anybody. Please!"

"I also said, if I want to."

"Please, I want you to want to. Haven't you punished me enough? You've proved your point. You've got your revenge, so will you please put an end to this? Please!"

Akim walked over to the bar in silence and, finding a bottle of scotch, poured himself drink. Susan watched in amazement and momentarily forgot her plight.

"I always thought that Arabs don't drink alcohol?" Susan remarked in a quiet tone.

"In public we don't but this is private, so private in fact that I need a little pick me up to see me through this discussion." Akim up-ended the glass.

"There's no discussion needed. I just want to get out of here," Susan pleaded.

"That can be arranged but there are conditions."

"What do you mean conditions? I have nothing to offer you. I have nothing, even these clothes I'm wearing don't belong to me."

"I am aware of that, seeing I selected them myself. I must say you look very charming and sexy in them."

"So that's it. You want to fuck me. Is that what you want?"

"When you say it like that, that is what I want but it is not a condition. I can fuck you when I want to, where I want to and how I want to, whenever it pleases me. I want a little more than that."

"You see me as I stand here. I have nothing left to offer," Susan replied humbly.

"Oh, but you have, my dear, you have lots more to offer."

"Like what?"

"Like offering me your hand in marriage."

Susan felt as if an electric charge of a high voltage had just passed through her body. Total disbelief at first, then followed by a nauseous spasm.

"Is this some sort of Arab humour? Are you making some sort of fun of me?"

"Hardly, my dear. You want out and I'm offering a way out."

"You can't be serious, first you get me in here and now you offer me a way out. That doesn't make any sense! Plus, you're an Arab and I'm a Christian!"

"Allah has provided a way round that. The reality is that from the first day I saw you at Uni I wanted you and I tried my utmost to get you, but you didn't want to know. I thought teaching you how to fly might get me closer, but no way. Then the idea came to me. If I can't get you in your place, I will get you in mine. So, what do you say?"

"I'm still trying to process the whole thing. For me to get out of here I have to marry you and what then? Do we buy a laundromat business in Sydney and live happily ever after?"

"Not quite like that. First of all, we would live in my palace in my country."

"You have a palace?"

"Of course, not as big as my father's, but when he dies it will be mine. Just a couple more years to wait."

"And what shall I be doing at this palace? Scrubbing the floors and picking up the camel dung for the cooking fires?"

"No, no," Akim said aghast, "nothing like that. You will be my number one wife and take charge of the servants."

"What do you mean your Number one wife? Have you got any others?"

"Only two, but they are nothing to me. They are business, political marriages arranged by my father."

"You have two wives, and you want to make me number three?"

"No, you will be number one. You don't understand. Westerners generally don't. My two wives are more like my servants, and as my number one wife they would be your servants as well. Allah says it is all right for a man to have more than one wife, but the wives are more like servants."

"I see, and do you have sex with your servants?"

Akim was a little taken aback by the question. "What do you mean?"

"I think it's pretty plain what I mean. Do you have sex with your two wives? I mean, do you fuck them?"

"Them, yes of course, I thought you meant the other servants."

"And if I became your third wife, would you still fuck the other two?"

"Well, I suppose, yes. It is my duty to keep them happy. It is Allah's wish."

"So, I would be your number one concubine and the others two and three?"

"No, you don't understand. It is you I want. It is you I wanted from the first moment I saw you. I want you to believe that."

"Oh, I believe that. Your every action so far backs that up," Susan replied, but running parallel in her mind was that all this banter was not going to help get her out of her present predicament. She thought of trying a different approach. "Akim I really believe you, but don't you see this will never work. We are from two totally different cultures. We think and believe in totally different things. The best thing you can do is to get me out of here. I'll forget this thing ever happened and we can still remain friends. Will you do that for me, please?"

Akim was still standing at the bar and was obviously thinking as he poured himself another drink.

"If I were to get you out of here, I would have to buy you back from Mr Mathew."

"What! You sold me to Mathew?" Susan interrupted him.

"It was a business arrangement but let me continue. I would have to buy you back. Say I would be prepared to live in Sydney with no other women, would you then marry me?"

For a moment there was a silence as Susan considered the proposal and then spoke.

"That wouldn't be possible."

"Why not?"

"Because you already have two wives, and under Australian law you are allowed only one. You would be charged with bigamy and sent to prison, and the marriage would be declared illegal and dissolved." As soon as she uttered these words, Susan regretted having said anything at all. It was the lawyer in her talking.

"I see," Akim said gravely. "That leaves us with only one option. You want to get out of here, then you will marry me here, right in this building, and we will go to my palace where you will be installed as my third wife."

Susan felt trapped and wished she had never said anything, especially about Australian law. She knew that back at home, even if she did marry Akim here, the marriage would not be recognised, and if Akim was in Sydney he would be spending his nights in Long Bay Jail rather than her bedchamber. She also knew that to become Akim's concubine she would be trading one jail for another. She knew enough about eastern harems to know that at best they are gilded cage prisons, and at worst they are just another term for female slavery.

"Akim, do you know what you are doing? Please reconsider your actions."

"There is nothing to reconsider. I have given you my terms."

"Yes, and by doing so you have turned yourself into a criminal, an international criminal at that."

"Me, a criminal, you must be joking!"

"It's no joke, Akim. First you arrange to have me kidnapped. That's a crime in every civilised nation on earth. Then you have me sold into sexual slavery to be raped by anyone who can afford it. That's even a bigger crime, and now you want to force me into becoming your sex slave. All up, any court in the civilised world would imprison you for life without the possibility of parole."

"You're talking a lot of nonsense. In my country this goes on all the time, and nobody bothers about it."

"Maybe not in your country but this is Slovenia, and the kidnapping took place in Australia. Add to that the illegal transportation of a human being, and all that adds up to an international crime and makes you an international criminal."

"So, I'm an international criminal now? How interesting." Akim chuckled. "Well, it looks like you don't like my terms, so I had better get what I came for in the first place. The time for talking is over, so now get onto the bed."

"No. Go to hell."

"What do you mean, no? Round here there is no such word. Now get onto the bed, or I will throw you on it."

"No!" Susan stood up and made a bolt for the door. Akim, who was standing near the bar, anticipated this and dashed to the door, blocking Susan's way.

"I'll say this one more time, get on the bed!"

Susan backed back a few steps, and when she was level with the bar, she grabbed the bottle Akim had used by the neck and smashed it against the hard marble top of the bar. The neck of the bottle remained in her hand with the angry shards of sharp, broken glass pointing towards Akim.

"So, what are you going to do with that?" Akim laughed, "Kill me? No, I don't think so."

"If you so much a touch me, and I'll stick this bottle in your face as hard as I can," Susan snarled.

"So, the kitten wants to scratch … you know, I've got a better idea." Akim carefully circled around Susan towards the curtains and display cabinet. He gently took hold of the hanging sash and pulled on it twice, "I think we'll have some company, any minute now."

Both parties stood, still squaring off but not saying a word. After what seemed like a long time but was only a few minutes, the door flew open, and Mathew entered the room flanked by Pepe and Mario carrying a small box. Mathew immediately noticed the broken bottle Susan was still holding.

"Looks like we have a touch of uncooperative behaviour," Mathew observed. "Are you all right, Akim?"

"Sure, I'm OK, but she could have done a bit of damage with that thing."

"I agree, nasty looking thing. Pepe!"

Pepe needed no further instructions. He went over to Susan and gently removed the bottle neck from Susan's grasp. Susan made no protest.

"Well, it looks like a little bit of corrective stimulation is called for in this situation, Pepe!"

Again, Pepe needed no further prompting. He walked over to the bed and came back with two pairs of handcuffs which he attached to Susan, one on each arm.

"Mario!" was all that Pepe said. Mario too knew exactly what was to be done, as he and Pepe dragged Susan over to the wall near the door. Susan looked up at the wall and saw the two steel rings she had noticed earlier. Now she knew their purpose.

"What are you going to do?" she asked fearfully as the corresponding ends of the handcuffs were inserted into the rings.

"We're going to make you a nicer person," Mathew replied, "Pepe, plug in Zippo, you know what to do."

"OK, Mr Mathew, at what setting do you suggest?"

"Try half power for starters, we'll see how she reacts."

"Your using Zippo?" Akim asked, a little amazed, "Why not the whip?"

"Akim, you have not been listening. I've told you a hundred times, whips are history. They bruise the merchandise and leave scars which take weeks to heal and most of our guests don't like the puss and the blood that sometimes dirties the sheets. With Zippo we get the same results without any mess, and it leaves no scars."

Akim watched quite fascinated as Pepe opened the box Mario was carrying. An electric lead was removed and plugged into a wall socket and another expanding lead had one end plugged into the box and the other end attached to what looked like a gun handle with a few flat needles protruding from what should have been the barrel. A trigger, just like the one on a handgun, complemented the handle.

First, Pepe approached Susan and pulled out the blouse from the pantaloons she was wearing and worked the blouse up to her neck, exposing her bare back. He then grasped the gun handle and placed the needle pack in the middle of her back. Pepe looked at Mathew who simply nodded. Pressing the trigger, he sent a wave of electrical current into Susan's middle back, causing her to writhe as the shock passed through her body. She would have cried out, but she couldn't, the electricity affecting her vocal cords. All she could manage was a barely audible groan. Pepe changed the administration point to her lower back to avoid possible burn marks.

The procedure and reaction of this form of punishment greatly excited Akim. It was as if he was deriving sexual pleasure from it.

"Do you think Pepe would mind if I had a go with Zippo? After all, it was me she was going to cut up with that bottle."

"Go for it! Pepe won't mind at all. I know for a fact that it's this part of his job he hates the most."

Akim made his way to where Pepe was and motioned that he would like to take over. Pepe looked at Mathew who nodded.

"OK, Mr Akim, you got it but keep moving it about, don't stay too long in one spot."

"Can I increase the dose?"

"You can but not on this one, much more and she die, and Mr Mathew don't like dead merchandise."

The whole torturous procedure lasted almost half an hour when Pepe called for a halt.

"Mr Akim, you stop now. She almost unconscious. Next thing, she die."

Reluctantly, Akin did as he was told.

"Well, that's that for the night," Mathew concluded, "Let's take her down and dump her in bed."

"Hang on, leave her there for a bit. I'll take her down in a couple of minutes, so you guys don't have to hang around," Akim suggested.

"As you wish, she's your date," Mathew responded, and after packing up Zippo the three of them walked out, leaving Akim with

Susan still spread eagled against the wall.

"So now you know how the system works," Akim said to Susan from the bar where he opened another scotch bottle and took a swig without looking for a glass. Susan's only response was a barely audible groan.

"You think this is over? Well, it's not over yet. I came here for a reason, and I'm not leaving until that is satisfied. He made his way over to the wall and put his hands on Susan's hips, gripping the sides of her pantaloons. In one sweeping movement he pulled them down to the floor level. Unbuckling his belt and sliding down his zipper, he let his trousers fall to the floor. Then, after a bit of shuffling about, he entered her and took her from behind.

It wasn't the best sex he'd ever had but he was satisfied. He'd shown her who was boss, satisfying his long-lasting dream to have sex with Susan. Maybe not in the best possible way, but the achievement was there, never mind the circumstances or the method. His only lament was that in his frenzy he had scraped and bruised his knuckles on the stone wall while squeezing her breasts as he was ravishing her.

Having dressed himself, he thought of leaving her there and have a staff member take her down, but then he remembered his words to Mathew, 'I'll take her down in a couple of minutes.' This was virtually a promise, and a real man never breaks his promise to another man.

CH 5. SOFT PILLOWS IN A STONE CAGE

The bed was very soft and comfortable but not capable of inducing sleep. Although there were no real physical effects from the electric current passed through her body, the pain Susan felt spreading through her came from the humiliating rape Akim had subjected her to. She still felt his angry thrusts into her and the degrading feeling she experienced. She was enraged with hate and loathing for him. The many times she reasoned with herself that there was nothing she could have done to avoid this brought little solace. The feelings of anger, disgust and violation lingered throughout the rest of the night.

Dawn was already in progress when Susan finally drifted off into what could be best described as exhausted semi-consciousness, but this state did not last long. She didn't know how or why, but some instinct made her feel she was not alone in the room. Opening her eyes, she saw the back of a man bending over a trolley. She must have made some sort of a noise as she reached for the silk dressing gown at the foot of the bed, because the man quickly spun around.

"Good, you awake," he said as he moved to one side of the trolley exposing some crockery and cutlery. "I bring you breakfast. First week here you get room service. Then when you OK, you eat in dining room with others, capiche?"

Susan studied the man, who looked vaguely familiar, then she remembered. It was Mario. She now recalled him fairly clearly. He had been with Pepe and another man when she was brought here. "Don't you people ever knock before entering a room?"

"No, no knock, is not allowed, er, how you say, is against rules."

"That's ridiculous, it's only good manners. Have your rule makers ever heard of good manners?"

"Si, but not for here, here rule is, no knock."

"I see, so anyone can just waltz in."

"How you mean 'waltz'?"

"Without knocking, you know, just barge in!"

"Oh no, not anyone, senorita. This special place, like er, er reception. Here only Pepe, Patra, and me allowed and Mr Mathew. When you OK, you go join others in south wing."

"Who are the others?"

"The ladies of course."

"Really! How many other ladies?"

"I don't count, maybe fifteen, maybe twenty. Why you ask?"

"Just curious."

"Well, you be curious no more. You ask too many questions. You eat breakfast and when you finish, pull cord once and I come to collect trolley," Mario was getting a little irritated as he spun round and left the room.

The breakfast trolley remained in the middle of the room. Susan stared at it for a while and then got up and wheeled it nearer to the bed and inspected the contents. It was a substantial offering; orange juice, cereal, several varieties of bread, scrambled eggs and bacon, two containers of marmalade and a cup of coffee. She didn't feel hungry but sipped a little of the orange juice and then finished the rest of it in two gulps. Her appetite returned to her in a rush. She was hungry. Devouring the scrambled eggs with relish, she spread the marmalade on the rest of toast and poured out the coffee. Thoughts of last night's events flooded her mind. So Akim was responsible for her present plight. The thought of becoming Akim's wife number three made her nauseous. How could he possibly hope that she would agree. Yet what was the alternative? There has to be some way out, there just has to be. As these thoughts raced through her mind the door opened, and Mathew entered the room followed by Patra and Mario.

Susan stiffened and braced herself instinctively feeling that this was not a social call.

"I see we've had a hearty breakfast," Mathew commented, as he inspected the trolley. "Good, we must keep our strength up, mustn't we?"

"Keep my strength up for what?"

"The work you were bought here to perform."

"You mean forced prostitution?"

"I don't like that word, my dear, I prefer 'courtesan'. Prostitutes are paid money, you, on the other hand, are not. Now I hope there will be no repeat performance of last night but that's up to you. You've had a taste of what's to come and believe me, that was just a small sample. We have many more ways of obtaining your full cooperation. Now here is your agenda for the rest of the day. Up to 3.00pm your time is your own. You can watch television or whatever. Lunch will be served at noon. At 3.00pm you will receive a visitor, an old Egyptian patron of ours especially selected, as he is not very demanding. You will address him as Mr Ali at all times unless, of course, he wants you to drop the Mr. Patra here will select your wardrobe. Then, at eight o'clock, you will entertain another guest, one you already know, Akim."

"What! Akim? I never want to see him again!"

"That may be so, but he seems to be quite taken with you, and that is all that matters. Now I must warn you. Any repeat of last night's performance and what you experienced then will be like a pin prick by comparison. I hope I have made myself absolutely clear?"

Susan remained silent, disgusted by what she had just heard. "What's that, my dear?" Mathew asked somewhat sarcastically, "I did not hear you say anything?"

"What would you like me to say?"

"I would like to hear you say that you have got the message and from now on you will cooperate with our patrons and be nice to them in every way."

"Mr Mathews," Susan addressed him as Mr, as did all his staff, "we have a saying in Australia that you can force a couple to marry but you can't force them to love the child."

"How philosophic of the Australians, but a waste of words here.

Besides there will be no child, not here anyway. With your breakfast you consumed enough contraceptive medicine to last a week."

"What! You laced my food?"

"No, we laced our food, you simply ate it. You must realise that a pregnant courtesan is of no use to us and therefore has to be disposed of in an untraceable manner."

Susan remained silent, shocked by Mathew's words but a little relieved from the thought of not falling pregnant.

"I will leave you now and hope I won't have to return later with more persuading toys. Patra will sort out your wardrobe for the afternoon and evening. You are to be ready a quarter of an hour before the appointed time. Come Mario, and take that bloody trolley with you. The damn thing should have been back ages ago."

"But, Mr Mathew," Mario protested, "she no pull the cord!"

"All right, just grab it and let's go."

***

Patra went to the wardrobe and started rummaging round the hanging garments. Having made her choice, she placed the articles on the bed. "This is a nice fully flared green skirt. This is for Mr Ali."

"Mr Ali likes to wear women's skirts?" Susan asked, regaining some of her lost sense of humour.

"No not. Mr Ali likes western women and the way they dress and especially blond, like you."

"I see, and what else does Mr Ali like?"

"He like western underwear, the bubbly, er, frilly type. I show you," Patra went to the chest of drawers and returned, "here, this pink petticoat, see how bubbly, er, frilly this is and this pink blouse. Almost see through but then not. This drive him crazy. Plus, you wear black breast holder and stockings. He go crazy."

"I certainly hope that's not going to happen."

"No, no. Not crazy like …" Patra held her index finger next to her temple and made circular motions. "Crazy like, er, like soft bread dough. No, Mr Ali very nice older man, everybody like him."

"Everybody but me," Susan thought to herself.

"Now, Mr Akim like what you had on last night so that fixed."

"Will I be virtually nailed to the wall again as I was last night?" Susan asked.

"I don't know, Mr Mathew say nothing to me about that, but Mr Ali probably tie your hands to the bed, he like that."

"I thought you said he was a nice man."

"He is, everybody like him and … oh! I see what you mean. Don't worry, he no hurt you, not Mr Ali."

Susan shrugged. "That's good to hear," she murmured.

"Now," Patra collected herself, "at three o'clock Mr Ali will be here at three o'clock and you must put on these clothes before he come, understand?"

Susan shrugged again and slightly nodded.

"Good," Patra continued, "Mr Ali drink no alcohol but he like orange juice. The bar fridge has plenty of that. He also like dried dates and Spanish anchovies, also in bar fridge."

"What, dates and anchovies at the same time? You're kidding, that's like sugar and salt mixed together."

"Sure, but that what Mr Ali like and that what Mr Ali get. So, when he here, you offer him what he like. Now, at eight o'clock you got Mr Akim and you already know what he like but please, not like last night, not good. Mr Mathew very angry and when he angry, no good for everybody."

"What do you mean?" Susan asked, "does he take his anger out on the staff?"

"Something like that. Last year one lady no want to cooperate at all. He, er, how do you say more than hurt?"

"You mean like torture?"

"Yes, that right, he torture her but no good, she just say no and no. So, he get Pepe and Mario and they throw her over the wall. Pepe and Mario never do anything like that before and they don't like it but he say do it or join lady over the wall."

"What! They threw her over the wall alive?"

"Yes, but not for long. Is a long way down and there are rocks everywhere. I think she die as soon as she hit ground."

"And did they just leave her there without checking whether she was dead or alive?"

"Yes, but not for long. Next day she was gone."

"How do you mean gone? Like crawled away or something?"

"More like drag away by bears or wolves, who knows? Next day she no longer there."

Susan felt a cold current run down her spine. At first, she thought Patra was telling her this in order to intimidate her, but the flat, nonchalant way she told the story convinced her that this was not the case.

"I go now," Patra announced, "Remember the things on bed you wear before three o'clock and the things on chair, before eight o'clock and for your own sake, do as our patrons tell you and oh! Here is your watch, someone took it off you when you fly here, I don't know why, we are not thieves here. I made it show Slovenian time, see." Patra handed Susan the small ladies' Omega timepiece and left.

***

Left alone, Susan inspected her quarters again, but nothing had changed. She fiddled with the television set and finally got a picture and sound, but it was all in a language she didn't understand.

"Watch television," the man said. "There's nothing to watch just foreign gibberish." Then, quickly, she realised that she was the foreigner here. "They must have cable or satellite, surely? There must be a TV program somewhere?" But search as she did, she couldn't find one.

There were no books or magazines in her quarters or any other items to stave of boredom. Rummaging through every drawer, she could find she found nothing of any interest. She knew her front door was not locked, and on impulse she went to it as if to test it. The heavy timber door was open, and Susan stepped past it into the dark corridor. Everything was much the same as it was last night when she first explored her surroundings, but the corridors must lead to somewhere. Then she realised she was only partly dressed in a dressing gown. Hurrying back to the bedroom, she found the clothes she had worn on arrival and changed.

Back at the corridor a thought flashed through her mind. "What if someone sees me?" Then, "What if they do? What are they going to do to me, escort me back to the room and then maybe lock the door? That would please Mario no end." To her right a lot of daylight streamed into the corridor, and she began walking towards it. After a few metres she came to a corner, and, turning right, the corridor opened to a pathway with a waist high stone wall acting as a protector from falling into the abyss below. A panoramic view of the Julian Alps came into view.

Susan crossed over to the protector wall and gazed out at the mountain crags almost in awe. She had visited the Australian Snowy Mountains a few times, which were very nice and picturesque but palled into insignificance when compared to what was confronting her. Looking down over the protecting wall was even more confronting. A sheer drop of several hundred feet or so, she estimated. Patra's report of a girl being thrown over the wall came back to her, and momentarily she linked her own fate to that of the past victims. Imagining the horror of being hurled over that wall if she did not cooperate was enough to bring on a small attack of nausea. She thought of her appointment with Mr Ali at 3.00pm. Surely, they would not throw her over the wall if she resisted his advances. No, they would simply torture her at first and then throw her over the wall.

"What shall I do?" Susan asked herself, "Either way. I can't win." Then something she said earlier to Mathew entered her mind, 'you can force them to marry but you can't make them love the child'. That may be it. They can rape me, but they can't force me to enjoy it." The thought fermented in her mind, and a solution of sorts was developing. "If I obey all the instructions but remain deadpan the whole time, they can't accuse me of not being cooperative, it's just the way I am. If I am asked to lie down, I will do just that and no more. I will not speak unless spoken to." She seemed to be making progress but then an alarming thought struck her, "But what if I am asked to perform fellatio on them?" The thought almost made her sick. "I suppose I will just have to do it, just go through the motions and think about something else, pretend they have stuck their index finger in my mouth. What's the difference, really? Besides, their finger is more likely to be dirtier than their prick especially when you consider what's under the fingernail."

For some considerable time, Susan struck up mental images of what could happen to her and how she would react. The main thing on her mind was survival. No matter what, she had to survive and investigate any and every opportunity of escaping. She looked over the wall at the rocky ground below. "That would be one way but only with a parachute," she mused. "I wonder if helicopters carry parachutes? Yeah, but once on the ground, then what?" She remembered Patra's mentioning the presence of bears and wolves. No wonder the place was not teeming with armed guards, the bears and wolves performed that service admirably and at no cost.

A cold breeze found its way from the from the peaks of the Julian Alps, still snow covered even though it was practically mid-summer. Susan shivered a little and drew her elbows closer to her body. The summer blouse she was wearing did little to keep the wind out. She decided to return to her quarters, as there was nothing more to be accomplished outdoors. As she walked through the door, she was surprised to see Mario in her room.

"Where you been?" Mario demanded, "I bring lunch but you no here." Mario stepped to one side and revealed the trolley behind him.

"It's not lunchtime yet, Mr Mathew said one o'clock!"

"Is lunchtime when I say is lunchtime. You eat now and then get ready. Patra will come and look at you, and if you not ready big trouble, capiche?"

Susan said nothing but approached the trolley and wheeled it to where she was going to eat.

"Good, you eat now and when finish, you pull cord once. As soon as you finish, capiche?"

"Yeah, yeah, I capiche."

"Good," Mario commented as he turned to leave the room and as he reached the door he turned, "Remember, you go pull cord once as soon as you finish, OK?"

"Fine, OK, whatever you say."

"Good, I go now," Mario replied as he left the room.

Somewhere in the back of her mind Susan recalled that for a lot of countries in Europe lunch was the main meal of the day. Slovenia it seemed, was no exception. On offer was a soup with dumplings in it, a stew that looked like Irish Stew but tasted nothing like it, two sausages on a bed of mashed vegetables, slices of rye bread, some biscuits filled with nuts which looked more like cakes, a pot of coffee and a small container of honey. Susan sampled a bit of everything but devoured the stew with relish. If nothing else, it looked like she would be well fed.

Wiping her lips on the provided embroidered, cotton napkin, she walked over to the wall where the sash was hanging and gave it a hefty tug, once only. Within a couple of minutes Mario entered and went straight over to the trolley. Seeing there was not much left unconsumed, he smiled at Susan.

"Was good, yes? You liked," he asked?"

"Yes, thank you."

"Good. Now you get ready. Patra, she come soon and look. If you no ready, big trouble."

"What's she going to do if I'm not? Have me thrown over the wall?"

"No not today. Later maybe."

"That's reassuring. I must say."

"What you say?"

"Nothing really."

"OK, I go now. Supper at 6.30, OK? Then eight o'clock Mr Akim, you got busy time."

"Don't mention that name to me please," Susan almost spat back, as she felt a chill run all over her.

"Why you no like him? He very nice man."

"Sure, like a rat with syphilis."

"No, he no sick. We check all customers. They have to be 100% OK. Sick customers bad for business."

"It's nice to know that you care," Susan murmured sarcastically. "Sure, no care no job. Anyway, I go now." Mario packed up the trolley and headed for the door.

Left alone again, Susan walked over to the bed where her afternoon and evening's wardrobe had been laid out for her. Inspecting the frilly petticoat, she wondered what to expect from Mr Ali.

"These were the vogue in the 1950s," she surmised, "so what's with this Mr Ali? Who knows, maybe he's trying to relive some of his past? The big question is how? I guess I'll soon find out. I suppose I'd better get changed or Mata Hari will throw a fit. Worse still, some electricity in me." Susan gathered up the laid-out clothing, wondering where it would be best to change.

Patra entered the room. "Is past two o'clock already. Mr Ali be here at three. I gave you your watch so you could tell time," Patra exclaimed, angrily.

"I was just about to change as you came in," Susan retorted.

"So, is good. You change, I wait and then bring Mr Ali in."

"What and stay around watching while he rapes me?"

"He no rape you, he just have sex with you. No big deal. You young women today so concerned about rape but will offer taxi driver sex to save paying cash."

"That may be so, but it is by choice, not force."

"Don't worry, Mr Ali don't use force, but he will report any lady who don't cooperate."

"You mean force after the rape."

"I don't understand that but no matter, here you do as you are told, and you have a nice life. It's up to you. Mr Mathew have no time for people who don't do as they are told."

Susan made no reply. She gathered the clothing which was put out for her and started for the bathroom.

"You can change here, no need to hide in bathroom. No one else here, just you and me," Patra laughed.

Susan hesitated for a moment and then returned to the bed and began to change. She didn't know why she thought to change in the bathroom, instinct perhaps. When she had finished, Patra looked at her and smiled in approval.

"Nice, you look very nice." Patra nodded.

"You might think so, but I feel like an upside-down wedding cake with the icing on the bottom."

"Does not matter what you like, is what Mr Ali like. Now you go and put on some makeup and comb your hair. You leave it long."

"I don't have any makeup, I don't even have a comb," Susan protested.

"In bathroom you will find all you need, including comb and brush. Now go and make ready but no hairspray, Mr Ali don't like hairspray. The smell that is."

In the bathroom, Susan pulled out a few drawers and discovered a treasury of makeup as well as other accessories to assist the art of face and hair decoration. She did not take long to complete the cosmetic transformation and left the bathroom only to find Patra waiting to make the final inspection. At first Patra nodded in approval and then suddenly stopped.

"The lipstick, no good."

"What! What's the matter with it?"

"Too pink. There's some very bright red lipstick in there, I know, I put it there, You go and put that on."

"Why? It doesn't suit me. It contrasts too much with my pale skin."

"It doesn't matter what suits you, it's what suits Mr Ali is what I think about."

"What does Mr Ali know about lipstick?"

"Probably nothing but he like bright red, specially on blond ladies and lots of it, so go wipe what you have off and put on bright red."

Susan was about to protest but quickly realised the futility of such a move and headed for the makeup mirror in the bathroom. Possibly as a form of latent protest, she gave the red lipstick tube a thorough workout, "If it's a tart he wants then a tart he'll get," she reminded herself, wondering at what sort of a person would like a scarlet lipped woman almost dripping in red wax and oil. "Is that better?" Susan asked Patra as she returned from the bathroom.

"Excellent, my dear, Mr Ali will love it." Patra nodded in approval. "And now for the final touches." She reached into her shoulder bag and extracted a wooden casket the size of chocolate box. Opening it, she produced a necklace with mounted red stones and a single red stone the size of a small hen's egg. "You will wear this round your neck while you are with Mr Ali and this," she picked up the large single stone between her two fingers, "you will place in your belly button. You will notice that it has been cut especially for that purpose. It will withstand a certain, er, a lot of surface activity but too much and it fall out. So careful you not lose it or there will be big trouble!"

"You're kidding! Trouble over a red bit of glass?"

"Red bit of glass to you maybe but a genuine ruby to those who know things. Also the necklace, real ruby."

"I don't get it! Real gemstones in what is after all just a brothel perched on top of a mountain?"

She didn't expect it or see it coming as Patra reached over and delivered a stinging, open handed, slap to her face.

Susan drew back, quite shocked, "What was that for?"

"That was to remind you never to call this place a brothel. Not to me or not to anyone. Do you understand that? This is a spa for some of the wealthiest gentlemen in the world who seek relaxation so that they are refreshed and ready to continue with their work. Sex is a natural part of relaxation and that is why you are here. Nothing is too good for our clients and a lot of them like to see ladies wearing good jewels, er, good jewellery. What do you think our client say if they thought our ladies were wearing fake jewels?"

"Sorry, I did not mean to be rude, but I still don't quite understand. What happens to the rubies?"

"Nothing happens to the rubies. You wear the rubies. When we say give them back, you give them back. Other times you wear emeralds or opals or even diamonds, but when you finish, you give them back."

"And what happens if one of the guests gives me a present, say a ruby to wear in my nostril?" Susan asked, somewhat sarcastically.

"That actually happens time to time. The procedure is simple. You wear it whenever you are with that guest, and when you finished you give it to me or Mr Mathew. If you try to hide it, Mr Mathew soon find out and you in big trouble."

"So, I get the picture now. I get to show it off and Mr Mathews gets to keep it."

"Good, we understand each other then. Now you prepare yourself. Mr Ali will be here in ten minutes, and you do as he says."

Susan clasped the ruby necklace in place but had trouble with the bellybutton gem.

"It won't fit! It keeps falling out," she protested.

"You're not doing it right," Patra laughed, "push your belly out; that's it, as far as you can, now squeeze in the ruby; good, now keep pressing on the stone as you pull your belly in. Good, that's it. Now you have got it."

***

It was almost a quarter past three when the door opened to Susan's quarters. Mathew entered followed by a very tall, skinny man, wearing a dark Italian cut suit, a white shirt but no tie. Both his hands were covered by off-white calfskin gloves and his right hand had a large, gold, onyx ring pushed over the gloved middle finger. His left hand carried a slender, black walking stick with a silver handle in the shape of an eagle's head. Susan wondered if the stick could play some part in Mr Ali's sexual deviations and felt a cold shudder run down her spine. Judging from his shock of almost white hair, Susan took him to be somewhere between 75-85 years old and looking remarkably fit.

"Susan, I would like you to meet Mr Ali," Mathew commenced the introduction, "He will be spending the next couple of hours with you. Mr Ali, I wish you a pleasant time and remember, if there is a problem, anything at all, just give the sash two tugs and we will be at your service."

Mr Ali nodded in appreciation, "Come Patra, we have other things to take care of."

"Well, Susan," Ali finally spoke after the others had left, "shall we sit down and talk a little?" His English was almost perfect but carried a slight eastern accent. "I believe you have some refreshments available."

"Yes, of course I have." Susan went to the bar fridge while Ali's eyes eagerly followed her, fixed on the hem of her wide skirt and the flash of petticoat protruding from it. In the bar fridge Susan found a silver tray with a jug of orange juice already on it and several rows of dates and anchovies decoratively displayed around the jug. She placed the tray on coffee table near Ali.

"Come, sit down next to me, my dear. Join me in a Spanish Date. That's what I call them. I find it remarkable how the anchovy brings out the flavour of the date. Try one!"

Somewhat reluctantly, Susan accepted the offer but regretted it immediately the uncomplimentary morsels attacked her taste buds. She had to pool all her strength to avoid throwing up. Ali watched her in amusement.

"The first one is always a little difficult," he commented, "but after you've tried four or five of them, you, you, how do you say, 'acquire the taste. After that, you're, er, you're hooked."

"If you don't mind, Mr Ali, I don't think I'd like to be hooked."

"Of course, I quite understand and please, no Mr Ali, just Ali will be fine."

"Thank you."

"There is no need for thank you, but there is a need for what shall we do now?"

Susan almost froze at these words. What she dreaded most, was about to happen. If she refused, she would be forced and hurt and eventually violated, of that, she was sure. Seeing there was no alternative she decided to do as she was told and chose the lesser of the two evils. "What would you like me to do, Ali?"

"Actually, very little. I would like you to go over to the bed and lie down on top of it. That is all. I will do the rest."

The freeze was really settling in, but Susan braced herself and walked over to the bed, kicking off her shoes.

"No, no" Ali cried out, "leave the shoes on."

Somewhat puzzled, she retrieved her shoes.

Ali then selected a chair and placed it by the bedside and next to it, a small occasional table with the tray of dates, anchovies and orange juice.

"Now, my dear, close your eyes and imagine you are lying in the shade of a palm tree in an oasis in the desert, or if you prefer, a boat drifting down a small river."

Susan did as she was asked but opted for neither, the palm tree or the river. She simply closed her eyes, dreading in wonder as to what was supposed to happen next. For what must have been like 15 or so minutes, but seemed like hours, nothing happened. Gradually, she part opened her eyes, but all she saw was Mr Ali sitting in the chair looking at her, one hand held close to his mouth and the other wrapped round a glass of orange juice. He seemed almost as if in a trance. She closed her eyes again and waited. A soft noise and movement on the bed mattress indicated Mr Ali had sat down beside her. She braced herself for what she thought was to come and with good reason. She felt a hand gently grasping her ankle, then slowly sliding it past her knee up to the stocking top of her thigh, at the same time working her skirt and frilly petticoat up to her waist. Then to her surprise Mr Ali pulled the garment down again to below knee level. A short pause and Mr Ali repeated the movement and then again, several more times. Perplexed by this curious behaviour, Susan wondered what next.

"That was most gratifying, Susan. Next, would you play a little music and dance for me."

"I don't have any music."

"Yes, you do. There is a cassette player under the bar with a cassette already in it. All you have to do is press the 'ON' switch. Would you do that for me please?"

"Sure," Susan got out of the bed and, locating the player behind the bar, switched it on.

The cassette player provided was foreign to her as was the sound coming from it. It was definitely Eastern, but that was as far as she could identify it. Still, it did have a swaying rhythm to it, so she did the best she could to interpret it in dance form. Casting modesty to the wind, she let her skirt rise in the swirls, much to the delight of Mr Ali who applauded each time it rose to reveal her stocking tops below the surf of lace created by the rotating and twirling of the dancer.

The music stopped, and Susan almost collapsed from exhaustion. A few beads of sweat appeared on Mr Ali's face as he motioned for her to return to the bed. He began to fondle her once more but this time from her breasts downwards. His hand, inside her blouse, soon stopped at the ruby in Susan's bellybutton. He loosened the garment to reveal the gem, gazing at it in delight and then started licking and kissing it. After a while, he ceased, choosing to rest his face on her belly. As time went by, nothing else happened, and Susan soon discovered that Mr Ali was asleep. She gently extricated herself from the awkward situation by manoeuvring herself from under his head without disturbing his sleep. By substituting a pillow for her belly, she let him sleep but left herself wondering at whatever next.

Nearly half an hour passed before Mr Ali stirred.

"That was wonderful, my dear. You have no idea how refreshed I feel."

Susan said nothing but managed a small smile.

"We must do this again soon. I will still be here tomorrow, so shall we say the same time?"

"I, er, I don't know," Susan stammered, "I, I er, have nothing to do with the plans here, I, er, merely ..."

"Don't worry, my dear, I will let Patra know. I'm sure she'll be most accommodating."

"As you wish," Susan uttered obediently.

"Good, that's settled then," Mr Ali concluded, finished his glass of orange juice and left the room.

***

When supper was brought to her, Susan felt all appetite leave. She was dreading the coming encounter with Akim and paced her room trying to decide of how she should behave. Akim was no Mr Ali and would not think twice at using brute force, even if he had to enlist outside help to reach his goals. Resisting him was useless. Appealing to his better nature was already on record and the outcome clear. The thought made Susan feel nauseous. She swallowed twice to avoid throwing up. Maybe there was the answer. Throw up all over Akim, that would at least convey to him a message. It would also guarantee a great deal of physical pain to her, of that she was certain.

No matter in which direction her thoughts turned, the end result stayed constant. She was going to be violated and that was that. Wryly, she kept recalling the adage, 'they can make you marry the person but they can't make you love the child.'

Not much of a solution but the only one presenting itself. She would submit, offering no resistance but also no cooperation. She would show no emotion and let her body become almost lifeless, limp in every other way except for breathing.

Changing into the wardrobe she had worn the night before, Susan wondered at what it was about clothing which aroused such different sexual feelings in men. Mr Ali and his fetish with frills and lace and Akim's attraction to pointed slippers.

***

It was almost 8.30 pm when Akim, wearing only a black silk dressing gown and shadowed by Mario, entered Susan's room.

"Good evening, Susan," Akim greeted her, "you look in better spirits than you did last night."

Susan did not reply. She sat on the edge of one of the lounge chairs looking past him, eyes fixed on Mario. Noticing this, Akim quickly said, "Oh him! I see. I don't think we'll be needing him tonight, will we?"

Susan said nothing.

"OK, Mario, you may leave us now."

"OK, Mr Akim, I go now, just please to remember, any problem just please pull the cord."

"And now please, Susan, would you pour me a drink? Scotch on the rocks would be nice."

Susan rose, went to the bar, prepared the beverage and handed it to Akim.

"That's better, no jagged bottle first," he quipped, "I think we've started to get along."

Susan said nothing and resumed her seat.

"Nothing to say," Akim asked, sipping his drink? "If I remember correctly, last night you were quite vocal."

Susan remained silent.

"I see. Like that is it? In that case, let's not waste any time. Get on the bed and lie down."

Susan did as she was told. Akim followed her and once in bed commenced to undress her. Susan did nothing to help or hinder. Having readied her to his satisfaction, Akim tried to kiss her but all he received was a closed mouth and clenched teeth under two lipstick covered cushions.

Angered but aroused, he tried to enter her, and, finding the point of entry too dry he used his own saliva to act as a lubricant. This worked, and penetration was achieved as was ejaculation a little later, but instead of sexual satisfaction, the only real result was frustration. "You're like screwing a dead tree," Akim exclaimed as he put on his dressing gown, "All that's in there are ants and sawdust. I know what you're up to, but it won't work. I'll be back and either have your clitoris yelling for more or have it removed forever."

***

Susan put out the lights and returned to bed pulling the cover up to her chin. It was quite a warm night, but she felt shivery and cold. An ocean of thought and tears engulfed her. "How long must I endure this?" Susan asked herself. "How long can this last? What is the end result? Will I ever see home again? Why me? What have I done? Why anyone? Why doesn't anyone help me? Where is the cavalry?"

Like a kaleidoscope, these questions took over her mind. Like leeches they clung to her, sucking at her strength, promoting despair and hopelessness.

"There is only one way," Susan resolved. "I must find a way to get out of here, there has to be a way. Edmund Dante, The Count of Monte Cristo found a way. Hmm ... but he was fiction. So what? The many daring escapes from prisoner of war camps were fact."

CH 6. LIVING BUT NOT LOVING

Akim returned to his quarters almost furious. Things were not working out as he had planned. He had expected Susan to be uncooperative first but was sure this was only a temporary and natural thing, and in time she would take stock of her situation and realise that life in Spa Shangrila could be quite pleasant and luxurious. He would have been far happier if Susan had resisted his advances and he had taken her by force. Actually, this was what he had expected and, in a way, looked forward to it. However, Susan's total capitulation took him by surprise, a surprise he was not welcoming. To lie there like a heap of camel dung, emotionless and motionless, not caring or feeling anything was almost like an insult if not a demonstration of moral superiority.

Changing into more suitable clothing, Akim proceeded to the guest's lounge, a reasonably large stone walled chamber in the complex, plushly decorated and carpeted with a stone-based and marble-topped bar in the centre of the room. Soft chairs and low tables took up the rest of the space. Akim noted about twenty men, all in the middle age bracket frequenting the lounge, five or so accompanied by young women. At the bar, two men were involved in a deep conversation, and opposite them Mathew was talking to Pepe who was also the barman.

Spotting Mathew, Akim approached him.

"Evening, Mathew," Akim greeted him quietly, "Do you mind if we have a word?

"Not at all, Akim. Pepe, get Mr Akim a drink. I did not expect to see you so soon! Any problems?"

"Well, yes and no, so to speak."

"I see. I take it your young lady may have something to do with this?"

"You may say so."

"Then why didn't you pull the cord?"

"There was no need to, there was no resistance, in fact, just the opposite, it was like screwing a corpse."

"I see, she just froze up," Mathew remarked, "This happens quite a bit at first, especially with virgins. They are frightened, that's all. Eventually they come good, but a fellow has to know how to press the right buttons. You know, work on the erotic zones and pretty soon she'll want to marry you."

"Not this one, I don't think. She hates me."

"Well, old boy, there is little I can do about that. You'll just have to keep on working at it."

"What if she doesn't come good, ever?"

"You can always drop her over the side, but you know the rules. The Board will estimate her value to us during her working life and present you with the bill. The choice is yours."

"Ha! And if I choose to ignore it?"

"Oh, come off it Akim! You remember Herr Spengler last year threw Musshi over the wall and refused to pay compensation? He ended up on almost the exact spot where Musshi did and then disappeared just as quickly."

"Sure, but Spengler wasn't part of the organisation, I am."

"Only via your father, not that that matters. Akim, you know us, and you must know we are a very democratic organisation, and the same rules apply to the executive as they do to the employ … make that the members."

"Yea, yea, I know about the rules but that's not what I wanted to talk to you about," Akim spluttered.

"What then?"

"Look, there must be a pill or potion or something which can be given her to heat her up?"

"I wish," Mathew sighed, "if that was the case, I'd have a pallet load of it in each bedroom. No, the best we can come up with is some knockout drops and all that achieves is a situation much like the one you are facing."

"I may as well throw her over the wall then and bugger the consequences."

"You're being a little over dramatic, Akim. Look at it using a bit of logic. She's only a girl. OK, I grant you, she is attractive, but she is just a girl. We have many attractive girls right here so why not take out your frustrations on one of them? Believe me the actual sex is the same with whoever you pick."

"You don't understand. We were students together in Sydney University."

"All right!" Mathew was now getting a little frustrated, "So puppy love turned into the real thing, for you anyway. OK, I get it, so why not try a softer approach? You catch more flies with honey than vinegar."

"What do you mean, a softer approach?" Akim's interest was aroused.

"The next time you see her, don't even try to shag her. Just talk to her. Let her know that you made a mistake in bringing her here. Tell her you thought she had the hots for you but was too shy to tell you. Tell her you will try to find a way to get her out but it's going to take a bit of time and lots of money. Tell her any bullshit you like as long as it sounds like you're a changed, contrite person. Bring her flowers, anything, and then try to shag her. By now she must realise that if she's unresponsive, she's blown her ticket out of here."

"You know something, Mathew? That might just work. I like the flowers touch but where do I get flowers here? There's no rose garden anywhere in the spa."

"The chopper flies in flowers for the guest rooms every week. I'll arrange for you to get some. Better still, why don't you go into the mountains and pick some wildflowers. There's still plenty there, and she'll think it's awfully nice of you to go to the trouble."

***

"Good morning, Eddy," detective Frank Henderson greeted detective Pike as he entered the meeting room and nodded to Phil Morrison and Annie Goodall already seated and waiting. "I'm sorry I'm a bit late, but I just finished tracking down a possible lead."

"Good for you," Dt Pike enthused, "That's one more than we have. Sit down and let's hear it."

"A few hours ago, I got a call from Darwin airport," Dt. Henderson began as he sat down. "Earlier, I contacted all our international airports and asked if they had noticed anything unusual in passenger behaviour or anything a bit strange. Darwin called back to say a coffin had been offloaded from a light aircraft onto a Malaysian international flight. According to the cargo manifest it contained the body of a young woman tourist drowned off one of our South Coast beaches and was on her way home for a family funeral. Her name was Svetlana Lubina, aged 24, from Slovenia. Apparently, her two brothers had flown to Australia to collect the body."

"Nothing strange in that," Phil Morrison interjected. "It doesn't often happen, but it does happen."

"I know that Phil, but why from Darwin? In the light of our investigation, I thought I'd better check it through, especially as I don't recall any young tourist reported as drowned during this period. After checking it, there is no official report of a drowning, male or female, for the last seven weeks, and why would a young woman from Slovenia go into our surf in the middle of winter?"

"That is a bit odd," Dt Pike observed, "but somehow doesn't seem to fit our case. Why would someone kidnap Susan, kill her, and then ship the body out of the country?"

"I agree, but there is a bit more to it than that. I checked with Immigration, and they have no record of a Svetlana Lubina entering the country. I also checked with the Coroners on the South Coast, and they had no drowning cases during this period."

"It does seem a bit fishy," Pike agreed, "But it lacks sense! Why kill somebody and then go to all the trouble to fly the body out of the country?"

"Maybe she wasn't dead," Annie Goodall joined in. "Maybe she was heavily sedated and placed in the coffin. I don't think airport officials go round sticking hat pins into bodies every time a coffin is in the cargo area and the paperwork looks in order."

"I think you've got something there, Annie. I think we had better have a closer look at this. This may be not our lady, but it is one hell of a good way to transport contraband. We'd better get all the relevant details from Darwin and, if necessary, send someone up there to dig for more details." Pike surmised and continued, "Seeing you dug this up Frank, you may as well follow it through."

"You mean me go to Darwin?"

"Why not you? Look, this may not come near to a bull's roar of finding Susan Bauford, but it may give us some interesting details and leads to other cases."

"You're the boss, Eddy. When do you want me to leave?"

"As soon as you can pack a bag and a toothbrush. In the meantime, I'll square it off with our treasury for the airfare and hotel vouchers and talk to my counterpart in Darwin."

"How long do you think I should be up there?"

"Depends on what you find out, doesn't it? Look, so far this is the only lead we have, the timing fits, and I'll give you ten to one that Susan's no longer in Australia."

"OK, but hadn't we better check with the Immigration Department formally to make sure this Svetlana is not a furphy? I mean, I only got this information over the phone."

"Don't worry, Frank, we'll check this thoroughly before you leave for Darwin, so all you now have to do is pack a bag and stand by while we do the detective work they pay us for."

***

Jim Bauford made himself a cup of tea, sat down at the kitchen breakfast bar to drink it. Under normal circumstances, Norma would have made the tea for him, but he had just returned home from the hospital having visited her. Only last night they were sitting down to dinner when she, quite suddenly, turned pale and slumped over the dining table. He immediately rang for an ambulance, and within minutes she was on her way to hospital. Jim followed the ambulance in his car, in the wake of the screeching sirens. Norma was rushed to the emergency department where two doctors and nurses were already waiting. While the doctors were busy attending to her, Jim was cornered by a hospital orderly armed with a clipboard and a lot of questions. In the rush of things, Jim had forgotten to bring her Medicare card as well the insurance documents, but as Norma had been admitted to the hospital earlier, the orderly could obtain the needed information from hospital records.

Then came the long wait. Minutes which seemed like hours went by before the two doctors addressed him. Norma had suffered a mild cardiac arrest and would have to remain in hospital for at least a day or two. The doctors also assessed Jim's condition and said he was fit to drive home.

The next day, it was mid-morning before he was allowed to see her. Sitting by her bedside, Jim noted that she still looked very pale and weak and spoke in short, gasping sentences. On consulting with her doctor, Jim was told that she should be all right but had to remain in hospital for a few more days if only to be sure she did not suffer a relapse. Having spent more than an hour with her, the medical staff suggested that Jim leave and let her rest to speed her recovery. Somewhat reluctantly, he returned home and made himself a cup of tea.

Slurping his tea, the way he did, would have received a severe reprimand from Norma. Jim slurped even louder as if commanding a reprimand to manifest itself, but none came. The telephone rang instead.

"Good morning, Mr Bauford, Dt Pike calling, how are you this morning?"

"Not really the best, detective," Jim responded and filled Pike in on the events of the night before.

"I'm very sorry to hear that Mr Bauford, I'm sure your wife will be alright. I was looking forward to seeing both of you, but I guess just one of you will do, if that's all right with you?"

"That's perfectly all right. I take it you have some news?"

"I may and I may not. It really depends on your answers."

"I see. Did you want to come here or would you rather I came in to see you?"

"No, no, I'll come and see you. I only rang to see when was convenient?"

"Most any time you like,"

"How about I drop by in an hour or so?"

"Fine, I'll be here waiting for you."

Jim replaced the receiver and went back to his tea, which by now had lost its warmth. He threw what was left into the sink and switched on the kettle to make another cup.

Slurping away, sitting in a lounge chair, the teacup firmly jammed on his index finger, Jim drifted off to sleep, spilling the rest of the tea partly on himself, partly on the edge of the chair and on the carpet. He was woken by the continuous ringing of the doorbell and a voice calling, 'Mr Bauford ... are you there? Mr Bauford...?'

"Coming...," Jim responded as loudly as he could and, ignoring the spilled tea, headed for the door. "I'm sorry, I must have nodded off," he said as he opened it. "Come in detective, I'm about to make another cup of tea. Would you like some?"

"Yes please, that would be nice," Pike answered and headed for the lounge. Shortly, Jim appeared with a cup of tea in each hand. Setting one down on the side table next to Pike, he settled down in a chair adjacent to Pike's.

"Now Dt. Pike, perhaps you'd like to tell me, what's on your mind?"

"Sure. Did your daughter, you, or anyone you know ever hear of a young woman, about 24 years old, named Svetlana Lubina? She was possibly a visitor or student from Slovenia, or have you had any dealings with anyone from Slovenia?"

"No, I don't think so. The name doesn't ring a bell, and I know most of Susan's friends. As for Slovenia, I must plead geographical ignorance. I have heard the name but have no idea where it is, but what has this got to do with Susan?"

"I have no concrete idea but at the back of my mind. Something is niggling and won't let go."

"I still don't understand where Susan comes in?"

"I know you don't, and I don't quite either. It's what we coppers call a hunch. OK, here's what we have. Two days after your daughter's kidnapping, a coffin arrives at Darwin Airport and is transferred to an international flight culminating in Slovenia. The coffin contains the body of a young Slovenian woman tourist who is drowned off the south coat of New South Wales and is sent back to her home to receive a decent burial. So far quite feasible. Then some suspicious bright soul decides to do a bit of checking and finds out from Immigration that there is no record of a person of that name entering the country. Further checking reveals that there has been no report of a drowning, male or female, during that period.

Now the question arises. Who was in that coffin, and was it a corpse or someone heavily sedated? The one thing we can be sure of is that the coffin contained a woman."

"What makes you say that? It could have been drugs," Jim suggested.

"Most unlikely. The plane was headed in the wrong direction, and if the body was male, it would have created an international enquiry."

"So, you think Susan may have been in that coffin?"

"It's a real possibility."

"But why?" Jim cried out, dismayed. "Why would anyone want to kidnap Susan, and how could she get to Darwin so quickly?"

"The why is simple. There is an international white slave sex trade located mostly in Asia. There are very rich Asian men who will pay enormous sums of money just to sleep with a white woman, and there are quite a few local villains who would charter a small plane and drop off a sedated woman at some lonely cove and offload her on a boat. That's been their usual way of operating. We have not struck the airport thing before, but it is feasible."

"That could mean that Susan's still alive?"

"Yes, if you can call it that."

"When will you know for sure?"

"I only wish I could tell you that, Mr Bauford. At the moment it's still only a theory, a pretty good one but a theory nevertheless."

"You will keep me informed on any further developments, won't you?" Jim asked. "My wife will be so happy to hear that there's a good chance that Susan's still alive."

"You can rest assured on that, Mr Bauford, the moment we have anything positive you'll be the first to know." Dt Pike finished his tea and was set to leave, "My best regards to your wife, Mr Bauford. I do hope she makes a good recovery and is home with you soon."

"Thank you, Dt Pike. I know she will be most pleased to know that there is a good chance Susan's still alive."

After Pike left, Jim returned to the lounge and recalled all that Pike had said. A light now appeared at the end of the tunnel. Here was hope, slim but nevertheless a hope. He knew Norma would get overexcited, and he now planned the best way to tell her without raising her hopes too high.

The phone rang in the hallway. Jim went to it and picked it up. "Hello."

"Is that Mr James Bauford?" a female voice asked.

"Speaking!"

"Oh, hello, Mr Bauford. I am Doctor Harris from the hospital. I have been looking after your wife. I'm very sorry to have to tell you that she passed away at 2.15 pm today."

"What! Can't be, I only last spoke to her his morning!"

"I'm so sorry, Mr Bauford. She had a massive heart attack only a couple of hours ago. We did what we could to revive her, but it was too sudden, too great. There was nothing more we could do. She died while we were trying to resuscitate her."

Jim felt himself go almost numb. His legs lost their strength, and he virtually fell into the small seat by the phone in the hallway. His throat went dry as his heart started to pound, and no sound came from his throat.

"Are you all right, Mr Bauford?" Dr Harris's voice could be heard through the telephone, "Mr Bauford, are you OK? Mr Bauford, say something."

Jim gathered his strength, "Of course, I'm not OK. You've just told me my wife died. Did you expect me to jump for joy? Swing on the chandeliers … mmfgh …hagh …. for Christ's sake …. my daughter's been kidnapped, my wife is dead and you … mfgh … gh … oh God …"

"Mr Bauford, listen to me. Sit down please, I'm sending you help. Hang in there, Mr Bauford. Help is on the way." Dr Harris left the phone off the hook and picked up another one, "Harry, it's Wendy, can you get a unit out to Putney? Get the address from the cardiac unit. Mr Bauford… his wife just died… he's taking it very badly. As far as I know he's all on his own.. bring him in.. I'll make sure he's alright and gets some help."

***

Dt Frank Henderson did not waste much time in Darwin. Three days after leaving, he was back in Pike's office with Dts. Annie Goodall and Phil Morrison already in attendance. After a brief 'welcome home' chatter, Pike called the meeting to order.

"OK, Frank, let's hear what you found out?"

"Quite interesting, actually, it seems that over the last year or so there has been a spate of drownings of overseas visitors and their bodies flown back for private burial."

"And I'm guessing they were all young women," Pike interrupted.

"You got it, Eddy. It would seem a lot of our tourist ladies are not much chop when it comes to swimming in the surf."

"Surely, someone on the ground staff would have checked if the contents matched the inventory records?" Annie asked.

"I asked them the same thing, and apparently in a couple of earlier cases they did and found the contents matching the inventory. After that they did not worry."

"You'd think they would though, wouldn't you?" Annie suggested.

"Not really," Frank retorted, "You must bear in mind, the ground staff are mostly handlers and store men, not policemen. When it comes to legal matters, they are more drug orientated."

"Either way, it is of no help to us now. What else did you manage to find out?" Pike asked.

"From their flight records I managed to find that the coffin was flown to Darwin in a small private plane from Bankstown Airport, almost a day after the abduction. It was a charter flight from a reputable firm, but I'll check them out later anyhow. From Darwin the coffin was put on an Air Malaysia flight to Penang International Airport. There the record stops. Penang is listed as the final destination."

"That's not much help to us," Annie observed, "As far as we know, the body was that of a Slovenian woman, so why would the final destination be Penang?"

"Who knows? From Penang it could have gone to a hundred different locations where officials turn a blind eye to almost anything as long as they feel a buck sliding into their back pocket?"

"All this is good and interesting but how does this help us?" Phil Morrison asked.

"I, for one, think that Svetlana Lubina is Susan Bauford," Pike said quietly.

"What makes you say that?" Annie asked.

"The timing fits. Around that time there are no other abductions reported, nor are there any drownings reported. There is no ransom demand, so it can't be the traditional kidnapping. A body of approximately the same age is flown to Darwin from Bankstown at about the same time as the abduction, probably heavily sedated."

"But all that time in a sealed coffin. Wouldn't she have suffocated from lack of air?" Phil asked.

"Not if the coffin had cleverly disguised air holes fitted throughout it, you know, hinges with holes in them but no screws. Possibly a raised cross on the lid with matching slits underneath, that type of thing. Even the bottom of the casket may be lined with air holes. Who looks at the bottom of a coffin?"

"You are probably right," Annie agreed, "but the question now is, what can we do about it?"

"Very little, I'm afraid, except to try and pick up the trail of the coffin from Penang."

"You mean one of us go to Penang?" Phil brightened.

"You wish! We have no jurisdiction in Malaysia, but Interpol have. It's time we had another chat with them."

***

Jim Bauford recovered from the initial storm of grief but not entirely. An inertia took over to the extent that he was in no shape to organise Norma's funeral. The social workers were preparing something small, but it was Eddy Pike who took things into his hands. When he had first heard of Norma's demise, he went to see Jim and was surprised by what greeted him. The man had aged ten years in only a couple of days. Pike notified some of Jim's colleagues in the racing fraternity, all of whom were aware of the tragedy of Susan's abduction and now, Jim's situation. They formed a small committee to take care of the funeral with refreshments afterwards at the restaurant in Randwick racecourse. It seemed like there were more mourners than flowers at the funeral. Ken and Ashley Barton were also in attendance, but Penelope stayed home claiming a sudden headache.

On top of the coffin, amongst the flowers, was a framed portrait of Norma and also one of Susan. A printed banner at the base of the portraits read:

"May they both meet again but much later than sooner."

CH 7. A HOUSE THAT'S NOT A HOME.

Mathew sat in a soft leather chair in his office enjoying a vintage Courvoisier cognac, his favourite. A perfect way to end a hectic day. The spa had become popular and in demand amongst the wealthy and famous. Matthew felt pleased with his achievements, he did not mind the challenges of the clientele and location. It felt good to be the Boss, and to have a degree of autonomy from the cartel.

Musing, he recalled how the spa began.

In a luxury hotel sauna room in Bern, five middle aged men had reserved the sauna exclusively for themselves after a gruelling meeting with their bosses; a syndicate of Americans covertly dealing in human trafficking, mainly young women, to stock their brothels in the USA as well as white slavery outlets in the Middle and Far East. The Americans were not happy, "You guys have gone off the boil," Jack Solomon flatly told them. "Since March, the merchandise you have sent us has been crap. We find 'the virgins' you delivered have had more screws than a dining room table. Other broads qualify to be grandmothers. Our Asian clients complain that the blondes start looking like skunks after a few weeks. This simply ain't good enough. We're losing customers and therefore money. Some of the broads are even violently uncooperative, which means that you guys have not softened them up enough. Some of them have tried to put the squeeze on our client's balls, and that is crippling for any business. Last month, we had two hellcats we had to liquidate and that ain't funny. A dead broad is no earner, but she has cost us plenty of greenbacks just to get her there. This means we have to streamline our expenses. To do this we are cutting your take by 25% per broad, and you will pay 50% of the cost of getting her on target. Any questions?"

"Si." Marco Rossetti put up his hand. "You say our selection is bad but what you want us to do? Walk up to each lady and say, 'scuse, we just want to look at your scalp to see dark roots or nits or something,' and do we say, 'please promise to be good when our customers jig a jig you, otherwise we not take you?'"

"Quite frankly, Marco, I don't give a crap what you tell them, just as long as the merchandise is worth the cost, and you keep the ugly ones yourself."

The meeting ended on that note, with the American bosses heading for the bar and the local head-hunters for the sauna.

***

"I think the Yanks are being bloody minded," Mathew Hudson observed as he threw some more water on the hot stones. "Next thing we'll have to ask the women to fill in application forms and then snatch the ones they pass for abducting."

"Splendid idea," Mato Rahal joined in, "I want one with three tits, the biggest one in the middle."

"I can fix that," Anton Novak offered, "In Slovenia we have plenty, but they all have horns growing from the head."

The small group in the sauna laughed and a great deal of tension eased.

"The Yanks think it is so bloody easy," Mathew continued, "Just put up a small table on a street corner and make a selection from the passing parade. Maybe we should try that, set up our own table independently and bugger the Yanks."

"Maybe that's not such a bad idea," Mato suggested, "As it is, we do all the dirty work, and the Americans take the biggest cut."

"I think it's a great idea," Walter Schmidt agreed. "We could set up a house right here in Bern."

"Oh, you'd like that, wouldn't you? You're Swiss and this is your hometown," Marco quipped.

"Hang on a minute, this may not be as crazy as it sounds. Maybe we should take a closer look at this," Mathew suggested, "Bern may not be the ideal place, a bit too much competition. We should look for something a bit more exotic, remote, exclusive, you know, like a resort, where wealthy gentlemen of leisure can relax and recharge their batteries in total security."

"The idea is good, but where would you find such a place? An island in the Pacific sounds good but it's too far and the upkeep, too expensive," Mato said, "Somewhere out in the desert is not much good either, only sand to look at. A house anywhere eventually attracts too much attention and there is always the danger of an escape and the next thing is the Gendarmes pulling the place to pieces."

"I have an idea," Anton Novak interrupted. "How about the Slovenian Alps? Many remote spots there, beautiful scenery and government servants who know how to look the other way."

"Not bad, but still problematic. To buy or build a chalet there, expensive and still under public scrutiny."

"Not really, there are many almost derelict monasteries in the alps. They were built by hermit monks and are now owned by the government. I am sure that finding the right government officials you could strike a good deal and all that you would have to do is re, re, redo it, you know like clean it up and adapt it. Besides, labour in Slovenia is cheap so the cost would be low."

Mathew thought about Anton's suggestion and then nodded as if in agreement.

"You know Anton, you might just have something there. An alpine, luxury, exclusive resort, safe from prying eyes and ears. Hmm, deserves thinking about. Clients coming in and staying for days or weeks. Not just a couple of hours. What do the rest of you think?"

"Sounds good," Walter agreed, "but where do we come in and how do we finance it?

"It's early days, but I suggest we take a look at the possibilities and then the costs. Everything above board, we pool the expenses, and each man gets a return on a percentage basis depending on the size of his contribution.

"That sounds fair enough, count me in," Walter conceded.

"Me too," Marco added.

"Sounds OK to me but only if we make 100% sure what we are doing," Mateo joined in.

"Fine." Mathew nodded. "It looks like we may have the start of a brand new adventure, and what about you Anton? You in or out?"

"Naturally, I'm in. The alps was my idea remember!"

"Good, then the next step is to set up a discreet meeting and get the ball rolling. The question is when and where?"

"We can use my warehouse in the south of Bern," Walter offered. "It's pretty nondescript and private, and as long as we all arrive separately, no one's to know."

"I didn't know you had a warehouse in Bern, Walter," Marco exclaimed.

"That's the good part about it, neither do the Yanks," Walter replied.

***

At about 11 am on a Sunday morning, taxis started to arrive in Berg Str in Bern. First to arrive was Mathew followed by Marco, Anton and Mateo. As host, Walter had gone to some trouble to welcome the delegates. Platters of finger-food were scattered round the large office as well as a portable bar, featuring a splendid array of beverage had been set up including a tea and coffee dispenser.

Following a bit of socialising, Mathew was quick to get things started.

"Gentlemen," Mathew began, "I take it you've all been to mass this morning and confessed your sins, so we have a clear week to amass some serious sinning. If you would like to find a seat at the table, we can get things started. Take any food or drink to the table you wish. This is Walter's church, not the Vatican, and please bear in mind that there will be no minutes taken of this meeting, so listen very carefully but take no notes."

As the members took their seats, Mathew continued, "I think we're all agreed that the location of our operation is to be in an alpine setting very likely in Slovenia. I think anywhere in Europe is out as it is too heavily trafficked and patrolled. The Slovenian alps are not but communication is harder and more costly. For us this may be a plus. However, we are looking to making lots and lots of money so a few bob more is not going to drive us to seek the dole. Seeing that it was Anton's suggestion in the first place, and he is a native of Slovenia, I asked him to come up with what information he can so you have a chance of making a decision. So, it's over to you, Anton."

"Thank you, Mathew," Anton replied but remained seated to respond. "As you know I am a keen skier and have been all over the Slovenian alps. There are a number of derelict monasteries, but one caught my eye. It is not too far from Ljubljana and close to the Austrian border. I don't know when it was last occupied but it is still in fairly good nick. The buildings on it are made of stone and a bit of spit and polish could work wonders. There used to be a road access to it, but the road now is only good for four wheel drives and donkeys. I think it would make an excellent resort type establishment."

"That may be so but how the hell do you get to it?" Walter asked.
"Mostly by helicopter or on skis."

"Helicopter! You're joking? That would cost an arm and a leg."

"It's expensive but doable, especially if you own the helicopter."

"I've had a look into this, Walter, and it's not as forbidding as it sounds," Mathew interjected, "especially as the guests would be paying around ten grand a day."

"Ten grand a day! You must be joking? Who would pay ten grand a day just for a bit of sex?"

"You'd be surprised, Walter. I can name you twenty people of the top of my head right now who would be glad to pay it and twenty more, if I have to think about it. We're talking about guys who spill more than that. These are guys who will think of nothing of spending."

$100,000 in a sanatorium right here in Switzerland where they can only fantasise about the nurses. In our spa in Slovenia they can actually fuck them."

"You've got a point there. OK, why don't we have a look at the place," Walter conceded.

"Thank you for that, Walter, and that brings me to the next point. Obviously, we are not going to rush into things, we need to research them and evaluate them. This is going to cost. I therefore suggest we each drop in, say, ten grand towards that cost."

"Ten grand, in what? Pounds. Dollars, Roubles?" Anton asked.

"Dollars, US Dollars as with nearly all of our dealing," Mathew answered.

"I think that's fair and necessary," Mato agreed.

So did all the others, and on that agreement a new cartel was born.

***

It was raining at Graz airport in Austria. Autumn had just begun, as the cold darts of wind reminded one and all. Mathew and Walter were standing at a window gazing out at Anton and Marco standing by a helicopter talking to a smallish man, with lots of arm waving indulged by both parties. Shortly, Anton left the man standing by the helicopter and joined Mathew and Walter in the small airport lounge. "OK, is all fixed," he told the other two, "I've explained to the pilot what we want. He was a bit worried about the thermals in the region, as he was warned about them by the Slovenian authorities when he sought permission to fly over the Julien Alps in Slovenia. I had to promise him more money if we struck dirty weather, so he was quite happy with that."

"So, what now?" Mathew asked.

"Now we board the helicopter and act like tourists."

The party went out to the tarmac and walked to the helicopter. Once there, they introduced themselves to the pilot, an Austrian well in his forties called Franz.

In the air, Anton sat next to the pilot and did most of the navigating.

He seemed to know exactly where he was going. Entering the alps, the weather changed dramatically as sunshine reflected from the snow-covered peaks, revealing a rugged vista of alpine canyons where fir and pine trees wore snowy mantles over their needle branches.

"There," Anton pointed out to the others, "that's the place I was telling you about. Can you head straight for it, Franz?"

Franz altered course slightly, and soon coming into view was what seemed like a conical mountain with the top cut off, allowing a wall to be built around it with several stone buildings erected in the inner perimeter.

"There's a compound just to the right of that building, Franz. Can you land us down there?"

"Sure, but no one told me about any landing," Franz protested, "Landings are extra, they'll probably charge me a fee, and it's not on my flight plan."

"Screw the flight plan, no one will ever know you landed. The place is deserted, you can see that for yourself."

"That's not the point. This was booked as a round flight, nothing was said about landing."

"OK, Franz, you've made your point," Anton said, quite exasperated. "What say we double your, no, triple your fee if you land us and give us an hour or so to look around."

"Cash up front, no paperwork?"

"You mean like now, before we land?"

"Ja, the extra as cash in my pocket. The original has to go through the books."

"OK, just hold on a moment, better see what the others think."

Anton turned to the others for confirmation.

"The little Kraut's got a point. We didn't say anything about landing," Mathew agreed. "We'd better pool a little cash together lads. We didn't come all this way for a haircut."

"What about Mato? He's not here but he's part of us?" Marco pointed out.

"We'll divide it five ways. I'll put in for Mato."

Wallets were produced and the desired sum cobbled together in two different currencies.

"I hope you don't mind, "Mathew said, handing Franz the cash, "It's a bit difficult to find a currency exchange up here."

Franz took the money, counted it and did a little mental arithmetic.

"Thank you, that's OK. I can stay on the ground an hour at the most and I have to radio my position to base, otherwise they will start searching for me."

"An hour is about all the time we will need, so just put her down as soon as you can."

Franz sighted the compound and, after circling twice, landed the helicopter on a cobblestone courtyard. Anton was first out, and the others quickly followed. Only Franz remained in his helicopter. Anton was right, the place was deserted and seeing this visit was his idea, he assumed the role of tour leader.

Inspecting the various stone buildings and their rooms, the touring party found the buildings old but structurally sound. They took photographs of nearly every one of them, from the outside and the inside. In the open air the scenery could not have been more alpine, a 360-degree view of peaks and troughs of snow-covered vegetation.

Standing next to a wall and looking down on the ground below, Mathew remarked to Anton, "How the hell did those monks manage to get all the building materials and stones to this place?"

"No one knows 100% for sure, but we think donkeys. Lots and lots of donkeys. They got strong backs and are very good heavy, so sure on their feet. A lot of the stone they probably quarried from the top of the mountain because originally it would have been a peak, not flat as is now."

"So, the monastery was built from its own material?"

"Something like that."

"You know, I'm beginning to like this place, especially the air. It's so light and fresh and crispy. This could be turned into a spa-like resort."

"That's what I've been trying to tell you."

"And you were right," Mathew agreed.

"Thank you and another thing, the privacy. Who's going to raid you here? There really is only one way in here, and that's by chopper and the quadrangle can only accommodate a few choppers at any one time. How can any other choppers land if our choppers, ours, are already there? They could start rebuilding the old road, but I don't think so as that was only built for donkeys and horses."

Franz watched his tourist party with great interest. He tried to fathom out the reason so many photographs were taken. To show friends at home? Pictures of rocks and old buildings and interiors? If they were Americans, he could understand that, but these men were all Europeans. He tried to suppress his curiosity, but it got the better of him. He waited for an opportunity and approached Walter, who was the only German-speaking person in the party.

"Pardon my asking, but why the great interest in a mound of rocks on top of a mountain?"

"We are looking for a site for a type of spa, er, hospital for people who need special treatment."

"But this is so remote. Surely, you would be better off on flatter ground?

"Possibly," Walter replied, "but we need the high ground, the rare, clean air and the peace and privacy."

"I see but the access? Really only one way, helicopter.
Expensive!"

"That's not quite the way we see it. Imagine a person coming to the spa is not at all well. If he came by road, it is a long gruelling drive. Also, a very expensive way to get there by an ambulance. But a flight to, say, Ljubljana or Graz and an immediate transfer to a helicopter direct to the spa, I think would prove to be the most economic."

"You have a good point there. You might even be better off having your own helicopters as you would need several, including one to haul supplies to your spa."

"Franz, you are a pretty shrewd fellow. Should we get this thing going, would you be interested in being our pilot and transport manager here?"

Franz remained silent for a short period. "On the face of it, yes, but you realise the conditions would have to suit me and then of course there is the money."

"The money is the easy part, and I am sure you would not be disappointed. The conditions we can discuss later if and when the need arises."

Franz did his best to hide his enthusiasm. He presently worked for the helicopter company on a casual basis and while the money was good when flying, the hours were sparse and unpredictable.

As the others were returning to the helicopter Franz conceived an idea.

"Gentlemen, seeing that all you wish to do now is to return to Graz, I think I may have misunderstood you. I thought you wanted to do many more landings and that is why I had to charge you extra. However, you have made only one landing and stayed here for quite a while, thus cutting my fuel costs. Therefore, I am returning the extra money I charged you as it was not being used up."

"That's awfully decent of you, Franz," Mathew replied, "but I think you have served us well and I vote you keep the money and this evening at the Schwartze Adler have a 'prosit' on us."

***

"Well, gentlemen, having studied the photographs, the maps and the estimates, are there any comments?" Mathew asked the newly formed group at a further meeting in Walter's warehouse.

"What worries me most is the access, virtually by helicopter only," Mato Rahal spoke up. "Couldn't we somehow put in a road? I believe there used to be one there."

"You couldn't be with us when we had a look at the place, Mato. Otherwise, you'd have seen what used to be a donkey track. It would be cheaper for us to have a fleet of helicopters than have a road put in, no matter how crude, and then there's the security angle, no unwelcome visitors or spectators. And no escape attempts from our workforce. There is plenty of room to increase the size of the quadrangle. Personally, I am sold on the idea, and I hope we can acquire the place at a reasonable price."

"And what would that be?" Mato asked.

"Anton!" Mathew called out, "tell Mato and now the rest of us what you told me when you got back from Ljubljana."

"OK. The land is owned by the government and not by the church. Four hundred or so years ago the monks didn't purchase it, they just built on it. As you know, Slovenia has had a change of government, and everything is a bit new to them. I had a meeting with the minister for the Interior and he was not keen at all to sell any part of Slovenia to foreigners, not even if we registered a Slovenian company with foreign directors. Well, I thought we'd wasted our time and money and got up to leave when the minister stopped me. It seems that while Slovenia was not prepared to sell, they still needed all the money they could get, especially foreign currency, so while he could not sell outright, leasing would be another matter. So, I brought back all the leasing papers with me."

"What?" Walter jumped to his feet, "You've committed us to a lease?"

"No. I just have the papers for us to look at and sign if interested."

"Sorry, Anton, please go on."

"OK, here's the deal. We can lease the mountaintop for 99 years, renewable, and wait for it…" Anton drew a figure on a large sheet of paper and held it up for all to see, "this is the rent for a year. Can you believe it? You can't rent an apartment in New York for less than that."

There was no need to take it to a vote. Everybody settled down to making plans in designing the world's highest and most luxurious sex slave gulag, but the hubbub lasted only a few minutes.

"Wait a minute," Walter suddenly asked for attention, "I think we may have forgotten something. The Yanks. Jack Solomon is still here and when his people in The States stop receiving merchandise, there's going to be questions asked, and pretty soon they will put two and two together and they are not going to like it."

"You are spot on, Walter, they are not going to like it. I've thought about it. What we are worrying about is them not liking what we are doing, and as a lesson them sending out a hit man to waste one or two of us. We have to nip this in the bud before it happens. We do this by sending them a message that should they send out a hit man to waste just one of us, we will arrange for a chap to return the favour and waste two of theirs and just to show we are serious, we will ask if they have heard from Jack Solomon lately."

"What! You are suggesting we waste Solomon?"

"I'm not just suggesting it. I'm saying it must be done. Jack is their bully boy and a danger to every one of us, and, being a man of Christian persuasions, I believe in doing to others as they would do unto you, just do it first."

"And you have a plan of how to do it?"

"As a matter of fact, I have."

***

Just before noon, Franz was already seated in one of the pews of Der Schwartze Adler in Graz when Mathew arrived alone.

"Good morning, Franz, it's good of you to see me at such short notice. Can we speak in English, or are you willing to put up with my German?" Mathew greeted him.

"Morgen," Franz replied, "English is fine. As you know all pilots must be fluent in English."

"Good, then that's settled, Can I get you something? Coffee, beer, Brotzeit? Anything?"

"A Mass beer would be fine, thank you."

Mathew opted for tea and when both were brought, he got down to business.

"Franz, you took us on one flight not so long ago in Slovenia and we all were generally impressed with the way you carried yourself. From what you may remember, we are setting up a specialised clinic in the alps and our only access is by helicopter."

"Yes, I remember very well."

"Good, then you will appreciate our need for a helicopter pilot."

"So, you will need my bosses to supply you with pilots and choppers on a regular basis."

"Yes and no. We plan to buy our own helicopters and have our own pilots and that's where you could come in. How would you like to be our head pilot, transport manager and adviser on all aerial matters? I think you will be pleased with the money and there will be bonuses, of course."

"Forgive me, but I am at a bit of a loss. Why me? You don't even know me."

"You'd be surprised, but I do know you."

"How?"

"Back on the chopper on the way back. You offered us the extra money back, but you weren't really offering our money back, you were making an investment. Albeit a long one."

"I did no such thing."

"Franz, if we are going to work together, we have to be honest with each other. There was nothing wrong with what you did, and I saw straight away that here was someone thinking of his future. So, what do you say?"

"What can one say after receiving such an offer?"

"One can say that there are not too many such offers floating about."

***

Mathew picked up the phone in his room and dialled Jack Solomon's hotel.

"Hi Jack, Mathew Hudson here. Glad to know you're still in

Bern."

"Well, you know, you get bogged down in business and there's always something else to do and Bern's a good a base as any. Anyway, what's on your mind?"

"You're not going to like this, Jack, but after you reefed some of the money from the other guys, they've sort of mutinied and have gone out for themselves."

"No kidding, nobody walks out on the business and enjoys a long retirement, you know that."

"I might, but there are those who don't. What's more, they plan to set up in opposition."

"That's a laugh. They could not set up two billiard balls."

"But they have, Jack, and it's a great concept and I think the family should know about it."

"OK, hotshot, so what do you want me to do about it?"

"I'd like to talk to you about it but not on the phone."

"So come on over. I'll be waiting."

"But it's just the two of us at this point. No one else, I think you understand why."

"Sure thing."

"Right, I'm on my way."

***

In Jack's hotel suite, Mathew accepted the proffered scotch and water and got down to business.

"The others think that you and the family are selling them short. They reckon the merchandise we sent you was just as good as it was from day one, but you want to up your end of the take."

"That's bullshit and you know it."

"It's not what I think that matters, Frank, it's what they think."

"OK, so what's your angle, why aren't you with them?"

"You've been good to me, Jack, and we've always been square with each other but the idea the others have got is a great one. I'm

116

not kidding, and I know you can use it. I'd like to stay with you."

"OK, so what's the idea?"

"We're still in the same business but from a totally different approach."

"So, tell me."

"I'd rather show you. That way you can visualise it better as I explain it."

"That shouldn't be too difficult," Jack conceded, "so what do you want me to do?"

"Take a ride with me in a chopper over the Slovenian alps and I will show you something which will make your eyes blink a million bucks at a time."

"Really hotshot, that sounds more like a bit of fun than anything else but OK make it happen."

***

"Here's what we're going to do, Franz. We're going to take a very sick American up in the chopper and fly him over the Julian alps. Somewhere along the line in some lonely chasm, the American will want to crap badly and I will gladly oblige him and ease him out of the chopper at about 3000 metres or so. Do you understand what I'm saying, Franz?"

"I understand perfectly, but on my flight plan how do I explain three men walk on the chopper but only two walk off?"

"Easy, as only two men will walk on, and two will walk off."

"How do you achieve that?"

"Again, easy. You will have to ID him and take him to the chopper, as I will have sneaked on board already, preparing some snacks or something. On the way back, only two men leave the chopper, just as your log requires."

***

A fine morning greeted both Jack and Mathew as they arrived at Graz airport.

"If you just wait here, Jack, the pilot's got your description and location. I'm just going to duck off and check on our order of supplies. A drop of scotch won't go astray at 15,000 feet."

Franz had no problem locating Jack and asked him to accompany him to the helicopter.

"What about Mathew?" Jack protested.

"Oh, he's just organising a little refreshment for the two of you. Totally illegal for the pilots, you know, but you enjoy as much as you can."

Cleared for take-off, Franz headed direct for the Julian Alps.

"So, where's this multi-million valley in the alps you are taking me?"

"It's not a valley, it's a mountain top, you ignorant piece of Yankee shit, but you'll never see it," Mathew called out from the rear of the chopper.

"What! What's got into you? And how dare you speak to me like that?"

"I'll speak to you in any way I choose, fatso, but right now I have no time to debate anything except that you just lost your power of debate." Mathew produced a snub nose .38 pistol and fired four rounds into Jack's body.

"I hope this sends a message to your fat-arsed pals. Franz, can you lower and bank the chopper a fair bit to starboard. I have a useless bit of cargo to ditch."

CH 8. THE PASSING OF TIME

Susan had only a vague idea of how long she had been on the rock. The weather, getting colder, gave her some inkling, as she watched the snowline creep down into the valleys. Christmas was just around the corner, but she didn't know which corner. Asking someone for the date was useless. All she was told was that it was a Wednesday or Friday. Even her clients were briefed to say nothing more than that.

She had grown to accept her fate when bedded by the clients. She even acted out the motions expected of her with nearly all of them, but not with Akim, which bothered him almost to distraction. Susan knew this, and she also knew that this was the only way to drive him to despair. By now, she almost enjoyed the moments.

As the weather grew colder, there was a noticeable drop in visiting clientele. This gave Susan and the other women more spare time to be bored. There were no social activities organised for the inmates, no common room to sit and talk, but there was a gym. This was Mathew's idea. No common room for the ladies to chat, eat and get fat but a gym and sauna room to stay slim. No food was allowed in the gym, but coffee and tea were available on demand.

Patra too made use of the gym, as she was determined to keep her figure, but whenever she was present a hush accompanied her. That annoyed Patra, as in a way she too was a hostage, deprived of the company of other women. Whenever she tried to strike up a conversation with another woman she was met with frightened, formal answers. Yes, no, fine and thank you, were the words which enjoyed the pinnacle of popularity. Even though Patra spoke four different languages, these words prevailed.

On the treadmill, designed for four, Susan was joined by Patra coming up behind her.

"Would you mind if I turned up the speed a notch?" Patra asked Susan.

Recognising Petra's voice, Susan replied immediately, "Of course not, turn it to whatever speed you like."

"That was not an order, Susan, it was a request."

"Whatever you say, Madam Patra."

"Tell me, what is it with you ladies? You talk to me as if I was Mrs Hitler or something. I work here just the same way as you do except, I do different things. I have never been unkind to you or hit you or anything?"

"Yes, you have," Susan blurted out.

"What! When? Oh yea, that time, but I had to, Mathew was watching me. I didn't hit you hard."

"No, but you still hit me."

"Obviously, not hard enough. You must understand, my job here is to keep you ladies in line, and that is not always easy. You can vouch for that."

"You have a job, and you get paid for it. I am forced to have a job I don't want, but I don't get paid even if I wanted the job. I am a slave, a sex slave," Susan was becoming emotional.

"You are right, of course, but look at it this way. If I wasn't here, there would be somebody else here. At least I can see to it that you are treated well. Besides, you may think of yourself as a slave, but you are not the only one. In a way, at times, I too am a sort of a slave here."

"You are kidding, aren't you?"

"Look, why don't we get of this stupid machine, have a coffee and just talk for a bit."

Thoughts flashed through Susan's mind at an amazing speed. Who knows where this could lead if she cultivated some sort of a friendship with Patra?

"That would be nice," Susan replied enthusiastically.

Both Susan and Patra left the treadmill and headed for the coffee dispenser.

Patra reached it first. Taking a cup, she turned to Susan. "How do you take your coffee?" she asked in a loud voice.

"White with one sugar," a surprised Susan replied, looking round the gym to see if anyone had heard. A few faces were turned her way. They had. Susan worried that her having coffee with Patra could be interpreted as having drinks with the enemy. She dismissed the thought.

"So what?" she thought, "if I can turn this to some advantage, to hell with them. They never responded to any attempts I made to be friends with them."

The two women sat down on one of the benches, facing each other holding their cups, as there were no tables on which to rest them.

"You were saying that at times you felt like being slave here. I find that hard to follow?" Susan began.

"Why does that surprise you? I am here every day, like you. Mathew give me my orders, and I have to carry them out. If I make a mistake Mathew will think of a punishment,"

"I understand that, but you don't have to stay here. You can always resign," Susan pointed out.

"Resign! Ha," Patra exclaimed, "and do what? What sort of job would I get? I have no skills. I have no family or husband. The money I saved would soon be passed through my stomach.

"Yeah, but you still have your freedom. You often go into Ljubljana in the helicopter, I have seen you."

"Sure, you seen me, but you have not seen me asking Mathew's permission every time I go, and every time he give me a list of things to do for him."

"But once you are in town you could take off for wherever you want."

"And go where? Sleep where? Do what?"

Susan was stumped, she had no answer, "I'm sorry I didn't realise that."

"You young girls! Many things you don't realise. You were

student before you come here, I believe?"

"No, I graduated university and was about to start work as a lawyer."

"I never went to school. When I was fourteen my father sold me to a brothel in Beirut. That's where I first met Mr Mathew."

"Really! I never would have guessed."

"Oh yes. I was in that brothel many years and then Mathew turned up. For some reason he liked me and became a regular."

"What was Mathew doing in Beirut? I always thought he was English?"

"He is, but he was living in Beirut dealing in arms, or so he said. Actually, I think he was doing more in shipping drugs than arms."

"So, you've known him for a long time."

"Yes, many years, and then one time he say he was going back to England and he take me with him."

"How could he do that? You belonged to the brothel, didn't you?" Susan asked.

"That's right, I did, but Mathew told the owner he would live a lot longer if he gave me away. Mathew had many connections, and the owner knew that, so he gave me to Mathew."

"That's fascinating, so whereabouts in England did you end up in?"

"In London. Mathew owned an escort service there and he got me to work there."

"As an escort?"

"Oh no, as manager. That's why I had to learn to speak English pretty quickly."

"You didn't speak any English before you went there?" Susan asked, quite amazed.

"Only a little bit from what I learned from customers in Beirut but mostly in London."

It was pretty clear to Susan that Patra was enjoying the opportunity to talk to someone of her own sex, and she decided to try and keep the dialogue going and look for any advantage which could prove to be useful.

"It seems to me that you and Mathew were a couple and should have married at some point or other?"

"Oh, we were a couple all right, and to some extent still are but marriage? Mathew use to say that marriage is for peasants who love Jesus, Christmas, birthdays and lollies, and he owned none of these qualities."

Although Susan was listening carefully, this biographical information was not what she thought was going to be of much use to her. Then, quite unwittingly, Patra handed Susan her boarding pass.

"So, I hope that you can see that there is a parallel between our two types of slavery," Patra almost sighed.

"I don't see that at all. You can get on board that chopper even if you do need Mathew's OK. I can't do that."

"It's not quite as simple as that," Patra replied. "It's more like telling a fish it can leave the water whenever it wants to, knowing that the fish will be back because it cannot survive out of water."

"I see what you mean, but the difference is that you can do it if you wish, I can't, I am much like a prisoner kept under lock and key."

"Nonsense," Patra protested, "your door is not locked, you know that. You can walk about the place freely. Nobody puts chains on you."

"No, but if I want to work in my off hours, I will be forced to work in the kitchen."

"So, you are telling me that when you are married and living in your suburban little house in Australia you would work in the kitchen only if you are forced?"

"No, that's not it. I hate kitchens and cooking. I would probably hire a cook if I could afford it."

Patra looked a little affronted. "Let me tell you something, Susan, in your lawyer's university they forgot to teach you one thing and that is that no matter what, we all have to eat. As you know, most of our food here is precooked and flown in, so what you really don't like is the scrubbing and cleaning?"

"You're quite right, I don't like it. I didn't spend four years at university learning how to wash dishes and scrub floors."

"Then why did you not tell me, I might find something else for you if why you don't like to be in the kitchen?"

"What! Tell you! That would be like telling a Nazi guard you don't like Auschwitz."

"So, they do call me Mrs Hitler?"

"Not that I have heard but you brought it up."

"Yes, I did, and I apologise, it is just that I see a lot of hate in the eyes of the women, but I have a job to do here. I didn't bring them here, but my job is to look after them."

"Then why not tell them that?"

"What good will that do?"

"You talk to them. They will talk to you."

By this time the other ladies had left the gym, leaving only Susan and Patra still talking.

"All right then." Patra looked around. "Why don't we start with you?"

"All right."

"So, you don't want to work in the kitchen. What would you like to do?"

"That's a good question. I'm a mental not a physical person. I like to work more with my head then with my hands."

"I see, you want my job."

"No, I did not mean that."

"I know that, so I have a proposition for you."

"Oh yes!"

"Yes. How would you like to be my personal assistant?"

"What? What does that involve?"

"Helping with the ordering and managing of provisions, maintenance requirements, fuel supplies and twenty other things which haven't come to mind."

"That sounds interesting, I think I would like that. Are you

124

serious?"

"Yes, very. You may not know, but around this place I have to run the economics while Mathew runs the politics. Sure, the money I get is good, but the time I get off is not enough."

"I can understand that, but if I am taking on this workload, do I get any of the money?" Susan asked.

"Don't push it, sweetie, you've earned enough trading stamps already."

"I'm sorry, I was actually joking."

"There's nothing funny about money. In any case, in the light of what we were talking about, come and see me after lunch tomorrow and I'll see what we can work out." Patra left her coffee cup on the bench and left the gym.

Susan remained on the bench, then rose to get another cup of coffee. Returning, she sat down and contemplated. "I wonder if that was the wisest thing to do?" She sipped her coffee thinking, "The other women will probably turn against me. Not that we're great friends as it is but if I play my cards right, I might just get Mathew. No, he'd never go for that, but I might fluke a ride into Ljubljana with Patra and then run like hell."

It was a sweet thought and heavens knows, she needed one. For the first time in months, Susan thought she saw a glimpse of light at the end of the tunnel.

***

Susan knocked on Petra's office door, and when ushered in was surprised how small it was, made smaller still by six four-drawer filing cabinets and two wall units. An average size desk with two telephones on it also featured an adding machine and stackable document trays. Large ledgers were pushed into one corner. Next to the desk was a floor-standing reading lamp, adjustable to suit the user. The desk had just one visitor's chair in front of it. The stone walls were softened by hanging drapes and cured animal skins.

"You said to come straight after lunch," Susan reported once inside the door.

"Yes, I did" Patra replied, "come in and take a seat. Now, take a look round you. This may not look much but it is the engine room which runs this place. Living on top of this mountain, everything we consume has to be brought in from the outside and depends on intricate purchasing and accounting.

"We have electricity here we have to generate ourselves. In cellar 3 is a generator and a spare one next to it. It requires petrol to run it. That petrol must be flown in by helicopter and stored.

"The kitchen requires lots of stores. Every steak must be flown in. The liquor our guests consume, even the toiletries, they all are flown in.

"Then there's the laundry, the showers and so on. At some time, they all have maintenance needs. So, we have a workshop full of bits and pieces. What I'm trying to say is that the helicopters we have are more than busy flying in all that we need, but we must have strict control or run the risk of financial collapse."

"I understand all that," Susan interrupted, "but what I don't see is where I can fit in?"

"Every single item we order must be verified and checked off as it arrives. At the moment, Pepe is doing that job, but he has long fingers, especially when it comes to the alcohol inventory. He is also lazy and has no idea how to keep a running inventory. I keep telling Mathew, but Mathew just shrugs his shoulders and says it is my responsibility, so I must do something about it. Well, now I am doing something about it. I want you to take over from Pepe. Do you think you can do this job?" Patra asked.

"I don't see why not. It's simple administrative practice."

"Good. Tomorrow I will transfer Pepe to maintenance, and you can take over. By the way, do you speak any other language apart from English?"

"No, a little bit of school French and German but that's about it."

"Hmm, that's too bad, but I guess it will have to do."

126

"Why do you ask that?" Susan queried.

"A lot of the invoices here are in different languages, depending on what they supply, but most product names are universal so a university graduate should be able to pick that up without too much trouble."

"I'm sure I'll be able to cope," Susan assured Patra whilst inwardly praying this doesn't jeopardise the job.

"Well. I suppose Pepe only spoke Italian, and that in some obscure dialect and a bit of English, so you shouldn't have too much trouble."

"Thank you, but just so I know, when I start this job, does that mean I no longer have to attend the evening selection parades before your guests?"

"No, it does not. Nice try, Susan, but if you don't like the arrangement, then you can't work here."

"No, no ..." Susan cried out in alarm, "I was only asking, you know, just to be sure."

"Good. Now, you are sure. You have one week to learn the job. I will explain to you what and how things are to be done and then it's up to you."

"Thank you, Madam Patra. I really appreciate what you are doing and hope you'll be pleased."

***

Patra was surprised how quickly Susan picked up the workload, and how clearly she understood what had to be done and how it all worked. She had even rescheduled the helicopter flights so that less time was spent on the ground and less paid out in landing costs at other airports. Thus, quite a lot of money was saved, much to the delight of Mathew. Franz, on the other hand was not pleased, and resented being shown up by a female and a sex slave at that. Nor, for that matter, was Pepe pleased. He felt that had been demoted, but when Susan confronted him with proof that he had had his fingers in the till, he accepted the situation as long as Susan kept her findings away from Mathew. Susan was quite happy to do this and stored this information in the knowledge that the day could come when she needed a favour. Her findings would be useful in calling in a favour.

"God," Susan thought when reviewing her situation, "I've become as bad as them. No, that can't be it. I'm virtually a prison trustee. I'm not here because I want to be. They are. Let that be the difference. Whatever way I can find to get me out of here can only be just."

***

It was with intricate care that Susan applied herself to the unpaid job. She quite enjoyed the change, but more than that, it gave her the opportunity to study the place and look for any possibility or anything useful to get her out of the place. She had full access to the kitchen, the bar, the laundry, the heliport fuel compound, as well as the maintenance workshop. The clipboard under her arm was like a universal key, opening the doors to let her check whatever she deemed was worth checking.

Mathew soon found out the change in Susan's status but for a long time made no comment. Then, on a Friday morning, he walked into Petra's office, finding both women engrossed in a ledger.

"Ah, conspiring on how to make my retirement a more pleasant one, I see." Mathew said as he entered.

"Hardly, Mathew," Petra replied. "You once told me you'd never retire."

"So, I did. Well never mind that. Susan, I hear you're doing an excellent job here. Good to see you're settling in well. Next thing I'll know is that you're after Patra's job!"

Patra winced a little if only to show that she did not think this comment funny.

"Actually, you're wrong," Susan intervened. "Yours is the one I'm after."

"No kidding, go for it my dear. Nothing like a bit of stiff competition. Talking of 'stiff' I dropped by to let you know your lover is back in Slovenia and will be visiting you in a week or so."

"What lover? I haven't got a lover," Susan protested,

"Of course, you have. Akim, the Romeo of the Balkans, and this time please, could you be a bit, just a bit warmer towards him?"

"I am as far as I can be, but how warm would you be to someone who's had you abducted on your wedding day?"

"Oh, I fully understand the circumstances, but a bit of acting wouldn't hurt, would it? I mean I get him the next day, slobbering all over me, and all because of your cruelty."

"That's rich, Mr Mathew. Which one is the one being cruel, the rapist or the victim?"

"That will be enough of that, Susan," Mathew ignored the question. "He's coming to see you and that's that."

***

While Susan enjoyed her newfound day job, the evenings were still quite horrible. Straight after dinner, she and the other women had to parade before the clients old and new, so that men could make their selection of a sexual partner for the night. Mario mostly presided these parades and issued printed room number tokens once a client indicated his desire. The client would then hand Mario an envelope with a note inside instructing what the lady should wear, plus his sexual preferences.

Not all clients attended the selections, as some had their favourites booked in advance. Quite a smooth, well-run operation but repulsive, nevertheless.

In a way, Susan was lucky. Mr Ali had taken a liking to her and was practically a permanent resident there. He liked to talk and apart from a little groping, spent a lot of time in her company. He was a very intelligent, highly educated, and a pleasant man. Susan actually grew quite fond of him.

Most of the time Mr Ali talked about himself, but on occasions he questioned Susan about her past and Australia in general. One time, Susan tried to develop the Australian narrative, suggesting he visit Australia and take her with him as his personal tour guide.

Mr Ali laughed at the thought. "What an idea, Susan. I can see you now, guiding me into your first police post."

"Oh no, Mr Ali," Susan tried to show she was offended. "I would never do that; you've been a friend to me here. Actually, the only friend I have."

"Thank you for that, my dear, that's nice to know and nice of you to say so."

"You must have some plans for your future, though? You can't spend the rest of your life in this place? For one thing, you must go broke soon at the prices they charge here."

"I don't understand. Why must I break something here? Oh, I am sorry, I see what you mean. I could spend the next hundred years here and still not, as you say, go broke?"

CH 9. A GLIMPSE OF HOPE

The job Susan had to do not only stemmed the boredom, but also actually increased her morale. Knowing how the place runs gave her the opportunity to see and evaluate a plan to escape. Her first thought was to stow away in one of the helicopters and run as soon as it's landed, but on closer inspection she could find no place to hide. The possibility of Patra taking her to Ljubljana was a comforting thought, but she had to admit this was a pipe dream. They would never trust her, even if she wore a collar and leash around her neck.

Franz, the Austrian pilot was a thought. She had caught him looking at her on a number of occasions when she was in the chopper pool checking energy supplies and measuring the petrol levels in each drum. A cash bribe was out of the question, but sounding him out as to possible sexual favours may work, but how does one instigate this?

The kitchen had two large pantries fully stocked with perishable and non-perishable food stuffs. A resident cook or chef presided here. He was a big, strong man in his middle thirties, moon-faced with a permanent stubble that he claimed was his beard. His name was Olaf, apparently an escaped convict from Zagreb. His qualifications as cook were unclear but seeing most of the meals were precooked and flown in, the only real talent required was to raise the temperature of the dish and apply some garnish.

At first, when Susan entered the pantry to see what stocks were to be ordered, Olaf would follow her in and try to force his attentions on her. Susan reacted as violently as she could and ended up using her knee to kick him in his testicles.

"You stupid cow," Olaf groaned, doubled-up in pain, "What did you do that for? I was only being friendly."

"I can do without that sort of friendship."

"You crazy woman, all of you! You all up here to fuck, so why not let your working friends have a bit of fun, or are we not good enough?"

"You are quite right; you are not good enough. When you can save up the 5000 or whatever bucks it is Mathew charges his rapists, then there is nothing I can do about it, but until then, if you try it again, I will squeeze your balls so hard they'll be like mashed potatoes. Do you understand what I am saying?"

"You one big cow, I'll report you to Mr Mathew and tell him I don't want you near my kitchen."

"Oh, by all means please do, and also tell him how you wanted to score a freebee and deprive him of his 5000 or whatever bucks. Tell him all that, or I have a better idea. I'll tell him."

Olaf said nothing while chewing over Susan's cutting threat, then, "OK, OK maybe this, this bit of a misunderstanding. Sorry, sorry, it won't happen again, I promise."

Without another word, Olaf walked out of the pantry, leaving Susan in a bit of a state of euphoria. For the first time, she had scored a victory. An end to the Balkans skirmishes it wasn't, but a victory, nevertheless.

It didn't take long for Susan to realise that neither the kitchen nor the pantry offered any avenue for escape, especially as the only means of escape was by helicopter. She thought again about winning the trust of Patra to the point that she could accompany her on a day trip to Ljubljana, but the chances of that happening were too remote as Mathew's agreement would be needed as well.

"Somewhere, somehow, there must be a way out," Susan kept on thinking. "Even Edmund Dante had to lavish in prison for 13 years before he escaped from Monte Cristo. 13 years! By then I will have lost most of my looks, so what happens to me then? I will be taken to some remote beach and let go? I don't think so, killed is more likely, or sold off to some Eastern Sheik as a slave. Tunnelling … tunnelling? No, forget the idea, there's no direction to go."

***

Autumn had already established its grip as the leafier trees attested. Only the conifers showed off their green needles, the rest displaying skeleton-like branches and twigs.

"It will get a lot colder, very soon," Patra commented to Susan. "I suggest you make inventory of our stocks of blankets and bedding supplies. Don't just count the cartons, count what's inside the cartons. I want a complete count, blankets, sheets, pillowcases, towels, soap, tooth paste the lot. Then we can start on the medicines. To do those you will need a key for the cabinets, so let me know when you get that far."

The next day Susan entered the supply room, armed with a clipboard and stock sheets. She looked around the various shelves and decided to start with the blankets and doonas. The cartons which were still sealed, she recorded the count printed on the side. The cartons which had been opened, Susan emptied them and counted the items as she replaced them. She worked methodically round the supply room making sure she missed nothing. On the top shelf of one of the bays, she counted eight cartons but could not see if any had been opened. A ladder at one end of the room became useful.

Of the eight cartons two had been opened. The cartons were heavily decorated with Chinese characters. Underneath in English, French and German was printed:

CHINESE SILK DOUBLE BED SHEETS
Made In China
Six sets per carton.

Somewhat surprised, Susan removed one set and inspected it. It was sealed in a clear plastic bag, but she could feel the smoothness of the fabric through the plastic.

"How about that!" she exclaimed loudly, and then to herself, "I'll be damned and all this time I thought I was sleeping on some sort of rayon. I suppose the pillowcases will be silk as well."

They were.

For reasons she couldn't explain to herself, Susan felt a lift in her spirits. She finished her inventory, handed the stock sheets to Patra and returned to her quarters. The first thing she did was to inspect the sheets on her bed.

"Well, I'll be damned, the same as in the cartons. Why would Mathew go to the trouble and have all the ladies' beds covered in silk sheets?" And then the penny dropped. The silk wasn't for the ladies, it was for the male guests."

***

Finding a willing and competent helper encouraged Patra to make the most of it.

"Talk to Franz and get him to give you estimate of what fuel we have and how much we'll need to carry us until March next year at least. Also, get a list of emergency spare parts we need for the helicopters to carry to see us through for the same period," Patra instructed Susan. "I hear we are in for a savage winter so we must be prepared."

"What do you call a savage winter?"

"Storms, plenty of snow and freezing temperatures. Also, not so many guests, but we still have to live through it."

Susan made a note of all of Patra's requirements and wondered if she should mention that Franz had an eye out for her but decided not to. She would fight her own battles. Then a thought occurred to her.

"For the coming winter, don't you think we should get some warm fleecy sheets?"

"I agree with you," Patra replied. "Just don't mention this to Mathew. He seems to think silk sheets are the sexiest things out, and to our clients they are a draw card. 'Put silk on the bed and the clients drop in on them like parachutists.' Silly man, but I'm not going to argue with him."

"I don't get it, but I suppose he's the boss."

"That he is but tell me, do you find silk sheets sexy?"

"They're nice, but I wouldn't call them sexy."

"Neither would I but Mathew, he's English."

"Ai! What's being English have to do with it?"

"The English are a bit strange. You know, when I was working for him in London, many of our English clients refused to take their socks off."

"Really! Why ever not?"

"I don't know, they were only too eager to drop their trousers and expose their 'willies' but their socks remained on, almost as though their toes were sacred."

"Did Mathew take his socks off?" Susan asked, and straight away wished she hadn't.

"Now you are being impertinent," Patra warned Susan.

"I'm sorry, I didn't mean to be. I was just being curious," Susan apologised.

"OK, but now you'd better get started. Oh, and by the way, he didn't."

Susan set of to find Franz, quite happy with the morning's outcome. Patra was losing her stony countenance, revealing the normal person inside her. Slowly, Susan was getting under her guard but how to put this to any benefit, she had no idea.

**

Franz was on top of the helicopters inspecting the rotor when he heard his name being called. Looking down, he saw Susan.

"Maybe she changed her mind about me?" Franz flattered himself as he clambered down from the machine. "Ach, you have come for me at last," he quipped in a jolly Austrian way.

"If I came for you that way, I'd be wearing a straitjacket. Madam Patra wants you and me. She wants some figures, and she wants them now."

"She is welcome to my figure any time, but I'd rather have yours."

"Hadn't you better discuss that with Mr Mathew?"

"OK, you win, and now we go and do some good work together."
As they walked across the cobblestones towards the motor pool
Franz queried, "OK, so what does Patra want?

"She wants to make sure we have everything we need during the
winter months, so apart from the obvious, anything you may need to
keep the motor pool running during this time, you let me know and
I will get it ordered in."

They both worked methodically and swiftly as Franz estimated
the fuel supply needs, and they moved on to the workshop. Susan had
never seen the workshop before and was amazed at the equipment it
housed. There were cabinets of various size, with pull-out drawers
containing screws, washers, nuts and bolts. Then nails of different
types and sizes plus other bits of metal items that made no sense
to her at all. The walls were covered by peg boards with silhouette
outlines of a variety of tools, showing which tool should go where.
At the bottom of the board, leaning against it was an array of battery-
operated power tools such as small saws, drills and sanding tools. A
wall cabinet revealed a stock of various batteries as well as chargers.
Part of one wall had reels of wire of different gauges attached to
them as well as reels of various strings. Next to them were coils
of rope, again of various types and diameters. In the middle of the
workshop stood a large work bench with vices fitted in the middle
and both ends. At one end of the bench, a freestanding electrical
bench drill separated a circular saw from the drill.

"Noah would have been thrilled to have all this gear when he built
the Ark." Susan commented, more to herself.

"Who this Noa, and where did he build the arch?" Franz wanted
to know. Obviously, Franz was no pursuant of Biblical mythology.

"Noah, the old man from the Bible who built the big boat."

"Ah yes, Noa the fisherman, I understand. Sometimes my English
not so good."

Clearly, Franz didn't understand, but Susan opted to let the matter rest.

"We now go to the materials store and then we finish," Franz suggested.

"We have a materials store?" Susan asked.

"Oh yes! When winter sets in you just cannot fly a helicopter to the city to buy one flank of timber to block up a hole the wind makes."

"I don't think you would do it during the summer either, would you?"

"No, but in the summer the wind is not so cold so it can wait."

***

The materials store was located directly below the main dining room, across the courtyard from the workshop. When they entered, Susan saw it was fitted with bays of racks which housed long timber boards as well as long timber slats of various widths. Another bay featured lengths of galvanised iron pipes as well as plastic tubing of various diameters. Sheets of thick glass were to be seen in another bay next to bags of cement stored at the same level. At the end of the room and sitting on the floor were two large stacks of roof tiles. Next to them, leaning against the wall was a short row of gardening tools.

"Some place you have here Franz. All that's lacking is a lawn mower."

"No need for a lawn mower, there's no grass."

"I can see that, I was only joking, but tell me, Franz, is it hard to fly a helicopter?" Susan asked, her heart skipping a beat.

"When you learn how to, it's much like driving a car. Why do you ask?"

"No real reason. I was just thinking, a lawn mower and a helicopter, in a way they are both choppers except that one has the blades on the top and the other on the bottom. One chops up the grass and the other the air, but the lawn mower is not hard to drive."

Franz was a little confused, "Ja, but lawn mowers don't fly."

"Could you teach me how to fly a helicopter?"

"I could but I won't."

"Why not Franz?"

"I would not like it for Mr Mathews to throw me over the wall." Susan made no further comment. Franz was not as dumb as he made out to be. In any case, she tried, although she got the answer she expected. But she had to try.

***

After her guest had left for the evening, Susan desperately tried to think of the use she could obtain from what she had so far seen, but nothing came to mind. She fixed herself a gin and tonic, taking it with her as she climbed into her bed, thinking. She fingered the sheets musing, "And I thought they were rayon. Silk, eh? Feels just like rayon, maybe a bit lighter. Anyway, what do I know about silk? Funny how there is such a big thing made out for silk. What did Patra say about silk? Let's see, something like, 'put silk on the bed and the clients drop on them like ... like, parachutists, that's it. I wonder what she meant by parachutists? What have they got to do with silk sheets on a bed? Oh well, maybe it's just Patra's understanding of English. Why would parachutists be attracted by silk?" Susan turned on her side, pulling the sheet to cover her shoulders when her own question sunk in. "Parachutes are made from silk!" I could sew some sheets together and drop off over the side." She was getting quite excited now, but then reality took over, "Yeah, but once I drop over the side, then what? Which way do I turn? Besides, I don't think the wall is high enough for the chute to properly open, and how do I pack and fold a parachute? A parachute may glide a little, but it would need more height than I get from this wall. Oh well, it was a good thought while it lasted. On second thoughts, what if it was a windy night and it could glide for a bit before descending? Yeah, and then land on the sharp end of a pine tree," Susan lamented. She pulled the silk sheet to

cover her shoulders. "And what the hell am I thinking, I don't need a parachute, the large door at the bottom of the wall is not locked, I can walk through it anytime I want to, but then what?"
Seconds later sat bolt upright in her bed.

"A glider … a hang glider." She almost yelled the words, "of course, I can somehow build one right here and with a bit of luck glide over to … to Italy, Austria perhaps, depends on the wind. It can be done, I'm sure it can be done." She settled again in her silk cocoon. Immediately, a warming and satisfying thought struck her. "To think that when Akim taught me how to hang glide he also handed me a method of how to get rid of him. All I have to do is build one and then fly it."

The exuberance over, the first question to arise was the 'how' and the 'where'. Starting with the frame, Susan began recalling her glider as given her by Akim. That came very easily. Before each flight, every glider pilot had to inspect their glider, looking for any defects, tears in the wing material and cracks or weaknesses in the frame. Thus, the skeleton was still emblazoned on her mind. She drew a rough sketch of the frame and had to add measurements. For proper balance and steerage, the wings had to be equidistant from the spine of the glider. She could roughly measure it out by pacing, but that was really not good enough, it had to be exact. Susan did not have a tape measure or even a ruler. This was the first setback but easily solved. She may not possess these items, but the workshop did.

There were going to be many of these sorts of setbacks, Susan knew, that but it was a start, piled up on a ray of hope. The task ahead of her was horrendous. First of all, she had to find a place to start the construction. Her room was out of the question for obvious reasons as secrecy was the prime consideration. Then, the materials required would have to be stolen so that they would not be missed or discovered in places they had no reason to be. Some tools were also needed, but they could be secretly replaced when not in use. Again, location became of paramount importance.

Looking round the courtyard, Susan took a mental note of every construction and evaluated its possibilities as a venue to build the hang glider. The result was disappointing. Every room was used for something and there were no convenient sheds to be had. The wine cellar did have a small cellar next to it which was empty, but it was too close to a major traffic area. Besides, to launch a hang glider she would have to carry it up some narrow stairs and possibly damage it in transit.

Her search for a construction venue was not going all that well when she noticed a large block of timber protruding from a hole in the wall directly under the apex of the roof. She had seen it before but then it was of no interest to her. Now she was more than curious.

"What is that thing sticking out from the roof over the main entrance?" Susan asked Patra at a convenient moment.

"You mean that boom thing?"

"Yes, that's the one."

"That goes back to when the place was first built, when the monks used to haul up their supplies from the ground by rope. There's one on the other side of the building as well."

"Isn't it used anymore?"

"Good heavens no. Today we have helicopters and winches and dumb waiters."

"If they're not going to use them why not take them down," Susan asked.

"Don't ask me! Bit of history, I guess. I don't know."

Susan asked no more questions, as she did not want this to be remembered as anything other than a casual conversation. As for herself, she became very interested in history.

***

Having decided on stealth, Susan waited for the opportunity to get inside the roof. It came soon enough on a Wednesday morning. Patra and Mathew were of somewhere in the helicopter. The moment they left; Susan was in the main building looking for an access to the roof. It wasn't too hard to find. A smaller staircase at one end led straight into the ceiling, which was covered by a timber floor one end to the other.

Although it was daylight, not much of it was getting through. The only source of light were the two openings on either side of the building, and they provided enough light to serve the whole area. As Susan surveyed, something grazed her hair. She looked up to see it was a single light bulb dangling from a cable attached to a beam on the roof. Looking at it, she found it had a toggle switch as part of the unit. She tried it and the bulb lit up. Surprised, she had a quick look around and switched it off. She could see two bed bases propping up a few old cupboards, two tables with broken legs and about six or seven chairs which had seen better days. Walking over to the two wall openings, she found she was looking down on some cobble stones from one and the outside wall from the other. Simple geometrics told her that this opening was looking down on the wall of the front door where the old road once was when the place was first built.

"Perfect!" Susan cried out almost aloud.

Having the tools for escape within reach, a strategy on deployment had to be implemented. It was obvious that construction would have to be on a 'do it when you can' basis. To avoid arousing suspicion, materials will have to be purloined, bit by bit, but first and foremost a quantity survey had to be established, and for this she required a scaled plan.

That afternoon, a tape-measure, a ruler and a small setsquare disappeared from the workshop.

The biggest problem was the frame. It had to be sturdy and remain rigid. The frame on her glider at home was made from aluminium, but this was not available. She had to choose between timber slats and rigid plastic piping. She chose the plastic, as she had noticed there were joiners available as well as T joiners and elbow bends. The risk of plastic joiners coming apart was more than possible but if clamped together by a small screw and a nut, it should hold together for some time. After all, the glider was to be used for one flight only.

The biggest problem Susan foresaw was in attaching the silk to the frame. Even if she had strong glue, it was bound to tear away under the heavy air pressure. This loomed to be a big problem. If a strut broke during flight, it was a serious matter, but the glider could be manoeuvred enough to make a landing. However, a torn wing sheet could force the glider into a spin and force a landing, probably fatal.

Susan wrestled with the problem and an idea came to her. She took one of the bed sheets from her bed and, spreading it out on the floor, measured it.

"More than enough material there," she thought. "If I double the sheet over, one side does not need any clamping or stitching, it's pulling the pressure against itself. I can then stretch out the sheet and anchor it to the base at the other side and roll it several times. It will make that base even stronger. Satisfied with her plan, she gathered up her sketches and, neatly folding them, went to her chest of drawers and hid them at the bottom of her underwear drawer.

It had been a long day, and she was tired. Her 'guest', having satisfied his lust had left around 10 pm. The moment he left, Susan retrieved her papers and sketches and commenced her scheming and was now ready for some sleep.

She was about to put out the lights when she remembered, "Christ! I nearly forgot, the tape, the ruler, the setsquare!" She got out of bed and fetched the stolen items from the table, putting them in another drawer.

"Tomorrow, I shall have to find an excuse to visit the workshop and see what is available in screws and nuts and scissors, I'll be needing scissors, but I don't recall seeing any there. Hmm, Patra, surely Patra would possess a pair of scissors?"

CH 10. THE FLIGHT PREPARATION

Putting all that she had observed and planned on paper, Susan reviewed her situation both from the success point to the weaknesses. She highlighted the weaknesses as well as the strength. The weaknesses were naturally the main worry. She could get caught constructing the hang glider. As yet she had no idea where or how she was going to carry out the construction or how to steal the materials she needed.

Assuming the glider was constructed and reasonably safe, the launch was the next worry. When leaping off cliff tops at home all participants would start off with a sprint and then launch themselves over the cliff face. At the Spa there were few suitable places to sprint and then leap, even though its altitude was high enough to provide space for a take-off. A possibility was right outside of Susan's room, a waist-high protective wall, about half a metre thick and flat enough to run on, but to launch off it would have to be a turn to the left or right, and she had never attempted this sort of take-off or come across anyone who had. The wind had to be strong and from the right direction. Another possibility was to attempt a kite-surfing tactic where the wind first filled the underside of the wings and then soared off, but she dismissed that thought seconds after conceiving it as too hard and mostly too dangerous.

Dwelling further on the subject, a thought flashed through Susan's mind. 'The Garbage Wall.' At the rear of the compound a section of the stone fence had been cut away and a wooden gate installed across the gap which opened to let all the Spa's garbage be dropped down in the chasm below. Because of its very nature, the drop zone was placed well out of sight, as no one was likely to tarry there, especially as it was next to a large pipe which emptied all the Spa's excrement and wastewater. Leading up to the gate was a narrow roadway used by trolleys carrying garbage bins. This roadway could be used as a runway to achieve lift-off. Susan made a mental note to inspect this site more closely. The thought of landing in a garbage dump did not worry Susan at all, as very little garbage was visible due to animal activity who must have thought it was manna from heaven.

By far the largest problem facing Susan was the construction of the glider itself. Even though it did not weigh much, she had to find secret places of storage, and this was not going to be easy. The wingspan of even a small glider was just over three metres.

For the framework Susan decided to use the plastic tubing. She would work out the quantity she needed and stash it until it was needed. A better idea still! Why not cut it to size and drill it where necessary and leave it where it is, until it was needed. Similarly nuts and bolts could be stolen a few at a time and stored as well as lengths of cables and rope. The silk sheets were the last item needed and should be attached shortly before the flight. Unfortunately, there could be no controlled test flight.

Satisfying herself with her plans so far, Susan thought about setting a date. Not that a particular date was important but more as setting herself a goal, because it was obvious that her escape attempt could only be made at night. Winter seemed the ideal time, as the ground would be snow covered and preferably moonlit, giving her some vision of the terrain. The direction was obvious. Anywhere but in Slovenia. Her rather scant knowledge of geography was greatly improved by conversations with Franz, a very proud Austrian who provided valuable information about Austria, even to its whereabouts in relation to the spa.

"Austria is very close to us here," Franz had told her, "About fifty kilometres due north from here, but if you want to walk it would be more like two hundred once you've climbed up and down the mountains."

"Can you tell from the air which country you have below?" Susan asked, "I mean by looking down can you tell if you are flying over

Austria or Slovenia?"

"Oh yes! Quite easy in daylight but not so good at night."

"Really? I can understand daylight being easier but it's still just mountains and valleys below, and they all seem to look the same."

"It's not just the mountains and valleys, it's the villages. When you fly over Slovenia the villages look to be quite poor, you know, drab. The moment you cross the border into Austrian air space, the villages seem brighter and well-kept, but the biggest difference is when you spot the churches, mainly the spires." Franz went on in some length describing church spires, leaving Susan regretting she could not take notes.

From a few middle blank pages torn out of a ledger, Susan drew a calendar showing dates for three months, November, December & January. He last week in January she shaded in with her pencil. Mathew did not permit calendars in the complex, reasoning that guests were here to have an enjoyable time and not worry about passing days.

A few weeks ago, Susan had asked Patra is she could see a calendar and Patra had explained the situation.

"That's ridiculous," Susan exclaimed.

"Maybe so, but for Mathew it has earned an extra $50,000 or so."

"How could that be possible?"

"Easy enough. A guest loses all track of time and stays two or three days longer. Mathew then adds the extra days to his bill," Patra explained.

"Don't the clients … sorry, guests complain? Surely, when you are paying out that sort of money, you'd expect someone to remind you your stay is over?"

"You seem to forget that to many of our guests, $1,000 for them is like one dollar is to us, and the service they get here is like nothing else in the world."

Susan hadn't forgotten, she simply found it hard to believe. As it was, she really did not need a calendar, she just wanted one as a goal setter and a memory jogger. The current dates she obtained from the radio and TV and drew up her calendar, blackening in the 26th January. This was to be her leap for freedom night, as there would still be plenty of snow on the ground to provide some light for navigating.

Although she had no map of her surroundings, Susan knew from discreetly questioning Franz, that Austria was some 50km due north and Italy about the same distance due northwest. Her flight plan was simple. Keep gliding until she was sure she was well over the border. Then look out for a larger village and an open field, suitable for landing. Once on the ground she would then seek out the nearest police station and surrender herself, claiming refugee status and asking to see someone from the nearest Australian Consulate or Embassy. She knew the police would have to cooperate by law, as her studies in International Law confirmed. It was the law and its usage which made Austria her first choice. Italy, she thought, could become quite complicated, as from what she had heard, they were ditherers, and she could be stuck in some Italian jail for weeks on end while her case was being investigated. Whereas, she felt, the Austrians would handle her case with Teutonic thoroughness.

That much having been done and decided left only one more thing to do. Construct the hang glider.

***

From that day on, Susan laid down a law for herself. Every day she must do something which is dedicated to her goal. Be it from stealing a few screws and nuts to stealing a length of plastic tubing and finding a place to hide it. She started drawing a skeletal plan of the wings, noting where fasteners were to be used as well as struts for strength and steering. Satisfied with that, she filed the drawing in the lower drawer of her chest of drawers containing her underwear.

She left the stealing of the silk sheets until last, as they could be used only when the wing frames were done, and she wanted to avoid any possibility of Patra finding out that they were missing.

On a couple of occasions Susan made a reconnaissance visit to the garbage wall. Very gently she peered over the top. As far as she remembered, the drop was deeper than the drops she had encountered before. The wooden gate sealing off the gap could be a problem by being just that bit too narrow, thus obstructing the wings. Susan measured the distance by crossing it, one foot directly after the other and memorised he count. On her way back from the drop site, she silently examined the proposed runway. She would dearly have loved to sprint down it but didn't dare in case of prying eyes. However, a mental measurement satisfied her, and as long as it did not ice over, it would meet the required standard.

***

Leaving her office, Patra was about to step out on the quadrangle, heading for the kitchen diagonally opposite, when she spotted Susan headed much the same way. Patra froze for a minute as she watched Susan pass the kitchen entrance and turn the corner building, heading for the garbage wall. This surprised her, and she decided to keep following Susan to see where this journey led. Peering round the corner of the kitchen wall, she was astounded to see Susan pacing out, measuring the width of the gap in the wall.

"Why is she doing that?" Patra wondered. "Surely she's not thinking of jumping? No, can't be that. She's up to something, though. Why come up to a garbage wall so furtively? Maybe she's checking out the place with a thought to meeting someone? Mario, maybe or Franz? No, they're both creeps. A girl like that wouldn't go for either. But she's up to something. I'd better keep a closer eye on her."

Susan began her accumulation of items needed for her escape kit. She decided to construct the hang glider in the loft or ceiling room where no one came and there was plenty of space and nooks and crannies to hide or disguise materials. The main attraction of the loft was the gantry loading section. When ready, the hang glider could be easily lowered to the courtyard, a reasonable distance from the garbage wall. To make sure it was still in working order, Susan passed a piece of rope through the pulley, which responded gladly, having been idle for such a long time.

For a week now, Susan had accumulated all the screws and nuts she had worked out she would need, plus a few more in case of malfunctions. These were hidden at great pains, mixed in with the underwear in her drawers. The bits of rope and cable she took up to the loft and scattered about, so they did not look like a cache. Now came the tricky part, the lengths of plastic piping she needed to construct the frame. The major problem here was that all the tubing stored was the same length. The glider frame needed long tubes for the outer frame and short tubes to strengthen the frame and keep the silk firmly to the whole frame. This meant that the tubes had to be cut to size and pre-drilled to accept the screws and nuts. So did the elbow joints and joiners used to secure them but they had to correspond with the drilled holes in the tube. After some careful thought she came up with an idea. Why not use one elbow joint and one joiner as a template. That way all the pre-construction drill holes will be uniform, making the whole operation simpler and much faster.

To Susan's surprise the stealing and cutting of the tubes went much faster than she had hoped. Almost as soon as her guest had left her, she would furtively make her way to the store house and workshop. Whenever a guest insisted on staying with her for the night, where possible, she plied him with drink and flattering attention. As soon as the alcohol claimed its victim, Susan headed for the workshop.

The cut tubes were piling up, and even when the offcuts and shavings were removed the pile was leading to a possibility of questions being asked. Now, as the opportunity presented itself, Susan carried the cut tubing in small amounts to the loft. The offcuts and shavings, too, could arouse suspicion and had to be disposed of, and the garbage wall gained another customer.

Patra noticed Susan in the quadrangle, carrying a canvas bag, heading in the direction of the garbage wall. Her curiosity aroused, she followed her at a respectful distance. She didn't get too far, as Susan was coming back. Patra backed up for concealment behind an arch in the side of the building. She noted that Susan was still holding on to the canvas bag. Susan passed by without noticing Patra. As soon as she was out of sight, Patra made her way to the garbage wall. Looking over the side there was nothing of interest to be seen on the ground below. Shrugging her shoulders, she pulled herself back and as she did, she noticed some black plastic shavings on the edge of the stonework. They seemed very fresh, and Patra had no doubt these had come out of Susan's bag but what for? What was Susan doing with plastic shavings and why dump them? She could have disposed of these in her own room, so why go to the garbage wall to do this? It made no sense at all except that she was up to something. But what? Patra decided to say nothing and resolved to keep a closer eye on Susan.

***

With the framework now almost complete, the final stage was now to be set in motion. The covering of wings with silk. From her measurements Susan worked out that she would need at least one sheet per wing, preferably two, to give it more rigidity and strength in case one sheet tore. This meant that two packs of sheets would have to be stolen practically right from under Patra's nose. The best time would be when she was away, but to carry two packs of sheets under her arms to the loft, she risked being noticed. One pack at a time seemed to be the best solution. Then there was Patra's ability to spot the missing gap of the stack in the storehouse.

Luck was with Susan. Patra announced that next week she and Mathew would be flying to Graz and returning the following day. She gave Susan a set of instructions of things she wanted done during her absence, which Susan gratefully received, as this would give her legitimate reason for being in and out of her office during the day.

That morning, Susan watched anxiously as the helicopter rose, and as soon as it disappeared from sight she went to Patra's office and the supply room next to it. She looked for the four-wheel housekeeping trolley and, finding one, went directly to the bedding shelf. There were two loose packs of sheets and some cartons. Susan ignored the loose packs and opened one of the cartons, taking out two packs of silk bed sheets. She closed the carton and pushed it back in its place. Now, a first glance would reveal that nothing was missing.

Wheeling the trolley over the cobblestones to the entrance of the loft was a little nerve racking, as the wheels of the trolley made quite a bit of noise, but she was challenged by no one.

Susan began feeling a little thrilled. For the first time she looked back on what had been done and what was still left to do. All the materials she needed had been stolen and stashed in relatively safe places. No one had reported missing items, and no one had reported strange noises coming from her room as she drilled holes in the plastic piping with a cordless drill borrowed from the workshop. She chose her room to drill the tubes because the thick stone walls that separated her room from the others made it fairly soundproof. Had she used the loft, the amount of free space there would have amplified the sound and the electric light bulb showed its presence to anyone below caring to look skywards at the loft. As a further precaution she performed the drilling in her bathroom, and, on completion, gathered every drilled plastic waste bit, and when sure she was not observed, emptied it over the wall the next morning. All that remained to do was to screw the whole frame together and secure it with the silk sheets. For this she still needed a pair of scissors.

To make sure she had enough time to do this, Susan conducted some dummy runs by timing herself as she screwed together a number of tubes. It was not the most scientific time and motion study, but at least it gave her some idea the whole process would take. Then an idea flashed through her mind. Instead of sewing the sheets on the frame, why not let the screws become anchor points for the silk sheet and use wire to secure areas where flapping was likely to develop.

Susan congratulated herself for the thought, as this would cut the assembly time by at least 50%. Then a sobering thought ran through her mind. The silk would have to be holed for the screw to pass through and once in flight could start to tear the silk, due to high wind pressure. This could also happen at many of the other screw points thus tearing the silk and sending the glider spiralling to the ground.

"This could possibly turn into a disaster," Susan reluctantly conceded. "Is the silk strong enough to resist high wind pressure without tearing? Ideally, I should have metal eyelets in the silk to pass through the screws. Now where the hell am I going to get those? There's nothing like that in the workshop, just screws and bolts, nuts, nails, washers. There's got to be something ... some way? God! To think I've come so far and am now to be stopped by nuts, nails and washers. Surely, there must be something in this God forsaken place that I can use? Let's see now, the kitchen. What has the kitchen got that I could use? There are bits and pieces there as back up for some of the appliances, but nothing like an eyelet or a washer or anything. Shit! Concentrate girl, there must be something ... did I just say 'washer'? ... Of course, I did. Washers, that's it! Clamping the silk down with a washer eliminates much of the pressure on the screw, and the risk of tearing becomes minimal."

Pleased with her newfound knowledge of physics, Susan set out for the workshop, clipboard under her arm. Whenever she embarked on a mission, stealing items for her hang glider, she made sure she always carried a clipboard. To any onlooker this suggested that she was going about on official business, so there was no need for speculation regarding her intentions.

The workshop carried a large range of washers of different sizes. Susan matched the ones she needed for her screws and counted out her requirements plus a few more, just in case. All she had to do now was to finish off the glider, and she was ready for take-off and hope for a soft snow landing in a field somewhere in Austria.

So far, she had been concentrating solely on building the hang glider without consideration of what else she needed. This now presented itself very clearly. It would be extremely cold battling the draughts and thermals through the alps, and her hands could virtually freeze holding the bar of the glider to navigate. Susan went through the wardrobe of clothing provided for her, noting some very nice garments but nothing warm. Not even a cardigan. There were, however, a good supply of culottes as well as long sleeve blouses. She could wear a number of pairs of these, but an anorak would be ideal. There were a number of garment substitutions which could be adapted but nothing for the hands. She thought of tying a hand towel round them, but this would hamper their dexterity and ability to control the glider.

"Back to square one," Susan thought, disappointed. "To think a pair of gloves can bugger up the whole thing. Back home I have about a dozen pairs, and it doesn't even get cold. I could ask if the gym has any, but they would be boxing gloves, useless. I'd be better off with welding gloves. Wait a minute, there is some welding equipment in the workshop. It must have gloves to go with it?"

It did. A pair placed on top of the welder and near it a drawer containing six pairs of brand-new welding gloves. Susan tried them on and took one pair.

***

"Mr Ali!" Susan exclaimed, "you haven't seen me for some time. Have you not been well?"

"Quite well, my dear, thank you for asking. I have been home attending to family matters. I have sons who are now nearing the difficult age. They are tired of playing with wooden swords and now want fast motor cars."

"I see, and you have been busy buying them cars?"

"Not on. How do you say it? ... not on your Nelly. I gave them a horse instead. It is better they learn to coordinate with a horse first."

"Did they like the horse?"

"Two of them did, or say they did, but the youngest one rebelled."

"Oh dear! So, what did you do?"

"I had him flogged. He's in hospital now, so tomorrow I must go back to see how he is. He is my son, you know, but I cannot stand insubordination. When he gets out, I'll give him a mule and then a horse if he's learned his lesson."

"Aren't you being a little hard on him? From what you say, he's still very much a boy."

"That he is, my dear, and that is why he must learn discipline even if it is through humiliation."

Susan let the subject drop. "Would you like some anchovies?"

"Yes, thank you, that's what I came here for and the other. And how have you been, Miss Susan? I haven't seen you for a while."

"Fine. Well, you know, nothing very exciting happens around here except winter is just about upon us and it's already very cold."

"Surely you can't be cold already?"

"Oh, I am. I come from a warm country, remember, and I feel the cold sooner."

"But you have plenty of clothing here, haven't you?"

"Yes, but it is all very flimsy stuff." Then a thought entered Susan's mind. "What I really would like is an anorak with a hood to cover my ears. When the north wind blows it really hurts my ears. I don't suppose you could get one for me?"

"I would love to, Miss Susan, but you know the rules here. The management frowns on us giving the ladies presents."

"Oh, I'm not asking for a present Mr Ali. I'd be happy to pay for it. Just to keep warm it would be worth it."

"And just how would you do that? Do you have American dollars?"

"No, but I do have a credit card somewhere here."

"A credit card you say. You would have to be next to me to make that purchase."

"It was just a thought, Mr Ali, no big deal. Now, what about those anchovies?"

***

Several days passed and no sign of Mr Ali. Susan began to wonder if she had offended him. But no, she was informed Mr Ali would be seeing her at 3.00pm on Friday, followed by Akim at 6.00 pm.

On the dot of 3.00pm, Ali presented himself. He was wearing a warm overcoat, although the weather did not yet demand it.

"How's your son, Mr Ali?" Susan asked the moment he entered her room.

"He's alright and very attentive. It's marvellous what a touch of a lash can achieve where words and logic fail."

"That's nice, so everything is fine?"

"In a manner of speaking, yes."

"Good to hear. Now why don't you take your coat off and I'll get you some refreshment."

"Thank you my dear," Ali took off the coat, revealing a fine all-calf leather anorak he was wearing under it. He then proceeded to take off the anorak.

"There we are, my dear. We're almost the same size so it should fit you."

Susan looked at him a little dumbfounded, "Mr Ali, I thought you were not allowed to give us presents?"

"Who said anything about presents? This is my anorak which I happen to forget to take with me when I leave, and the next time I come here, I forget I ever had an anorak."

"Mr Ali, what can I say except thank you. You really are a darling. I'll get the anchovies."

***

Akim was at Susan's door sharp at 6.00pm.

"Well, Susan!" Akim addressed her, "I see you are pleased to see me as always?" He added somewhat sarcastically.

"Oh yes," said Susan, "it's like seeing a robot. As a matter of fact,

154

I think I'd prefer a robot."

"I see. Well, you just may change your mind, as I think I have some good news for you."

"Oh goody! You are sending a helicopter to take me out of here?"

"Actually, I may well be doing that."

"Really, tell me you are not joking!"

"I am not joking. Last week I had a serious discussion with my father. He is in agreement to buy you out of here, and as a director of this enterprise he can do that and will do that to please his eldest son."

"That would be like a miracle come true, but why should he want to do that?"

"I just told you, to please his eldest son."

"This is unbelievable," Susan was almost in awe. Instantly, thoughts flashed through her mind of the weeks she had spent on building that hang glider and out of the blue, this? "I don't understand, all this time and your father will let me go? Just like that?"

"No, not just like that. I had to plead with him and convince him that I love you and always have."

"And that was the reason you had me kidnapped and brought here?"

"No, no. You don't understand. You were to be married that day to another man. Should that have happened, I would have lost you forever. My religion forbids me to court a married woman."

"But it allows you to kidnap one and sell her into slavery?" Susan cut back sharply.

"In a way, it does. I had no active part in the kidnapping. All I did was agree to the proposal, and I did insist that you be handled with care and not harmed."

"Really! The gallantry blows me away. Did you really think I would thank you?"

"In time, yes. Life can be beautiful in the East."

"How long before the helicopter gets here?"

"As soon as the money has been paid and the terms settled."

"Terms! What terms? You never said anything about terms!"

"I have already explained the terms to you. We get married, and you will live in my palace where you will have a handmaiden as well as servants to grant your every wish."

"What! And share you with your other wives. What kind of marriage is that?"

"You still don't understand. My wives are more like servants. It's not like European marriages. These wives were chosen for me for business and political reasons. You will be the top wife. Wife number one and the other wives will be your servants."

Susan remained silent for a while, thinking, "This really means I'd be exchanging one prison for another, but there would be more opportunities to escape, or would there? I can cover a lot more distance in the alps using a hang glider than I can on foot in a desert, and I don't think I could sue for a divorce." Whilst all this was machinating, a further thought came to her mind and she asked out loudly, "If I agree, would I also have to convert to Islam?"

"Hmm," Akim was caught unawares, "I don't really know. I haven't even thought about that, but I suppose you would. In any case, that's no big deal."

"It is a big deal. I was raised a Christian and from what I know of Muslims, women are treated badly, and the only right they have is the right to do as they are told."

"I would never treat you badly, Susan, you know that."

"What I know, Akim, is that so far you have had me kidnapped, transported me to a foreign country, imprisoned me, beaten me, raped me, and more if I think about it. There seems to be evidence of some bad treatment there, wouldn't you say?"

"That was just to get you here. Some restraints had to be used, but once you become my wife, it will never happen again."

"Tell me something, Akim, when you say you would fly me out of here, I can see that, but when we land what then?"

"What do you mean, 'what then'? I don't understand the question."

"It's simple. I don't have a passport or any other documents. How do I get through immigration and customs without documents?"

"Oh, I see what you mean. Much the same as when you came here. You will be sedated and placed in a coffin. I will claim you are my sister killed in a road accident, and your body is coming home for a proper Muslim burial. Don't worry, it will be all taken care of."

Susan cringed inwardly but said nothing. She shuddered at the thought of another escape plan's door closing.

"Akim, you surprise me, and you have given me much to think about. Next time you come, could you bring with you some pictures of your palace and its surroundings. I would like to see what it is like. To make it easier when I get there."

"Of course, I understand, you Western women are very fussy about things of this nature," Akim conceded, happy at the thought of having gained a victory.

***

For Susan this was a signal to become airborne before Akim's next visit. It was possible that he felt encouraged by Susan's relenting tone, and with that to spur him on, she could once more find herself in a coffin, drugged and heading for somewhere north of Aden. Now, all there was left to do was to screw together the glider's frame, cover the wings with silk, then take an almighty leap and hope for the best. Through her dummy runs she had timed how long she needed to finish the glider and added an extra hour for contingency. Next was to listen to the radio for weather forecasts to determine the time for departure.

The first snow had just fallen, and the forecast for the next few days promised to be sunny and mild, To Susan, this was like a sign from heaven. She scheduled one evening to finish off the framework and take off the following night, but she still needed the scissors to cut the silk. Patra was still in her office when Susan entered on some pretext to check some figures. Browsing through a ledger she innocently asked. "I don't suppose there's a pair of scissors anywhere here I could borrow?"

"What do you want scissors for?" Patra asked.

"To trim the ends of my hair, they're starting to split."

"You don't have to do that yourself. Ask Bertha from housekeeping to do that for you."

"I didn't know Bertha was a hairdresser!"

"She isn't. She trims most of the girl's hair here, and she's no too bad at it."

"All just the same, I'd rather do it myself. I've always done it myself ever since I was a little girl."

"All right then," Patra opened the lower drawer of her desk and withdrew a wooden case. "Which do you want? I suppose it's the pointy ended ones."

"Yes, they'll do splendidly, thanks."

"There you are then. Just leave them on my desk when you've finished." Patra handed Susan the scissors and left her office.

"God, that was easy," Susan said to herself. "If everything else turns out as easy, I'll be home and hosed."

***

That same evening after her guest had passed out from excessive alcohol intake, Susan headed for the loft. Her plan was to assemble the hang glider to the ready-for-take-off stage and leave it in the loft until tomorrow night when its inaugural flight would take place.

Once inside the loft, she laid out the cut tubing pieces on the floor, one by one, until they formed the unsecured shape of the glider. From her skirt pocket she produced two small ring spanners, freshly liberated from the workshop and went to work. Within an hour, the glider was starting to take shape. Susan was glad to see the washers sink into the silk material, and she was now sure that without them the material would have started to tear.

Working now with a great will, she started to install the control cords. She didn't hear the loft open but could not mistake Patra's deep voice.

158

"Making someone a Christmas present, are we Susan?" Patra asked sarcastically.

For a moment Susan's innards went numb with shock, as she saw Patra's figure in the doorway clad in a long black dressing gown. She virtually lost her voice but recovered enough to spew out, "Patra! ... How did you know... find me?"

"I've known for a while that you were up to something. I just didn't know what. As a matter of fact, I still don't. Just what is that contraption? Some sort of a sleigh for Santa Claus?"

"No, it's not." Susan was sure Patra would find out sooner or later. "It's a hang glider."

"What is the purpose of this glider thing? Are you going to keep it as a pet and hang it on a wall or something?"

"You know better than that, Patra. I was going to fly to Austria with it. I hear you can get an excellent apple strudel there for Christmas."

"Fly! ... Fly in that thing? Are you insane?"

"I have spent many happy hours back home flying in one of those things."

"And you think you can fly to Austria in that?"

"With the right winds assisting, most certainly. I may not be able to pinpoint the exact landing spot, but I will get there. Would you like me to give you a demonstration, right now?"

"Sure, like I was born yesterday," Patra scoffed, "and you built it all by yourself?"

"Yes, I did," Susan regained control but still trembled with disappointment, expecting Mathew and a couple of helpers to next appear in the doorway.

"How can you be sure it will fly?"

"It will fly all right, but the question is for how long? If the frame withstands the wind buffeting without snapping, it will probably fly to London. The pilot will probably break down first."

"How do you know all this? I thought you were studying law in Australia?"

"I was, but hang gliding was my weekend hobby. Actually, it was

Akim who taught me."

"Akim! Our Akim?" Patra questioned, almost in disbelief. "Yes. Our Akim."

"How do you get this thing to fly? From what little I know, you need a vehicle to tow you in the air or something like that."

"That's a glider plane you are thinking of. This is a hang glider. All you need is a cliff with a good drop and a few metres clear running space to build up some momentum."

"So that's what you were doing at the garbage wall, measuring it up for distance?"

"You were spying on me?"

"Of course, I was. That's my job. Now, assuming you get to Austria, what then?"

"Then I go to our embassy in Vienna and get them to repatriate me home." Susan thought she may as well reveal the truth, as making up stories seemed pointless.

"Your embassy will want to know all about how you got into this situation. What will you tell them?" Patra asked, finding a reasonably sturdy chair and sitting down in the doorway.

Susan knew what Patra was getting at. Offering some sort of lie would only be insulting Patra's intelligence.

"I would tell them all I knew about getting here, which actually isn't all that much, as for most of the time I was heavily drugged."

"But you must know where you are?"

"Sure, somewhere in Slovenia, in the alps."

"Then how do you know where Austria is?

"Due north of here. Franz told me. OK, Patra, you caught me, so what now? Report me to Mathew and enjoy watching me get a thorough beating?"

"You're way ahead of yourself, girl. I'm not going to do any of those things. I'm going to help you get out of here."

Susan was transported to several seconds of disbelief, stunned and open mouthed.

"What? ... What did you just say?"

"I said I was going to help you get out of here."

"That's what it sounded like ... I don't get it ... you ... why?"

"I have my reasons, many of them, but you must first settle into the idea."

"I still don't understand. Why would you want to help me? I have no way of repaying you, you must know that."

"Once you get out of here, there are certain things you can do to help me."

"I still don't get it! What can I do?"

"You can help get me out of here."

"What! How, I mean why, I mean just the other day you and Mathew were in Graz. You could have stayed there and not come back."

"I could have, but where would I have stayed? On a park bench? I told you earlier that I too am as much a prisoner here as you are. Sure, I do get more privileges but nonetheless I am still a prisoner. A prisoner of Mathew, well kept, but on a short leash."

"I still don't understand."

"All right, I'll go through it again. In Beirut Mathew became a regular client. When he went to London, he bought me from the brothel keeper and took me to London with him to manage a brothel he owned there. In London Mathew got me pregnant, and I gave birth to a daughter. I was never given the chance to be a mother to my own daughter. Mathew took charge of her, and the day she turned 16 he raped her and installed her into the brothel as a sex worker."

"You're kidding? A father rapes his own daughter and forces her into prostitution?"

"I know it's hard to believe, but Mathew is a suave, well-mannered monster. I am here on this rock only because Mathew promised to do other things to my daughter if I didn't stay with him. He never breaks his promises."

"That is quite horrid to hear but I don't see where I fit in as a help," Susan interrupted.

"I know you don't, but here is what I can see happening. Once you tell your story to your government, they will bring it up with the Slovenian government which is about to open its first embassy in Australia in February next year. The Slovenians will not welcome any scandalous publicity as the spa is leased by them and not owned by the cartel. My guess is that they will shut it down faster than you can blink.

There will be other repercussions in London, and I want you to get my daughter out of there before that happens."

"To be perfectly honest, I'd be glad to help, but I don't see what I can do."

"You'll think of something, I am sure of that. Anyone who can think of this plan of escape can think of something else just as good."

"How do you know that once I'm out of here, I'll actually contact you again?" Susan taunted.

"I don't, but I don't think you will abandon me, as you have that one thing that most of us here lack."

"Really, what's that?"

"Integrity."

Both women remained silent for a while, probably reviewing the situation. Patra broke the silence.

"When were you planning to make the jump?"

"Tomorrow night."

"So soon."

"Not too soon from where I stand."

"Why at night?"

"I have a client booked for the evening. As soon as he goes or passes out, I plan to go."

"You don't have a client tomorrow, I'll see to that, so when would you like to go?"

"About eight would be OK."

"Eight o'clock it is then. Is there anything you still need?"

Susan thought about it for a few moments, "A pair of warm slacks or jeans would be of great help."

Patra looked Susan up and down, "I just may be able to do

something there. Anything else?"

"Not really, except help carry the glider to the garbage wall."

"How sure are you that that contraption will fly?"

"Pretty sure. It meets with all the standards Akim taught me."

"Akim?"

"Yes, Akim knows a lot about hang gliding."

"Ah ... now it start to make some sense. He teach you to glide and wants some sex as payment. You say no, so he kidnap you for here. Now I understand more than before. Typical Arab! But how do you know this thing will fly?"

"It will fly all right, but the question is for how long? If the screws don't weaken the struts it can go for a long time, but in any case, it should be good for one flight."

***

Around noon someone delivered a pair of black corduroy slacks to Susan's room. Trying them on, the fit was close enough for the purpose.

The weather forecast was for a dry night with winds freshening. This could be either good or bad news. It was dependent on the degree of freshening. Freshening to gale force could end up in disaster.

Close to 8pm Susan made her way to the lot. To her mild surprise, Patra was already there.

"I see the slacks fit you, I'm glad. I also brought you a couple of sandwiches you can keep in your pocket in case you get hungry," Patra informed Susan. "So, what happens now?"

"Now, we get some rope round the glider and attach it to the rope on the gantry, then gently lower it to the ground."

"Right, but just before we do that, I have something else for you."

"Really! What?"

Patra reached into her skirt pocket and pulled out a pouch the size of a human fist.

"In here are some precious stones, all best quality. Also, inside is a paper with a London address on it. When you get there, go and see them. Tell them I sent you, and they will give you the best available price. I suggest you put the pouch round your neck and tuck it in your bra."

"Thank you, Petra, but why are you doing this?"

"To be able to help my daughter you will probably incur expenses. Use them as you see fit."

"I don't know what to say, Patra. I mean, we are both on the opposite sides of the fence. How do you know you can trust me?"

"You have just confirmed that. As I said before, you have integrity, and I would gladly give my own life if I could rescue my daughter from the life which lies ahead of her."

"If everything goes all right, how will I contact you? I don't think using the spa as an address is a good idea."

"You are quite right. When you look into the pouch you will find another piece of paper with the name 'Anton Brak' from Beirut on it. He is my friend, and he will know what to do."

"But what about the jewels? Won't Mathew find out they are gone?"

"Probably, but I have a cover story for that."

"Really, and what is that?"

"I'll tell him you stole them when you escaped. Now, let's get this jigsaw puzzle over to the garbage wall."

It was light work lowering the glider, and Susan was glad to learn she could have managed it easily by herself. At the garbage wall she lifted the glider, then, grasping the handlebar with both hands, she nodded to Patra and began her sprint. As her feet left the rocky surface, the glider dipped and looked like it was headed for the ground. This momentarily horrified Patra, who was observing from the wall, but then the falling contraption evened out, catching a wind reflecting off the rock face and started to gain height.

Soon, only a dark figure could be seen as the white bed sheets blended in with the snow-capped alps.

CH 11. THE FLIGHT

As the glider was descending, Susan realised there was wind on the rock face itself, ricocheting away from her approach. She had to get into that air stream, or her flight would have a short and catastrophic ending. She manipulated the handlebar as much as she dared and used the rest of her body to guide the glider. Close to panic, she dared not look down. She knew she had to concentrate. Using her body as a rudder, she flipped hard to port, perhaps a little too hard as she recognised the danger of going into a spin. She tried to pull the wing up as much as she could and, much to her relief, received assistance from an updraught which shunted her away from the rock face with a force Susan had not experienced before. The updraught made it possible for Susan to gain height, and as it melted into the prevailing wind higher up, she was able to set course from the stars she had been watching regularly for some weeks before the flight. She had never flown a glider at night before, as her club in Australia were not in favour of it, mainly due to bad visibility, but here in The Julian Alps it was almost a pleasure, as the snow cover provided a near needle-sharp panorama of what was below. Susan inspected the struts of her glider for any signs of weakening or tears as much as she could from her prone position. Everything seemed to be in working condition, much to her relief. She released one welding-gloved hand from the handlebar to check the pads of her knees. From one of her bras, she had fashioned a pair of kneepads which were now strapped on. Her glider lessons earlier had taught her that in the event of a forced or sloppy landing, the knees were the first to suffer injury. The homemade pads were happily in their place.

Soaring through the alps, Susan almost forgot the reason for her being there, but a reality check soon reminded her. She tried to look at her wristwatch to see how long she was airborne but gave up. The watch was on her wrist inside the welding glove. To try and take the glove off would risk losing it, thus exposing the hand to the extreme cold surrounding her. She cursed her lack of forethought, and now, having to pay the penalty by losing track of the time, she needed to reach the Austrian border. From her height, she spotted an opening in the mountains which was probably a valley, and, on approaching it more closely, the valley seemed to flatten out, suggesting a continuation into a long pasture. Looking at her navigating stars, she concluded that she had just about reached Austria. It was decision time. If she flew through the valley and the terrain remained flat, she would seek a suitable spot, and if she could see any lights, land and hope that it was Austria.

As she neared the valley, she saw that it was one of three valleys with two of them leading off the central one. She prepared to lose height as she came closer and at the opportune time entered the first valley. It was not long before she was lined up with the meeting point of the first of the other valleys. A wind shear hit the glider with some considerable force, causing the glider to suddenly gain height and then just as suddenly drop. Alarmed, Susan took evasive action and steadied the glider up to the time she struck the meeting place of the other two valleys. Once there, thermals took over the management of the glider, buffeting it severely like a loose sheet of paper in a storm. It was more through sheer luck than flying skills that Susan managed to steer the glider through the main valley. As she left the raging winds behind her, Susan heard a high-pitched flapping sound coming from one of the wings. Looking up, she saw a piece of silk torn off the wing and flapping ferociously, tearing at its next securing bolt. There was nothing for it. She had to land as soon as possible or fall out of the sky. Fortunately, she was almost out of the valley, and ahead of her lay a large snow-covered field. The wing had lost more of its silk cover, and Susan knew that very soon this loss of balance would put the glider into a spin and propel it to the ground. Susan prayed she would have enough time to make a passable landing, but in vain. The glider started to spin just before touching the ground, leaving it out of control with enough velocity to make it crash into what looked like a snow mound but, in fact, was a stack of pine firewood covered in snow.

***

Otto, Lemi, Uli and Wolfgang were all young lads in their twenties. They were playing cards late into the night in their log cabin adjacent to the main farmhouse. It was specially built for them and lovingly named, "Der Herren Schloss," which whimsically suggested that ladies were not to enter. Stocked with a good supply of beer, some schnapps and a warming fire, they were prepared to greet the dawn, as it was then a holiday, and they could sleep for as long as they chose to.

"What was that?" Lemi suddenly exclaimed.

"What was what?" Uli asked.

"I heard it too," Otto joined in. "Sounded like some sort of a crash."

"Don't be silly." Wolfgang discounted the thought. "There are no roads out there so what's to crash?"

"Had to be something to make that much noise. Why don't you take a look, Lemi?"

"Why don't we all take a look," Lemi countered.

"Yeah, it might be an Italian invasion," Otto suggested.

"Always the smart-arse, Otto, but I suppose we'd better take a look."

The four of them donned their overcoats and filed out of the log cabin.

"I don't see nothing," Uli said, looking around, "everything looks normal."

"I agree," Otto concurred.

"It's gotta be something," Lemi protested, "that was quite a loud noise we heard, and it wasn't the sound of one hand clapping.

Something got clobbered. We just have to find out what."

"No need to," Wolfgang announced, "take a look at that woodpile we stacked on Wednesday. It's come apart, and there's some white thing sticking out on the side of it."

The four of them began tramping through the untrodden snow towards the disturbed woodpile.

"Well, kiss my arse. It looks like some sort of glider has slammed into our woodpile," Uli exclaimed, being the first to reach the spot. "And look, there's someone underneath it. Jesus Christus! Help me get some of this crap out of the way."

The four young men worked quickly, clearing the timber and bits of the now-shattered hang glider away, exposing Susan.

"It's a woman!" Uli announced.

"God in heaven, what's a woman doing out here at this time of night? Is she dead?" Wolfgang asked in awe.

Uli, who was closest to her head, leaned across and after a short pause, looked up and said, "I think she's still alive, she just took a short breath, and I think she tried to cough."

"That's something. Take her pulse."

"Where do I find that?"

"Don't you know? It's under her wrist or try the blood vessels on the side of her neck or, never mind. Move over, I'll do it." Wolfgang decided to trust his own judgement. "I can feel a pulse but it's very weak. Anyone got their mobile handy?"

"I've got mine in my pocket," Otto volunteered.

"Good. Ring 'Emergency' and get an ambulance, and I suppose you'd better phone the coppers as well."

"What do you want the coppers for? Demolishing a woodpile?"

"Don't be so stupid, Otto. We don't know who she is or where she's from. For all we know, she might be an alien."

"What! An alien? I don't think so, not if she used that contraption as her spaceship."

"Otto, will you please make the calls and stop dithering, I don't want her dying on my father's farm."

***

The police arrived before the ambulance. Two officers were patrolling nearby when they got the call. They had to leave the patrol car in the farm's courtyard and proceed the relatively short distance to the woodpile on foot. Both were young men about the same age of the four card players.

The driver of the police car took one look at Susan and immediately took off his greatcoat, covering her with it. He looked up at the four card players as if to say, "Couldn't one of you gotten her a blanket?"

As if guided by mental telepathy, Lemi asked, "Should I get a couple of blankets to put over her?"

"Yes, that would be of help," the policeman replied.

The ambulance arrived only minutes after the police. Two paramedics alighted and opened the rear ambulance doors, extracting a folded-up stretcher and a large black bag and traced the policemen's footsteps to the woodpile.

"How did she get to be here?" One of the paramedics asked.

"We don't know for sure," Lemi replied. "We were in the cabin playing cards when we heard this crashing sound. We went outside for a look and there she was."

"And none of you know her? You know, like an old girlfriend or somebody's girlfriend, anything like that?"

"No. Never seen her before in my life. None of us have."

Having made a cursory examination of Susan, one of the paramedics gave her an injection and started to prepare her for removal.

"Will she be alright?" Lemi asked.

"Hard to tell. She's unconscious now, and, as long as that does not translate into a coma, she'll probably pull through, but at this moment it's hard to tell. There's a team of medicos at the hospital waiting for her to be brought in, so I guess it's up to them."

Manoeuvring Susan as gently as possible onto the stretcher, the paramedics loaded her into the ambulance, and, after a brief conversation with the police, they left. Lemi and the others prepared to leave, but one of the policemen stopped them.

"One moment before we go, we have to write a report, so is there somewhere we can go inside? We have to ask you quite a few questions."

Once inside the log cabin, one of the policemen produced a notebook.

"I will need all of your names, addresses and so on plus a statement from each one of you of exactly what happened," the policeman informed them, "so let us start with you." He looked at Lemi, who only too willingly produced his driver's licence as well as other information when it was asked.

"And you say you have no idea who this woman is?"

"No, I have never seen her before in my life. I don't even know her nationality. She could be German, French or Italian for all I know, but I am sure she is not Chinese."

"Have any of you seen, met or have any knowledge who this woman might be?" The policeman turned to the others but received a negative response. "Would any of you know or have any idea why she was flying over this farm?" Again, a negative response. "Very well then, this will be all for tonight. You will probably be contacted from someone in the department, in a few days' time."

"Excuse me, officer," Wolfgang spoke out. "Could you tell us to which hospital the ambulance took the woman?"

"To the Unfallkrankenhaus in Graz, why do you ask?"

"We might want to find out how she is or maybe who she is?"

"I see, well I'd leave it for a few days. I don't think she'll be in any condition to receive visitors just yet or ever. When you do call remember to give this number 3752; that's the police case number. Quote that and the staff will give you an update."

**

In a public ward of Graz Hospital, Susan slowly opened her eyes.

At first all she saw was white, reflecting off the screens around her bed. "Where am I?" was the first thought going through her mind.

The answer did not come immediately. She closed her eyes and fell back into a light sleep. A few minutes later her eyes opened again. "Where am I?" she asked again, this time taking her time to study her surroundings. "Am I alone?" she uttered with all the strength she could muster. "Hello, is anyone else there?"

"Sie ist wach!" She faintly heard a woman's voice say and presently one side of the screen was opened by a woman in a nurse's uniform. "Gott sei dank, Sie sind wach! Ich rufe den arzt."

Susan did not quite understand what the nurse said, but she was pretty sure it was German. A great feeling of relief passed through her. She had no idea where she was, but she was sure it was somewhere in Austria.

"Gruess Gott," a mature man, with a stethoscope round his neck said, "Ich bin Dr Jungman. Wie heissen Sie?"

Susan did not understand the question, all she could contribute was, "Where am I?"

"Aha, English, ein vorschrit," the doctor surmised. "Bitte rufen Sie Dr Spengler," he asked the nurse. "Er ist auf English vorbereitet."

Dr Spengler arrived within a few minutes.

"My name is Ernst Spengler; I work here as a doctor. What is your name?" he asked Susan in English.

"Where am I?" was all Susan could answer.

"You are in a hospital in Graz. Now we must know your name and where you come from. Can you tell me that?"

"Yes, thank you," Susan replied gathering some strength. "My name is Susan Bauford, and I am from Sydney, Australia."

"Australia!" Dr Spengler exclaimed, "Australia! What is a young lady from Australia doing in a hospital in Austria, all smashed up?"

"I didn't come directly from Australia. I came from Slovenia."

"Even more fascinating. By autobus, car, plane, snowskis?"

"I came in on a hang glider."

"I see, this gets better as it goes along. Young lady, would you like to rest a little more and rethink of how you got here. There are two policemen in the hospital cafe wanting to talk to you as soon as you are fit to talk."

"Good, I want to talk to them. Please send them in."

Dr Spengler dispatched the nurse to fetch the policemen and remained at Susan's bedside studying her medical chart at the foot of the bed.

***

Captain Dob Eicher and detective Sep Dichter approached Susan's bed. The captain spoke English and the detective looked as if he understood it.

"Miss Bauford," the captain addressed Susan, "the doctor here tells me that that is your name, but we have no way of knowing that this is the truth. We found no passport on you or any other travel document. No business card, no diary but a pouch full of some interesting jewels. We would like to know exactly who you are and where you come from and even more so, where did the jewels come from? It is worth a lot of money as you probably know."

Susan then recounted how she was kidnapped and brought to Slovenia. She described the spa and how she worked to escape it. The only thing she couldn't tell the captain was where she crashed, as she had no knowledge of that.

"That's quite a story, Miss Bauford. I'm sure the Brothers Grimm would find it hard to improve on that."

"You don't believe me?" Susan cried in dismay.

"That you come from Australia, very likely, but the rest of it is rather hard to swallow. That you built a hang glider out of bits and pieces, and someone handed you the jewels because they trusted you? Come now, Miss Bauford, you must think I have a little birdie in my head."

"I see. So, what happens now? Are you going to send me back to Slovenia?"

"Without a passport or other travel documentation, we can't send you anywhere except to one of our luxury type prisons. While you convalesce, you will remain here under police protection, and you will receive some officials for further interrogation."

Much to her surprise, Susan summonsed a burst of angry energy as she sat bolt upright in her bed.

"You will do no such thing. I will have nothing to say to any interrogator you care to send. You will, however, contact the Australian Embassy in Vienna and ask them to send out a consular official, who will in a short time confirm my identity."

"Are you giving me orders, Miss Bauford?"

"Yes, I am, captain. I am a graduate lawyer in Australia and am familiar with international law which is also your duty to uphold. You cannot hold me under arrest forever before I face one of your courts, where I will immediately claim that my international rights have been violated and call on everyone present here as a witness to the fact."

Captain Eicher, for a moment, was dumbfounded.

"Very well, if that is your wish, it shall be done but you will remain here, under police protection until such time as we resolve this matter."

***

It took two days before someone from the Vienna Embassy visited Susan. His name was Victor Craddock, 31 years old and looking every inch a career diplomat. He was tall with a lock of blonde hair threatening to obscure his vision.

"Now, Miss Bauford, you are going to make my life a little difficult in establishing your identity."

"Difficult but not impossible I hope," Susan murmured.

"Good heavens no, it's just the time these things take to get verified. Now your name. I've heard that name somewhere before. Wasn't there a Susan Balforth, something like that, a young bride kidnapped on her wedding day some months ago?"

"There was, and her name is Bauford, and you are looking at her."

"Well, I'll be buggered, oops, sorry for that. We were asked by Interpol and our crowd back home to keep our eyes and ears open, in the off chance that name cropped up anywhere. That was in our Jakarta Embassy just before I got transferred to Vienna. It is you, isn't it?"

"Look at it this way, Mr Craddock, how many brides get kidnapped on their wedding day and have the same name as mine?"

"Point taken, but it is still incredible, but what is the situation here? Are they looking after you?"

"Very well, I have to say."

"And what about your injuries, how bad are they?"

"Actually, I have been very lucky. As you can see, I have a dislocated shoulder and enough cuts and bruises all over to see me through the rest of my life, but, as I said, I've been very lucky. Now all I want to do is to get out of here. Plus, I want to ring my mum and dad and my fiancé. They must be sick from worry."

"That's one problem easily solved. If you can remember their number we'll phone them now, and I don't think they will care if its three o'clock in the morning in Australia," Victor produced a mobile phone from his pocket and Susan dictated the number. The response was disappointing, all they heard was a recorded voice saying, 'the number you are calling has been disconnected ...'"

"I don't understand." Susan looked puzzled. "I know the number by heart. It's always been our number, ever since I was child. Maybe you mis-dialled?

"That's possible, let's try it again." Both of them fell silent as they listened for the response and again heard the recorded voice, "the number you are calling ..."

"Something's wrong!" Susan exclaimed, alarmed.

"Maybe not, Telecom are always updating and changing numbers and after three months or so, declaring them disconnected. I have an idea. The Sydney police are bound to have a record of the abduction in their 'unsolved' cases file. The moment I get back to Vienna I will fax them and ask them for a report."

"Thank you, Mr Craddock, that should clear things up and restore my identity."

"Now, is there anything else you would like to add? Something you may have overlooked or if you have a better idea. Recount to me all the events which took place from the time of your abduction to present day. I will record them on my cassette recorder and have them typed up later. Is that all right with you?"

"Certainly, I'll be glad to." Susan agreed.

"Wow! That is quite a story," Victor commented, when Susan finished. "It commands my deepest respect."

"Thank you," was Susan's quiet reply.

"Now, here is what is going to happen. I am going to have you declared an Australian refugee in Austria, under the protection of the UN and Australian Government. You will be transferred to a hospital in Vienna where you will remain until fully recovered and then we will see how best to repatriate you home. How does all that sound to you?"

"Like a dream come true, would you believe, and if I may ask, would you please try and contact my parents and Ashley, my fiancé, and let them know I'm all right. I'll give you their home addresses, but I can't remember Ashley's phone number. I had it on my phone and only had to press 11 to talk to him. Could you do that?"

"Consider it done, and the moment we get a reply I will send it to you."

***

Detective Eddy Pike was beaming when he entered the detectives' conference room. Frank Henderson and Phil Morrison were already seated. Annie Goodall squeezed past Eddy and pulled up a chair. Eddy, slowly and a little pompously, sat down at the head of the table placing on it a manila folder.

"I have a terrific announcement to make," he said, taking some sheets of paper from the folder. "I have some great news for you, all on these few sheets of paper."

"If it's about the takeaway lunch shop changing their menu again, I don't want to know," Phil Morrison quipped.

"Very droll Phil but no cigar. Early this morning the Super called me into his office and handed me a fax from our Embassy in Vienna. It looks very much like that Susan Bauford has been found in a hospital in Graz, Austria."

Shouts of 'what' and 'you're kidding' echoed throughout the room.

"Settle down," Eddie continued, "it's all there all right. A lot of the information matches what we have already. She's even identified the names and addresses of her parents and fiancé, Ashley and other things like dates and personal information. I have made copies of the fax to pass them round. Please read, and we'll take comments afterwards."

The room fell silent but marked with exclamations of 'holy shit, bloody hell, unbelievable' etcetera as everyone eagerly scanned the pages of the fax.

"It has to be fair dinkum." Annie Goodall was first to finish reading the fax, "Even though it's incredible, it slots in with what we know already."

"Thank you, Annie, my sentiments exactly. The question now is, where does this leave us?"

"I suppose one of us will have to go to Austria and escort her home," Phil offered.

"You wish," Eddy replied. "This is now a diplomatic matter. She has no passport or papers, and we can't issue those. Once she does get home, we can question her and see if we can do something about her abductors, and I guess we'll be working closely with Interpol. In the meantime, it's up to the stiff shirts in Canberra to bring her back."

"This reads like a thriller," Frank Henderson observed. "All that is missing, is the car chase. The media will go ape-shit when they get hold of this."

"No, they won't, Frank. All this is strictly classified." A chorus of 'what' and 'you're kidding' filled the room.

"I don't get it," Annie asked. "This has got to be the greatest international story of the year and you say it's classified?"

"Yes, and I repeat, classified. Here is what we have, Annie. An international cartel running a white slavery brothel in Slovenia. One woman manages to escape. Just one, and the only witness. This mob are cashed up and can probably pull lots of strings. How much do you think her life would be worth if every newscast in the world would run the story?"

"Yes, you're right, of course," Annie replied. "Bloody Slovenians. We should declare war on them or send an aircraft carrier or something to drop a few bombs on them."

"Annie, the place is in Slovenia, but it is not run by Slovenians."

"So what? I still reckon we should send an aircraft carrier."

"Annie, we haven't got an aircraft carrier."

"Well then we should get one."

CH 12. THE FALLOUT

For quite a few hours, no one at the spa, with the exception of Patra, was aware that Susan was no longer with them. It was Pepe who first raised the alarm. He wheeled in her breakfast trolley as usual, and, not finding her there, thought nothing of it. He left the trolley near the bar, assuming Susan was in the bathroom or just stepped out.

An hour or so later, when no alarm bell was heard, he returned to Susan's room ready to collect the trolley and admonish her again for failing to tug on the bell cord. As he walked into Susan's room, he noted the breakfast trolley was exactly where he had left it and the dishes were still on it, untouched.

"Miss Susan," he yelled out. "Why you no eat breakfast? You all right?"

He failed to get an answer and tried again and received the same result.

"Miss Susan! You OK? I'm coming into the bathroom to see if you OK."

Very gingerly, Pepe opened the bathroom door. He looked around but saw no one. Puzzled, he scratched his head and wondered what to do. Wheeling the breakfast trolley back to the kitchen, he passed Patra's office, and as the door was open, which it nearly was all the time, he left the trolley and went in. Patra was already at her desk, leafing through a ledger.

"What is it, Pepe?" she asked. "What do you want?"

"It's Miss Susan, Miss Patra, I bring her breakfast but she not there, I thought maybe she with you?"

"She's not with me, and what do you mean, she's not there?"

"She gone somewhere, she not there. I bring her breakfast and she not there. When bell not ring for some time, I go collect trolley anyway, but she not there and she don't eat nothing. I look round and even check the bathroom but she not there."

"Maybe she went out for a walk or something. Get some fresh air?"

"Is too cold for fresh air," Pepe protested.

"Well, she's got to be somewhere. Get Mario and someone else and look for her and look over the walls just in case there's been an accident." Patra added, just in case the rising hang glider last night had been a figment of her imagination.

More than an hour passed before Pepe returned with Mario in tow.

"She's not anywhere we can see," Pepe reported. "We look everywhere but nothing."

"That's not possible. She's got to be here somewhere," Patra lied. "There's no way out of here except by helicopter. Are both helicopters here?"

"Yes, Miss Patra," Mario assured her. "Saw them just a few minutes ago, and anyway, she can't fly a helicopter."

"Really, Mario, and how do you know that?"

"Well, if she could, one helicopter would be missing."

"Correct, so where is she?"

Both men simply shrugged their shoulders looking a little sheepish.

"I suppose we'll have to let Mr Mathew know," Patra concluded, "Mario, you had better go see him now."

"Me!" Mario exclaimed. "Why me? I know nothing about this until Pepe told me."

"You're in charge of the grounds so it's your job, Mario. Take Pepe with you, that way Mr Mathew may not hit you."

Both men left reluctantly. Patra took a mirror from her desk and freshened her makeup. She knew it would only be minutes before Mathew would be storming in.

***

"What have you done with Susan?" Mathew shouted at Patra as he entered her office with Mario and Pepe a respectful distance behind him.

"I have done nothing, she's just disappeared?"

"Disappeared, my foot! No one disappears from here unless I say so. She has got to be here somewhere, there's no other way out. Have the place searched immediately."

"We have already done that and nothing," Mario pointed out.

"Then do it again. This time thoroughly. Search every corner and every room. Look into every cupboard and garbage bin big enough to hold a person, is that clear?"

"Does that include our guest's rooms as well?" Mario asked.

"Yes … tell them you are looking for … for stone shrinkage or something, just make sure you look."

Mario and Pepe did not wait to be told twice, and Mathew turned to Patra.

"How could something like this happen? You're in charge of the women here. What have you got to say?"

"What can I say? The whole thing is a mystery to me," Patra lied.

"Who was she with last night? That may tell us something."

"Offhand, I'm not sure. Let me look at the register." Patra reached in her desk and tabled a foolscap size ledger, "Let's see now. Five pm to seven pm, Mr Ali."

"And then?"

"Then nothing. I assume she went to bed."

"You assume? You mean you don't know. Did anyone see her after 7 pm?"

"How would I know?" Patra lied again. "It's your job to know," Mathew insisted. "She may have gone to the gym."

"Have you asked any of the girls in the gym?"

"I don't know who was in the gym last night, and it's not part of my job to keep records of who is at the gym and who isn't. Besides, I only found out a short time ago that she was missing."

"All right," Mathew conceded, "but you had better find out who was at the gym and ask some questions and make sure you impress upon them that if they tell lies, they will receive the most extreme of punishments."

Mario and Pepe returned to Patra's office with no triumph showing on their faces.

Well?" Mathew asked.

"Nothing boss," Mario reported, "nothing. We looked everywhere. Nothing! She just disappeared."

"Rubbish! People don't simply disappear. She must have found a hiding space! She's hiding here somewhere! She's bound to get hungry soon and come out to get some food. Warn the kitchen to look out for any food missing."

"Maybe she go out through the main door," Pepe suggested. "It's not locked, you know."

"I know that, but she would not last for more than a few hours. You know that and so does she … wait a minute, maybe she's lost her marbles and thought she could walk out. Mario, you and Pepe go out the door and check the snow round the place. If she did go out that way, she would have had to leave footprints in the snow. See if you can find any footprints," Mathew ordered.

Both Mario and Pepe were only too willing to oblige.

"She has to be here," Mathew continued in a ranting manner. "Except by chopper, this place is escape proof. What am I saying? Both choppers are still here, we just have to find her."

"Yes, and before four this afternoon," Patra suggested.

"Why then?"

"Akim is coming to see her then, and you know what he's like."

"Shit! That freak, he's like a lovesick puppy licking his arse for stimulation. He's even asked his father to buy her back for him. He's going to be impossible to deal with, and that means we'll have to be lenient with her when we find her."

Mathew was back in his office when Mario and Pepe came to report.

"Nothing boss, absolutely nothing. Not even animal prints near the garbage wall."

"I didn't think you'd find anything. All right, keep on looking and look for anything unusual and unless you find her, call for a general staff meeting at eleven o'clock in the gym. I want everybody there, understand, everybody. We'll close the doors and one of you make sure none of our guests come near it. The last thing we want is to alarm them."

***

As there was no trace of Susan, the eleven o'clock meeting went ahead in the gym, as scheduled.

"One of our ladies, Susan, has gone missing," Mathew informed the gathering, "As you all know, the only way out of here is by air, and that did not happen. This means that she has to be here somewhere. Now, if any of you know anything about this, I want you to speak now and nothing more will be said."

"I want to know any detail, no matter how small. When we do find her, we will find out if anyone else was involved, and the consequences will be severe, so speak up now."

An uncomfortable silence took over the gym. No one spoke. "… No one! A person disappears from here, and no one has seen or heard anything. Remarkable! Virtually unbelievable. All right, you can go now. If anyone has anything to say, I'll be in my office all morning," Mathew informed the staff. "Oh! Not you Franz, I want to talk to you."

"Sure boss," Franz replied, "what can I do?"

"You can tell me you have thoroughly checked the choppers; I mean the insides?"

"Sure, boss. The moment Pepe told me she was missing, I checked both choppers."

"Yesterday, you had to fly to Ljubljana to pick up a guest. Is it possible she could have been in the chopper, wrapped in a blanket or something? You know, on the floor between the seats."

"No boss, not possible. Part of the pre-flight check is to inspect the interior. If there was anything on the floor, I would have seen it, especially a bundle that size."

"Yes, I suppose you couldn't miss it. All right, Franz, you can go now." Mathew released him and lapsed into thought, "It has to be Franz, he's the only means of escape, but why? Why would he want to help her? Maybe she bribed him but how? She had no money. Maybe sex. Naw, Franz would not be that stupid. He'd want more than just one nookie on the seat of a chopper. Hang on, maybe he's had a few already and this was the pay off? Possible, very possible."

Mathew considered other possibilities, but none of them made any sense. It had to be Franz.

Mathew flicked on the intercom on his desk, "Patra, please come to my office now!"

"How well do you know Franz, our pilot?" Mathew asked as soon as Patra was seated in front of his desk.

"What? … Apart from 'hello and goodbye, I hardly know him at all. Why do you ask?"

Mathew then expounded his theory about Franz.

"It's possible, I suppose, but highly unlikely. I mean, why should Franz take such a risk?"

"Men are prone to take big risks for something they want."

"Yes, I suppose they are but Franz?"

"Why should he be an exception? We all know that the only way out of here is by air and that requires a pilot. In case it's missed your attention, we don't have too many of them running about here."

"Maybe there is another way to get out of here by air," Patra suggested.

"Another way? What are you talking about? There is no other way!"

"Maybe there is and maybe there isn't. Have you ever heard of a hang glider?"

"A hang glider? What the hell are you talking about? We don't have any hang gliders here."

"I know that, but one could be made."

"Again, what the hell are you talking about?"

"I'll tell you. About a week ago I discovered some bed sheets were missing from the stockroom. At first, I thought someone had stolen them but then I thought, who would want to steal bed sheets? I put it down to an error in our stock sheets. Just now I checked the stock sheets and true enough, two sets are missing."

"So, what? What have bed sheets got to do with Susan disappearing?"

"Just this, Susan was working in the stockroom and our sheets here are made of silk."

"So, what?"

"Parachutes are made from silk, that's what."

"Are you suggesting Susan made a parachute to get out of here? That's ridiculous, all she had to do was to walk out the main door," Mathew mocked.

"I didn't say she made a parachute, but she could have constructed some other device, like a glider of some sort or a hang glider."

"Maybe, but then she'd have to learn how to fly it, but I haven't noticed anyone flying round the place with wings strapped to their back."

"She didn't have to learn; she already knew how."

"What are you talking about? She was a law student in Sydney not a test pilot."

"That she was, but her only sport or hobby was hang gliding."

"How do you know all this?"

"She told me herself. One night at the gym we were talking about keeping fit. She remarked on how having to be fit is vital when hang gliding. I asked a few more questions and found out she was well practised in the art."

"She'd need more than bed sheets to construct a gliding thing.

"Where would she have found those?"

"I have no idea, but as they say, if you look for it hard enough, you'll find it. She found the wings in a cardboard box."

Mathew leaned back in his chair, "You know the way you put it almost makes sense."

"Here's another news snippet. Guess who taught her to fly?"

"Don't tell me, it was The Red Baron."

"No, closer than that, it was Akim."

"What? Akim who? Our Akim?"

"The very one."

"This is unbelievable. Maybe he helped her build the thing?"

"That's most unlikely."

"On the face of it but consider this. Akim has been trying to have his father buy her back from us, and maybe the old man baulked at the price. This may be one way for Akim to solve his problem."

"Sounds fine in theory," Patra agreed, "but Susan can't stand Akim, so why should she change one prison for another?"

"Could be she thinks escaping from Akim's place could be easier, so she plays along."

"Anything is possible I suppose. In any case, you can ask him yourself. He'll be here this afternoon."

"Don't worry, I plan to, but I still like the theory that Franz is behind all this better. It would have taken her months to build this glider. Somebody would have noticed something. Besides, she's a mere slip of a girl. It's hard to imagine she could build this thing on her own.

"Have Franz come and see me immediately. I have a few more in-depth questions to ask him."

In answer to the summons, Franz was soon standing in front of Mathew's desk, waiting to be asked to sit down.

"Franz, I want you to recap on your movements yesterday," Mathew commanded, leaving Franz standing.

"I already told you. I flew into Ljubljana to pick up a guest."

"What time was this?"

"Somewhere between eight or nine in the evening."

"Why so late?"

"That was to do with the guest's incoming flight. He only landed on an Alitalia flight at ten."

"So, when you took off it was quite dark?"

"Of course."

"When you started the engine, could not somebody have crept up to the chopper and sneaked in and remained on the floor?"

"I would have heard the door open."

"No, you would not. The rotors were going, and you know the noise they make."

"I suppose it is possible, but I would have known when we landed."

"You just said 'we', when we landed."

"Sorry, I meant when I landed."

"Did you check the passenger side when you landed?"

"No, I already checked it before take-off."

"I see," Mathew said, contorting his gaze into one of anger, "Franz, I don't think you are telling me the truth. Have you spoken with Susan, you know, socially, often?"

"No not really ... just the once that I remember."

"When and where was that?"

"In the stockroom ... no ... in the workshop but that was some time ago."

"What did you talk about?"

Franz tried to remember, "Oh! I know now. She asked me if it was hard to fly a helicopter, and then she asked me in which direction was Austria and how far?"

"And what did you say?"

"I think I told her, but that was about it."

"Franz, I think you are lying to me. I think you made some sort of a deal with her and last night bundled her into the chopper and flew her to Ljubljana."

"What! Are you crazy? Why would I want to do that?"

"Because she offered to let you screw her a number of times, and last night was the pay off."

"That's crazy. If I wanted a screw so badly, all I have to do is go to Graz. There are no shortages there, and, believe me, the Graz ladies just love pilots."

"That may be so, but, as we both know the only way out of here is by chopper and you are in charge of choppers, and last night only one chopper was used. Yours."

"I have no idea how she got out, but it was not in my chopper."

"Be that as it may, Franz. Right now, I have a problem. My partners will want to know what happened and how it happened, and guess what I will have to tell them? I will have to tell them, and I will, that all the evidence points to you; as it indeed does," Mathew then opened his desk drawer and produced a snub nosed .38 handgun. "So now I will have to shoot you and say that when confronted with the evidence, you attacked me, and I had to protect myself. Sorry, Franz, but that's how it goes."

A feeling or terror ran down Franz's spine and then, immediately, calmness took over.

"In that case we will both have to die."

"What are you talking about?"

"Do you remember an American gentleman, a Jack Solomon if I remember correctly."

"Yes, what about him? He's dead."

"Yes, and I watched you kill him."

"Thanks for reminding me and giving me another reason to shoot you."

"Yes, but in this case, I also shot you."

"I don't follow?"

"I shot you shooting Solomon and then heaving his body out of the chopper. Thanks to a security camera fitted in the chopper, I have it all in black and white. Pity, I would have preferred technicolour, but black and white will have to do."

"You're lying. You would have had to hand the security photos in at the end of your flight."

"I did, but I handed in a blank chip and told them there was a malfunction with the camera. I had an idea the original could have its uses someday. Well, now it has."

"And just what do you think the cops will do when they find out just how long it's been laying around?"

"Who said anything about the cops? It's going straight to Jack Solomon's family."

"And now it's resting in some lawyer's office, I suppose?"

Mathew considered this threatening information for a moment or two. Could be Franz was lying, but then, the time for him to invent this story was far too short. Mathew had no choice but to give Franz the benefit of the doubt. He slowly returned the handgun to the desk drawer.

"It looks like a sort of stalemate, doesn't it? All right, but for my own curiosity, how did you smuggle the girl out of here?"

"For the hundredth time, I didn't. Why would I want to? She's just one of the girls here."

"Then where is she?"

"I don't know. As a matter of fact, I don't remember seeing her in the last four or five days."

**

At almost precisely 4.00 o'clock Akim walked through the door of Susan's room without bothering to knock. A bit miffed at finding it empty, he settled down to wait.

A ten-minute wait got too much for him. His sense of self-importance was offended. He got up and paced the room for a short while as anger mounted. A few more minutes slipped by, making Akim even more annoyed. Working up a rage, he left the room and headed straight for Patra's office.

"Where's Susan," he shouted, as he stormed into the office. "I had a 4.00pm appointment with her and she's not there. It's almost 4.30 now. Where is she?"

"She's not here," Patra calmly replied.

"I know she's not there. I've just come from her room. It's empty, she's not there, and I have a 4 o'clock appointment with her."

"When I said she was not here, I meant we don't know where she is. She has disappeared."

"What! What do you mean disappeared? How can she disappear?"

"That is what we are trying to find out," Patra replied and reached for the switch on the intercom, "Mathew, Akim is here in my office, I thought you might want to talk to him."

"What have you done with Susan?" Akim demanded to know as soon as Mathew entered the office.

"I thought you may be able to tell us," Mathew replied.

"Me! How would I know? I had a 4 o'clock appointment with her. That's all I know."

"And that could be a clever cover."

"A cover? A cover for what?"

"I'll tell you shortly, but first I want some answers to some questions."

"What questions?"

"When and where did you first meet Susan?"

"About a year or so ago, in university in Sydney."

"And while there you taught her how to use a hang glider, in fact you are a hang glider enthusiast yourself."

"Sure, what of it?"

"Why did you teach her how to hang glide?"

"She seemed interested, what of it?"

"I think you sold her the idea because you wanted to get closer to her. I mean like, get in her pants."

"Maybe, but not like that. I loved her and sure I wanted to be with her, but she didn't want me."

"And that's why you had her abducted and sent her here?"

"No, it was not like that at all."

"Then tell me how it was."

"OK. I thought that if I brought her home, she would get to love me. I thought of kidnapping her but that costs money. I asked my father for the money, and after a while he said yes. I told him I needed the money soon as she was about to be married. I could not have a married woman in the house, as that is against our law.

"I started learning her movements and also those of Ashley, the man she was going to marry. Ashley knew Susan's father was a bookmaker with lots of money, and Ashley was in financial trouble; so was his father. Ashley thought that Susan's father would help him out of his financial problems, but he said no. Not until he was dead, anyway. I was sort of friends with Ashley, mostly through the hang-gliding club.

"One evening, he had drunk a bit too much, and he told me his troubles. That was my big chance. I told him there were ways of getting money. This was an opportunity, and I told him I could help him, but he had to give up the idea of marrying Susan. He jumped at the chance. We planned the whole thing so that no blame could be attributed to him. He readily agreed, if it covered his debts. What better way was there? Who would ever suspect a groom of complicity when his bride is carried off on their wedding day?

"It all went like clockwork except that my father double-crossed me. Instead of flying her home, he had the flight altered to here. I was furious with him, but what could I do. He was my father.

"He told me that he had done me a favour, as now I could always screw her here as much as I wanted to, and he would pick up the bill."

"That's quite a story, Akim," Mathew remarked, "and do you know something, I believe you, plus it opens up much of what we were thinking.

"Tell me something, just how good was Susan at flying a hang glider?"

"She was good, very good. I was surprised. She just took to it and enjoyed it."

"That's what I thought. Now tell me, how long did it take you and Susan to build a glider here, and where did you store it?"

"Build a glider here? What are you talking about? How could you possibly build a glider here?"

"I was hoping you would tell me that."

"I didn't build anything here. This is ridiculous, build a glider here! From what? And why should I want her out of here?"

"One question at a time, please. I know for a fact that your father had no intention of buying her out. As to materials, silk bed sheets come to mind plus various bits and pieces scrounged from around the place. Now I am not saying it was the Rolls Royce of gliders, more like a Volkswagen but nevertheless something that can fly."

"You think I did this? It's ridiculous, I mean, why would I? If my father did not come up with the money, where would I take her from here?"

"Then maybe you could tell us where Susan is now?"

"How should I know. I came to see her here, remember?"

"Sure, a wise ploy to throw anyone off the scent."

"What scent? I don't really understand what you are talking about. What has me teaching Susan how to hang glide have to do with anything?"

"Quite a lot. Let me ask you something. If you wanted to get out of here, how would you go about it?"

"There is only one way, by helicopter. That's how I go, and that is how I leave."

"Right, by air and we know now that it was not by helicopter, so that leaves only one other alternative, a glider of some sort."

"So, you think she left by a hang glider which I built for her. You think I did this only to have her killed? You think I am as stupid as all that?"

"I said nothing about having her killed, where does that fit in?"

"Obviously, you haven't ever flown in a glider, especially round here in the alps."

"You are right, I haven't, but so what?"

"Flying above the alps is OK, but you can't stay there forever. Sooner or later, you must land."

"Yeah, yeah we know that, get on with it," Mathew prompted.

"Right, when you try and land in alpine country it is always dangerous. You have to deal with the thermals and wind shifts. The winds whip through the many valleys and are violently strong. Just ask your helicopter pilot. Often, when they meet, they create an uplift so powerful they can smash you into a rock face and there is nothing you can do about it. Even less if you are in a homemade glider where the steering mechanism is always the weakest point. Then there is visibility. Flying at night, you can never tell what is in front of you, clear air or a rock face."

"So, what you are saying is that if Susan did leave last night by hang glider, there is a strong possibility that she is either splattered over a rock face or crunched up somewhere on the ground and by now covered in snow or chewed up by hungry animals."

"That is what I am saying. Believe me, I have been flying gliders for many years now."

***

Shortly after the meeting, Mathew instructed Franz to fly over the nearest route towards Austria the next morning to try and spot any wreckage. Franz returned a couple of hours later with a negative report.

***

Worse news for Mathew was still to come.

Later that afternoon, Patra reported to Mathew. "I hate to tell you this, Mathew, but a good part of our precious stone holdings are missing."

"What! What do you mean missing?"

"Gone, not here. I started to get the jewellery for tonight's business, and I saw half or so of it is missing."

"Are you sure? Where do you keep it?"

"In the bottom drawer in my desk."

"You are supposed to keep that sort of thing in a safe."

"Sure, but I haven't got a safe. Remember, I asked you for one, and you just laughed and said that no self-respecting thief would climb this mountain just to steal a few baubles."

"As a matter of fact, I do. You are quite right, but who here would have the nerve to steal them? Wait a minute … just wait a minute. First Susan disappears and then jewellery disappears. It's all starting to make sense. Susan did build that kite thing and then knocked off our jewels to exchange for something she didn't have, cash. I only hope she did slam into a rock or something. This is going to be very difficult to explain to my partners."

CH 13. AUSTRIA

For the first time now in many months, Susan enjoyed the luxury of relaxation despite her injuries. Her collarbone was reset and was knitting well without causing her any pain. The cuts and many bruises were another story. They ached with the slightest movement, especially the bruises.

Susan adjusted her body, looking for a pain free spot. "Strange that mum and dad's phone number had changed," she reviewed once again. "The telephone was part of dad's business. Maybe the police will have their new number? It would be great to hear their voices again, and Ashley? I hope that the police have found him at home, and he will phone soon. He'll get such a surprise."

Susan's thoughts now turned to Ashley, "Funny that I haven't thought too much about Ashley or mum and dad for that matter. I suppose that during that period I was too busy with my thoughts of escaping. I hope he hasn't given up on me and got himself a girlfriend. No, not my Ashley. We'll get married as soon as I get back and in the same church. Won't the rector get a surprise? He'll probably lock me up in the vestry until it all over, just in case ..."

Susan continued her musing, as through her door appeared Victor Craddock with a posy of bright yellow wattle in his free hand.

"Hello, Miss Bauford. How are you feeling today? I brought you some flowers, I hope you like them."

"Mr Craddock! These are wattles. Where on earth did you get them? Wattles don't grow in Austria."

"I know but they do in Australia."

"But how did you get them here?"

"I stole them from the Embassy."

"What?" Susan laughed, "you stole them from the Embassy. Does the Embassy grow wattles?"

"No, not as such. The ambassador has them flown in with other diplomatic stuff to decorate the foyer, you know, the 'Australiana' touch, flora and fauna. If he got his way, he'd have kangaroos hopping round the foyer and saltwater crocodiles guarding the strongroom."

"And you stole from the Embassy?"

"Well, not really, I had to ask his permission, and he actually thought it was a good idea."

"In that case, please thank him from me and thank you."

"Right, then let's get down to it," Victor pulled up a chair and sat down by Susan's bedside. "The good news first. We have researched the background of your identity and it matches with what you have told us. So, the embassy can issue you with an Australian passport and the government will repatriate you back to Australia at no cost to you. I have here a few documents for you to sign and then I will ask you to pack up whatever things you have here and come with me to Vienna where we will place you in a safe house until you are fully recovered."

"Did the doctors here say I am fit to travel?"

"Short distances yes, but for long ones you will still have to convalesce."

"What about my jewels?"

"Oh yes! The police have found no record of it being stolen, and they have returned it to you. It is waiting for you at the embassy. It was the Vienna police who did the investigating, and they have your address listed as care of the embassy."

"Thank you, Mr Craddock. At least that's a weight of my mind."

"Good, but now I have some bad news. I'm afraid I have to tell you from a police report we have from Sydney that both of your parents have died."

"What! When? Was it something to do with my kidnapping?" Susan exclaimed in shock.

"The report says 'from natural causes', but I suspect the kidnapping did contribute to it."

Susan remained silent for a short while and then burst into tears and convulsive sobbing.

Craddock put his arm around her and let her cry. It took a while, but finally Susan regained her composure.

"I'm sorry, Mr Craddock."

"Nothing to be sorry about, after what you have been through, I feel like having a good cry as well."

"I don't understand. Up to a few months ago I was a happy person. I was going to be married and now my life is a bucket of shit. ... Sorry."

"Don't be sorry, it's all behind you now. Once you get back home you can resume a normal, well almost I suppose, a normal life."

"And Ashley? Have you been able to contact him? I have been dying to get a call from him."

"Not as yet. It seems that he is away or something. I had a call from a detective Pike from the Sydney police to say he personally went to the address you gave. It seems that he is in charge of your case. He was also quite insistent in wanting to talk to you, but I told him you were not well enough to talk to him. Do you know him at all?"

"No, I've never heard of him."

"Good. For the time being, I would rather you don't talk to him."

"Why's that?"

"I'm not at liberty to tell you too much at the moment until we have a clearer picture of events."

"What do you mean, a clearer picture?" Susan asked, a little annoyed, "I have told you everything I can. Do you think I am lying or something?"

"No, not at all. It's just that Interpol are involved in your case as well as the Slovenian Government. They all want to talk to you. They say that a place such as The Spa Shangrila does not exist in Slovenia, and Interpol just want to talk to you."

"I don't mind talking to either of them. I have nothing to hide, so I would be happy to talk to them."

"I am not suggesting for a moment that you are hiding something. As your government we have your interests at heart and are taking no chances to you being compromised in any way."

"What do you mean, 'compromised?' I was kidnapped, raped and tortured. How much more compromised can it get?"

"You may be in danger of losing your life."

"What! That's ridiculous. I am here under your protection."

"At this point, I can't tell you much except this. The Slovenian Government is about to open its embassy in Australia in February. If news of this spa being in their country leaks out to the media, they will be severely embarrassed. Our guess is that they will quickly shut down the spa with as much force as it takes. They will arrest the staff there but not all the culprits, as it is obviously a cartel run by Americans, Germans, Chinese, who knows? You are the only credible and star witness. When news of this leaks out, and it will, what do you think the cartel will do to try and stop you from giving evidence?"

This had never occurred to Susan as the shocked expression on her face made evident.

"Do you really think it would go so far?"

"Don't you?"

"Yes, I suppose they would go so far. What do you suggest I do?"

"For the time being you will be under our protection until such time as you are completely well. After that you are free to do as you please, but we will assist you all we can."

"Thank you. So, what happens now?" Susan asked.

"Now, we will get you discharged from here and then take a scenic drive to Vienna where you will meet our ambassador and familiarise yourself with your new lodgings."

"What about the cost of my stay here? What do I do about that?"

"Don't worry about that. The Australian Government will take care of that?"

***

"I heard on the grapevine that there is some sort of a scandal brewing in Slovenia," a voice speaking in German was overheard by Marco Rossetti as he sat dining alone in his habitual bistro in Rome. He was fluent in German, and, on hearing Slovenia mentioned, he pricked up his ears and tried to move in a little closer.

"Really! A scandal in Slovenia," replied the fellow diner, also in German but with a heavy Italian accent, "and I thought that scandals in Slovenia arose only when their men went to bed without taking off their socks?"

"Ja. But this one could be a lot juicier. It seems some foreign girl escaped from what seems to be a white slave sex camp somewhere in the Julian Alps."

"Is that so? What happened?"

"I'm not sure. I was on duty at Graz station at the time when a newspaper phoned for more details. Their crew had listened in to a police patrol radio broadcast directing the patrol car to a crash site on a farm. When they got there, an ambulance was already on its way to a hospital. They followed it and at the hospital heard some rumour of the girl having escaped from some sort of sex camp in Slovenia. They wanted to interview the girl, but before they could some foreign embassy people arrived, and a security blanket was thrown over the whole thing. I think they call it a media blackout."

"Sounds intriguing. Probably a Russian spy or something like that?"

"I don't know. I was due to go on leave the next day, and for a while I was afraid they would cancel my leave, but no, here I am, salute!"

Marco digested what he had just overheard and became a little worried. Back in his apartment he was still not at ease and opened up his phone.

"Hello, Mathew, it's Marco here … fine, fine, tell me? You haven't had one of your girls go missing? … No, no, I mean missing … like in gone, disappeared, escaped? … Aha, no kidding … Well, one was found in Austria, a bit banged up but living and yelling about a sex slave camp. I don't know for sure but here's what I heard." Marco then went on and related what he had heard, "I don't know, I can only tell you what I overheard. I'm pretty sure that the Austrian was a cop, but I don't know about the other fellow except that he was definitely an Italian and a close friend of the Austrian ... What's that? Tomorrow? No, I can't make it tomorrow but the next week is OK ... What's that? ... No, that's not a problem as long as Franz is there to pick me up ... OK I'll see you then."

***

Mathew put the phone away and commenced to work up a rage. Furiously, he swatted his desk, making papers and stationery items airborne and fall to the floor.

"The bitch," he cried out loud. "She didn't get killed, she made it to Austria." Mathew began pacing the floor.

"She's probably with the Australian government right now, singing her head off. But that is Australia, this is Slovenia. They are not going to go to war over this. Hmm, but then we have American, German even Indian nationalities here. If the shit hits the fan, they will all be screaming their heads off. Damn it, we must stop her from talking. Actually, she can talk all she likes, she just must not turn it into evidence. We could claim she agreed to the kidnapping for money and staged it herself. Akim would back that, or I'll make bloody sure he does. His father's a shareholder."

Mathew picked up the intercom from the floor and almost automatically flicked Patra's extension.

"Come to my office right away," he ordered.

"What's up?" Patra asked as she entered and watched Mathew pick up papers and other bits on the floor.

"The bitch made it, she's not dead."

"Which bitch is not dead? I don't know what you are talking about?"

"Susan, she made it to Austria, a bit scratched up from what I hear but she made it to Austria."

"I'm gla ... I mean I'm sorry to hear that but how do you know?"

"I know, I just know, so let's leave it at that. What matters now is what to do about it. She's with the Australian embassy right now so this means that the Slovenian government have been informed unless I am very much mistaken."

Patra, though initially shocked, thought on her feet and quickly replied. "So, what? What's the Slovenian government going to do? You haven't broken any laws here. The girls cannot be described as prostitutes as they make no money out of it. So, they grant a few favours to a few well known business people, so what? There are times when sex is the best medicine. We have dossiers on all the girls' backgrounds and families, and we can tell them what will happen to their families if they make the wrong noises, so what are you worried about?"

"The police! I'm worrying about the police. Do you think they will just stand idle and twiddle their thumbs when they know there is a glory-making case waiting for them to get their mitts into?"

"Which police? The Austrian police? You have committed no crimes in Austria, so how can they charge you? A bit far and expensive for them to get involved. OK, there was the abduction, but you didn't do it. You were here all the time that was taking place so how and with what can they charge you, and more importantly, how are they going to prove it? Susan can't testify, she was unconscious the whole time."

"All that makes a lot of sense, Patra," Mathew remarked, quite relieved. "We shall just have to fight it out."

"And don't forget, we have entertained some super rich clients who may not wish to have their names mentioned in public and be only too happy to apply a bit of pressure where it's needed."

"You're a cunning fox, Patra, I never knew that, but I can top that with a brilliant stroke of my own."

"Really, and that is?"

"Susan really did not escape from here. She ran away after she stole a whole lot of our precious stones."

***

The cadmium plated Mercedes pulled up at the entrance to the Australian Embassy and parked diplomatically if not legally.

Victor opened the car door for Susan and reminded her, "We won't be here for long. I'll just introduce you to our ambassador. He's looking forward to meeting you and then take you to your quarters."

"How do you know he's available?"

"He's available all right. I phoned him before leaving Graz and gave him an expected time of arrival."

They walked through the foyer past the reception desk to the elevators and took one of the two to the second floor. When the door opened, they were facing another reception desk manned by an attractive middle-aged lady.

"Hi, Barbara," Victor greeted her, "we're back. Is he in?"

"Of course, he is, and expecting you," she replied and reached for the intercom switch. "They're here, Mr Mannering."

"Good, send them in please."

The receptionist pressed a button and a heavy timber door swung open.

Seated at an L-shaped, large desk was a middle-aged man, greying at the temples, wearing a pinstripe dark suit.

"Mr Ambassador," Victor opened as he and Susan stopped at his desk, "may I present Miss Susan Bauford. Miss Bauford, Ambassador Charles Mannering."

"Miss Bauford, delighted to meet you." The Ambassador rose and proffered his hand, "You must be the bravest lady I have ever come across."

"Thank you, sir but I'd hardly call it bravery, more like desperation."

"Quite. Please sit down and I will explain the reason I had you brought here." Both Susan and Victor sat down on the visitor's chairs.

"What we have here is a rather delicate diplomatic and criminal situation. Slovenia is about to open its first embassy in Australia next month. If your story breaks in the media, it will be a big one and an international one. Big enough to send the blood of some of our hotheads boiling. People discern from the media mostly what suits them, so this could lead to protests and even rioting. Not at all the sort of things we want to see at the opening of an embassy on our soil. Slovenians in Australia could become subject to attacks, that sort of thing. This, of course, would result in more media attention internationally. Do you see what I'm getting at?"

"Yes, I do Mr Ambassador, but surely you are not asking me to forget that this ever happened?"

"Good God no! What I am asking, for the time being, is that you do not speak to the media until such time as we have the situation resolved."

"Would you please explain in more detail by what do you mean, resolved?"

"Very well. We know that the Slovenian government is not involved, but we also know that there are behind-the-scenes, criminal forces profiting from that enterprise. When we are in a position to expose them, then the media can have its field day."

"That could take ages, years even, and through all that time there are women held captive there and raped regularly. What about them?" Susan felt the blood rising in her head.

"I understand your concern, and I can assure you that the police have given this their number one priority."

"The police! What police? The Australian police cannot enter Slovenia, nor can the Austrian police."

"You are quite right, they cannot. But Interpol can and do."

***

Vasco Visjak, the current Minister for the Interior, became quite infuriated after he finished reading an epistle newly received from the Australian Embassy in Vienna.

"Josko," he called out to his aide in the adjoining office, "spare me a minute now, please."

"Yes, Minister," was the quick reply, as Josko rose and entered his boss's office.

"Sit down, Josko, and read this, this note I just received and tell me what you think?"

Josko studied the document, becoming more angry as he perused it.

"This is a lot of rubbish! Where did they get all this from? We don't have a white slave camp in the alps!"

"I'm aware of that, but the Australians seem to think we do."

"Could this be a covert move, something to do with the opening of our embassy down there?"

"I don't see how? What do they have to gain?" the Minister asked. "If they didn't want us there, all they have to say is no. It's their country."

"Maybe they want to embarrass us, you know, soften us up or something?"

"Maybe but why? We've always had good relations with Australia, that's why the embassy."

"Just a moment, Minister, may I see that note again?" Josko asked. "Aha, I read it correctly." Josko nodded, having reread some of the document, "See here, it refers to a 'white sex slave camp' in the Julian Alps and on the next page it goes on to say, 'she escaped from the spa with the aid of a hang glider'. The spa, Minister not a sex camp. So, which is it?"

"A spa … didn't we lease a mountain top or something in the Julian Alps to some crowd who wanted to convert it to a health spa or something, this was quite a while ago?"

"We did indeed, Minister, I remember it now. It was an international group who wanted to buy a derelict monastery and turn it into health spa. You told them that, as foreigners, they could not buy real estate in Slovenia but they could lease it."

"That's right. I offered them a 99-year lease. Interesting, I expect they have paid all rents on time otherwise we'd have heard more about it. Any idea of what's been happening there?"

"Not really, Minister, except that I see their helicopters every now and again. You can't mistake them, they have, 'Spa Shangrila - Air Bus' signs in large letters painted on both sides."

"Would not they be subject to health checks by the Department of Health?"

"Ordinarily yes, but to get there you have to go by helicopter, which is very expensive, and seeing the spa was for rich foreigners only, they sort of didn't bother."

"You mean you didn't inform the Department of Health?"

"No, Minister, they were foreigners catering to foreigners …"

"And they thanked you with a little present."

"Nothing great, just a tip like any waiter gets."

"Oh, Josko, you people are something else. When you do it, it is a tip. When we do it, it is corruption. Well, that's the world I suppose. You must have a file on the spa, you know, copy of contract, rental receipts, location, that sort of thing?"

"Of course, we do."

"Will you bring it to me, please. I'd like a closer look at it."

"Of course, Minister. I'll be right back."

***

Vasco went through the file a number of times and made some notes and summonsed Josko again.

"I've read through the file, and while its contents are all in order, I am not disturbed by what it says but rather what it doesn't say."

"I don't follow," Josko protested.

"I'll go into that later. It says here that the resident CEO is one Mathew Hudson, an English national, and we have a contact number for him. This Mathew Hudson, have I met him?"

"Yes, Minister, you have, but just the once at the signing of the lease."

"Hmm, I don't recall it but no matter. Get hold of him and tell him I want to see him right away ... now. Make an appointment for him and let me know. Also impress upon him in the strongest possible terms that failure to comply could result in a couple of helicopter loads of our police landing on his courtyard as well as the cancellation of his lease. Oh, and ask him to leave his helicopter at home. We will send him one of ours."

**

For days now nothing more was heard regarding Susan's flight. "Perhaps she's decided to say nothing and simply buggered off, back to Australia," Mathew confided to Patra in his office.

"Wishful thinking," Patra replied, "I'd say she's still in a hospital somewhere in Austria, doing her best to recover. I think this is not the end, just the beginning. There's bound to be some fallout."

"Maybe, but you said yourself there was nothing to worry about."

"Mathew, I gave you defence plan, not a 'get out of jail free card'."

"Yes, and I appreciate that, but it's still very quiet. I just hope it stays that way ..."

As Mathew was talking his telephone buzzed. He picked it up.

"Mathew here ... oh, nice to hear from you, Josko. What can I do for you? ... I see, and who's this? ... the minister! What does he want? ... Tomorrow? No, I can't... he is! That sounds more like a promotion rather than a bollocking ... I'm ... I see, that leaves me little choice ... no of course I'll not disclose our arrangement ... fine, I'll see you tomorrow."

"What was that all about?" Patra asked.

"That was my government contact. It seems the Minister of the Interior wishes to see me."

"Why?"

"He didn't quite say. Some irregularities or something."

"Irregularities, my foot. We both know what about."

"Can't be all that bad. He's sending a government helicopter to pick me up."

"Maybe it's for a one-way trip."

"I don't think so. If that was the case, he'd send a chopper full of cops. No this is government courtesy."

***

Mathew didn't even have time to sit down as he entered the Ministry. "The Minister will see you now," Josko told Mathew, leading him to the Minister's office.

After exchanging formalities, the Minister asked Mathew to take a seat and excused Josko from the room.

"So, what can I do for you, Minister? What's this all about?"

"First of all, you can tell me just what is happening at Spa Shangrila?"

"Much the same as usual. You know, we get guests eager to relax and take in the mountain air."

"And what are the ladies doing while the gentlemen are airing?"

"We have no ladies; the guests are male only. When I say we have no ladies, we have a few staff members of the female persuasion,"

"Yes, we know, and one of them left your premises using a hang glider. Couldn't you afford to send her by helicopter?"

"I don't know anything about that. What's her name?"

"We don't know her name, but we do know she is of Australian nationality, now in the hands of the Australian Embassy who claim she was raped whilst in your care."

"Raped did you say? I wonder by whom, certainly not me."

"I did not say you, but I did say raped and on a regular basis. Is this your idea of a health spa?"

"This is a serious allegation, Minister. Do you have proof of any of this? Results of a rape kit perhaps?"

"You know we don't, but we do have this." The Minister handed Mathew the communique from the Australian Embassy, "Please read it and let me have your comments."

Having read it, Mathew tossed it on the Minister's desk. "Sheer political propaganda. The Australians must be having an election or something and this is to create some sort of diversion."

"How would an incident like this be an electoral diversion?"

"Quite simple, really. One candidate has to be of Slovenian extraction for the opposition to claim that he cannot be trusted."

"Then that would be valid too for anyone of German extraction. Sieg Heil and all that. Now, there are other irregularities I'd like your comments on."

"You're the boss, go for it."

"You had a lot of renovating to do after you signed the lease, I assume?"

"You bet we did and at some cost."

"But you did not read the terms of your lease, did you?"

"You mean the small print."

"No, the ordinary print where it clearly states that all structural alterations and renovations must comply with the country's building codes and must be inspected by a qualified building inspector and passed by him before occupancy can take place. Can you produce the certificates of approval?"

"No, but this applies to local development, not way out into the alps practically out of the world," Mathew protested.

"Mr Hudson, then please show me where on the contract the Julian Alps are exempted. The contract clearly states Slovenia, and we are very much part of the world, part of Europe in fact."

"OK, so we made a mistake, fine us and take a little for yourself."

"Mr Hudson, did you just offer me a bribe?" The Minister shot back, almost outraged.

"No, no. I'm sorry, a bit of English humour, quite harmless, I assure you."

"Very well then. We now come to another matter. As you say, you were opening a spa, a sort of medicinal refuge for which you need to be licensed and regularly inspected by an accredited health inspector. That is also in the lease. Can you show me your licence and inspection certificates?"

"I don't have them on me, but we must have them somewhere back at the spa."

"Oh, and tax returns, you do have copies of those?"

"Well, yes but ..."

"Yes, I know Mr Hudson, they're back at the spa."

"Minister, I was told to bring nothing, just myself."

"Yes, I am aware of that. That is why we had better go back to the helicopter which brought you here and go back to the spa and have a good look."

"You can't do that, well not right now. I am a busy man, and I am entitled to some notice."

"I am the Minister for the Interior, and I can do that. As for notice, I have given you notice ... now, or would you prefer a police escort?"

***

As the government helicopter wove its way deeper into the Julian Alps, Mathew noticed another helicopter bearing on the same path.

"Why is a chopper out there shadowing us?" he asked of no one in particular.

"It is not shadowing us," the Minister explained. "It is following us."

"Why?"

"Because it contains six armed policemen who have been sent along for my protection, in case we encounter any surprise activity."

***

Franz was busy checking his helicopter when he heard the whirling, pulsating sounds of chopper blades. Puzzled, he climbed into the cockpit and watched two helicopters circle and finally land in the quadrangle. He watched as Mathew got out first, followed by the Minister, then turning to the other machine he watched six armed, uniformed policemen disembark.

"He's gone mad. What the hell for does he want coppers here? Could be that Susan's disappearance, he's still hot under the collar about that."

***

"Where would you like to begin, Minister?" Mathew asked.

"Why don't we start with your office first?" Turning to his police escort, Vasco directed: "Four of you search the area for anything out of the ordinary and report to me. Two of you come with me."

Approaching the doorway to his office, Mathew suggested, "please go in and make yourselves comfortable. I'll be with you in a sec, I just have to get to the toilet, otherwise your stay could prove to be most disagreeable." He limped along the corridor to a toilet and closed the door behind him. He waited a few seconds, then opened the door just a crack. The corridor was empty. They had obviously entered his office. Taking a deep breath, he ran to the nearest exit, across the quadrangle to where Franz's helicopter was standing. Jerking the door open, he was glad to see Franz still in the cockpit.

"Happy to see you still here, Franz, I thought I saw your shadow as we landed. Can you fire this thing up right away?"

"Sure thing but why?"

"Just do it. Once you're airborne I'll explain everything."

"But I haven't lodged a flight plan?"

"Fuck the flight plan, Franz, just get this thing in the air or would you rather spend the evening or a few years in a Slovenian jail?"

Franz needed no further convincing. The rotors spun into life and the aircraft rose to a height convenient to set a course.

"Where to, boss?"

"Austria but not Graz. Look for a small, private airfield or a flat piece of ground. We can ditch the chopper and get a taxi or a lift or something."

"I've got no money on me, boss, so forget the taxi."

"Don't worry about that, I've got plenty and access to more. Right now, the main thing is to get lost. Damn that Susan. Who would have thought that she could bring down in one night, that which took us years to build?"

CH 14. MOPPING UP

"Josko, I want you to organise at least three helicopters, large ones, you know, the ones that can carry troops and have them fly here as soon as possible," the Minister ordered on the telephone. "Yes three. Even then that won't be enough, but there is not enough landing space available for more. There's a lot of personnel here who have to be evacuated … yes, I know the police won't have troop carriers, but the army has … ring the secretary for defence and let him know. I will take full responsibility. I haven't got his number, or I'd ring him myself … well if he does, give him my number and have him ring me here… I'll have the map coordinates from our pilot ready as soon as you ring back to confirm … tell him I have declared this a Priority II situation, no make that a Priority I."

Vasco hung up the phone and turned his attention to Patra who was sitting opposite him while he occupied her seat behind her desk. "Now, Miss Kurri, I understand from the others that you are in charge here."

"Hardly in charge. When Mr Mathew is not here, he has instructed me to be the caretaker."

"And what exactly does that involve?"

"Nothing really, I carry on with my work as usual."

"I see, so you are in fact an employee."

"Yes."

"I'd like to know the circumstances of how you found this form of employment?"

"Not much to tell," Patra replied.

"I'd like to know anyway."

"I've known Mr Mathew for a long time, mostly in London when one day he asked me how would I like to work in a spa in the alps.

The thought of getting out of London appealed to me, so I said OK."

"And when you got here did you know beforehand what was happening here?"

"Not before I got here, and only then I found out part of my job was to arrange sleeping rosters for the women with male guests."

"And you were happy with that?"

"No, I was not, at first I was outraged."

"Then why did you not leave?"

"You are joking, aren't you? How could I leave?"

"The way most people do. You hand in your notice and go."

"Mr Visjak, you can't be serious, or maybe you are having a joke at my expense."

"I don't follow, I'm not joking."

"Mr Visjak, just how long do you think I'd be breathing if I tried to walk out, carrying with me the knowledge I have observed? Look, the moment I started this job, I became a slave here just like the women brought here."

"That may be so. We'll soon clear this up when we speak with your boss."

"How are you going to do that? You've just let him escape." The Minister felt the sting of these words, "I hardly let him escape, but he won't get far, Interpol will soon pick him up."

"Good, you can question him then. Can I go now?"

"Not just yet, I have a few more questions."

"What about?"

"You would probably be the best person to answer this one. How many women were involved in this operation? I mean, how many women are detained here?"

"It varied but between 15 to 20. Right now, about 15, no make that 14, one escaped."

"When you say 15 to 20, that means that some women were released."

"You could say that. Some of them lost their head and became useless. Others left with their guest who paid a price to take them."

"What happened to the mentally affected ones?"

"I don't know. They were taken away by helicopter, but I don't know where. I assumed to a mental institution."

"More likely thrown out of the helicopter somewhere over the alps."

"I don't know."

"All right, now. I believe you had an escape from here. Was it just the one woman or were there others?"

"Just the one."

"And how did she manage that? From the look of the place, unless she had wings, I'd say it was pretty near impossible."

Patra fell silent for a short period but then in a soft voice said, "She had wings."

"What? Could you clarify that?"

"She secretly built a hang glider."

"You are joking, how could she do that? Where did she get the materials to construct something like that?"

"Silk bed sheets and plastic tubing. She somehow managed to cobble together a frame and stretched the sheets over it."

"That's quite fascinating, but how do you know this?"

"I saw the thing when she finished building it."

"You saw it completed and you did nothing about it?"

"I did do something about it. I helped her carry it down to the garbage wall and watched her take off in it."

"Are you saying you helped her escape?"

"Yes, I did."

"Why?"

"I knew that her escape could lead to my escape."

"I don't follow."

"I knew that if she made it, she would go straight to the nearest Australian embassy and tell them everything. In fact, that was her plan. She told me that would lead to people like yourself being here, asking a lot of questions. With you here no one would dare touch me. I could leave here with you, and the boss would be in prison, and I could be free."

The Minister digested what he had just heard but was not sure if the story was believable.

"Can you prove any of this? You must admit it sounds a bit like a tall story.

A young woman held in captivity secretly constructs a hang glider from bed sheets and scraps and soars out over the alps. To do that she would need specialised technical knowledge. Now, where would she get that? Our reports show that she was a newly graduated lawyer, not an aerodynamics engineer."

"I am aware of that, but I know for a fact that while at university, hang gliding was her sport and hobby."

"Even so, that does not make her an expert in constructing gliders. If, as you say, you helped her, with what? I take it you are no expert. Do you fly gliders yourself?"

"No, I don't."

"I see. I'm afraid all this is a little thin."

"I can only repeat what I have told you."

"I'm afraid we would need a little more than that."

"Well, there is no more than that. What else can I tell you? Wait a minute, when Susan was found she would have been searched for any documents she may be carrying. They would have found a pouch of precious stones on her."

"From what I understand, they did, but what has that to do with anything?"

"I gave her those stones."

"You did! Why?"

"She had no money, and if she made it, she was going to need cash, so I told her to take them and sell them at the first opportunity."

"Really, and where did you get them from?"

"From the collection of jewellery and precious stones we keep here at the spa. Mathew insisted we use them to make the women more attractive, you know, alluring. I stole them."

"You stole them? Would not that have put you at great risk?"

"Not really, I told Mathew that I discovered the theft, and he assumed that Susan had stolen them as part of her escape plan."

"Neat, very neat, but it's not me you have to convince. Our police will handle that, and I think Interpol will also be interested."

"I am aware of that."

"Good." Just then the Minister's phone buzzed, "Visjak. Oh, hello, Josko, how did you go? … Good, three of them… oh! How did the media get wind of this? Leaked! … Do you know who? … No, you tell them nothing, nothing you understand. Until we have completed clearing this thing up, it is a media blackout."

***

"Hello, my name is Vasco Visjak. I am the Minister for the Interior. Please take a seat. I'd like to ask you a few questions?"

"Thank you, Mr Vis … vas …" replied a middle-aged, obviously, American, gentleman.

"Visjak, and you are?"

"My name is Adrian Podmore."

"Really! Any connection to AP Industries?"

"You could say that. Actually, I own the company."

"So, then I take it you are here for health reasons?"

"Health reasons, nothing. Nothing wrong with my health, I just want to keep it that way."

"And just how do you go about doing that?"

"None of your damn business, sonny."

"I am the Minister for the Interior."

"That doesn't make you a doctor. I talk to ministers all the time. As a matter of fact, I own shares in a few of them."

"That must be very rewarding for you but if you refuse to talk to this Minister you will find yourself talking before a judge in one of our courts of law."

"What the hell are you talking about, fella? I've done nothing wrong. Why should I talk to a court?"

"Mr Podmore, in Slovenia we call complicity to abduction and multiple rape a serious crime. You don't have to say anything. If you remain silent, the court will hear the States' evidence and pronounce sentence on that, which in your case would be somewhere between 16 to 20 years in one of our resorts, except nobody calls them that."

"This is outrageous. I have done nothing wrong and raped nobody. I want to talk to my lawyers." Adrian reached in his pocket for a phone.

"Your lawyers? You mean you have two of them?"

"Better than that, sonny. I have a whole firm of lawyers working for me."

"In that case, you had better call them, but before you do, just one more question. How much were you paying for your stay here, you know, per day, per week?"

"If you must know, about five thousand bucks a day plus."

"And you never knew the women here were sex slaves kept here against their will?"

"You said just one question!"

"I know, sorry, but I would like an answer."

"Of course not. How was I to know? Nobody ever said anything about that."

"Thank you, Mr Podmore." Vasco then turned to one of the two policemen in the office, "Officer, will you please place this man under arrest. He's coming back to Ljubljana with us. Send in one of the other guests."

Momentarily alone with the other policeman, the officer commented, "Nice going, sir but I think he will get off free, with a lecture from the judge."

"What makes you say that?"

"Not enough hard evidence to convict him unless some of the women name him and even then, it's still a bit iffy."

"That may be so, but there is a harsher penalty he faces from his family and peers. That is why the arrests are vital. Once this story goes to the media, these guys will see just how hard it is to find a bushel under which they can hide."

***

Including Podmore there were another six men staying as guests at the 'spa.'

Vasco interviewed them all separately, and, not surprisingly, discovered they all had similar stories. All of them were wealthy. All of them had a firm of lawyers at their disposal, and none of them knew anything about sex slavery. All of them were there to breathe the alpine air, and all of them proclaimed their innocence vigorously. All of them were placed under arrest.

***

Charles Mannering called Victor to his office at the embassy in Vienna.

"How's our glider lady coming along, Victor?"

"I was going to try and corner you sometime today and talk about it."

"Well, now you can. What's the verdict? I understand you saw her yesterday?"

"I did and I would say she has just about made a full recovery. I think she's ready to travel."

"Good, the sooner we get her out of here the better for all of us." The ambassador opened a desk drawer and produced a small, blue plastic wallet, "I have her passport here, and a one-way, open air ticket to Sydney and $400 in cash. She'll need at least that for expenses once she gets home. Also, there is a government voucher covering her for medical expenses should any of the existing injuries she sustained give her further trouble."

"That's very generous, sir."

"I hope so, I would have liked to see more but you know Canberra.

Mention money and they all fall on their swords. Oh, and there also is the phone number of a detective Pike from Sydney CIB. He's the cop appointed to handle her case from day one. He's been pestering the embassy for Susan's phone number so he can talk to her, and I told him that when she's well enough she will ring him."

"Good, I'm glad that's sorted. When do you suggest I drive her to the airport?"

"I leave that up to you and her. Let me know the details later."

***

Victor drove out to Grinzing, a fashionable suburb of Vienna on the border of The Vienna Woods. The Australian government had purchased a cottage there, where it was used as a safe house as well as a venue for diplomatic visitors when privacy was an issue.

Susan was the sole occupant in the cottage at the time, except for a private nurse visiting on a regular basis making sure the food larder was well stocked and all medical procedures followed.

Victor arrived at the cottage and from his attaché case produced a bottle of champagne.

"Hello, Miss Bauford, would you mind putting this in your fridge? We'll have a celebratory drink after you hear my news."

"Sounds exciting, Mr Craddock," Susan replied, taking the bottle. "Where would you like to sit for this revelation?"

"The dining room table would be excellent. Among other things, I have a couple more papers for you to sign."

"Would you like a glass of wine now or later?"

"A little later, thank you. The wine needs to regain a little of the chill it lost in transit."

Victor sat down and put the blue plastic wallet as well as a manila file on the table.

"Would you like some tea and a slice of strudel?" Susan offered further hospitality. "It's really delicious. Apparently, there's a bakery just down the road from here so the nurse has been getting it for me regularly."

"Maybe later with the bubbly, thank you. Strudel with champagne complement each other very well, but now can we get down to business?

"Oh! Before I forget, there was someone who came to the embassy two days ago and asked if we could tell him which hospital you were recovering?"

"What? That's not possible. No one else knows I'm here. What did he look like?"

"I did not see him but from what the receptionist told me, he was middle aged, obviously English and had brown hair."

"My God, that sounds like Mathew. What did the receptionist tell him?"

"Nothing, she told him that this was classified information, and that it is the embassies' policy never to reveal this sort of information to anybody unless it goes through the proper channels."

"Thank God for that!"

"All the more reason to get you safely back home. Now, here is your passport and other bits and pieces plus a few papers to sign verifying that you have received the papers."

Susan laughed, "I have to sign some papers to say that I have received some papers. Next thing you'll tell me that I have to sign another paper verifying that I have signed the papers."

"Canberra is very strict about verifications. Even our parliamentary members have to sign verification, verifying that they stayed awake throughout the sitting in the House."

Now, pay attention, note that the airline ticket is left open, undated and unreserved. As there is no direct flight from Vienna to Sydney, you will have to go via London. We will get you on a flight from Vienna to London and connect with a Qantas flight to Sydney. From there you are on your own. A detective Pike from the CIB in Sydney has offered to pick you up from Sydney Airport and drive you home, but before I give him your flight details, I need your er, er, verification."

"That's not a problem. Actually, it suits me very well, providing I can do one thing."

"What's that?"

"Stopover in London for a few days."

"Why? I thought you'd be wanting to get back home as soon as possible."

"I do, but I promised someone I'd return a favour, and I can do that only in London."

"That sounds mysterious."

"It's not really, and I think it is something you should know. There's a woman at the spa called Patra, I don't know her other name. She is in charge of a number of things there, but she too is there against her will. She was the person who could have prevented me from escaping, but instead of that she helped me. I'd like that to go on record in case she is charged with anything. I promised her I would find her daughter in London and talk to her. That's why I'd like to stopover in London."

"Miss Bauford, after what you've been put through on that mountain top, I don't think you owe anything to anybody."

"Then we will just have to agree to disagree. She's also the person who gave me the gems to exchange for money, because she thought I would need the cash."

"I see. I suppose that puts a more serious tone on it. Look, I can't see any reason why you can't have a stopover except that you will have to contact Qantas yourself and book your flight home."

"I expect I won't find that overtaxing."

"No, somehow I don't think you will." Susan signed the 'verification' documents. "Anything else I have to sign?"

"No, that about does it. They will keep some clerk back in Canberra busy for at least a week. Oh yes! One more thing. I have the phone number of detective Edward Pike of the Sydney CIB. He's been pestering us constantly, wanting to talk to you. It's up to you whether you talk to him or not. Just bear in mind that Sydney time is 8 hours ahead of Austria."

"Pike, isn't he the one who was going to locate Ashley for me?"

"That's right, he's the one."

"Has he said anything about Ashley?"

"Not that I know of."

"That's very strange. He's got to be home sometime, surely!"

"In that case give Pike a ring and put a bit of pressure on him."

"I will. I'll do it tonight."

"Good. That bottle of champagne should have regained its drinkable temperature by now, so what say we have a glass and drink to a successful outcome and a safe journey home."

"With pleasure, I'll get the bottle and some glasses and the strudel."

"Fine, and if you will excuse me for a sec, I've just got to fetch something from the car."

Susan found some champagne flutes, as well as the strudel, and placed them on the table.

Victor returned quickly, carrying a small suitcase. He placed it on a chair.

"This is for you from the staff at the embassy."

"Really, why? I don't quite understand."

"It's really quite simple," Victor started to explain. "Airlines are very suspicious of anyone travelling without any luggage, as are hotels. So, we decided to get you a suitcase to spare you any embarrassing encounters. Then we thought you would feel pretty stupid walking about with an empty suitcase, so the ladies at the embassy thought it might be a good idea to fill it with some clothing and stuff you might need, seeing you don't have a change of clothing. They got a good idea of the size you take from me, so there you have it! You are now a bona fide traveller."

"I don't know what to say." Susan was overcome with surprise and emotion. "Thank you and thank your staff very much."

"Believe me, it was a pleasure, so here's to a good future, Miss Bauford, and a happy homecoming."

"What's with the Miss Bauford?" Susan asked sipping her

drink. "Please call me Susan."

"In that case, I have to insist on being called Victor."

***

In the early hours of the morning Susan called Pike's number. To her surprise the call was answered promptly, and she was connected right away.

"Detective Pike," he answered.

"Mr Pike, my name is Susan Bauford, and I am calling from Austria. I believe you have been trying to contact me."

"Susan? Susan Bauford? The kidnapped bride!" Pike was surprised and also amazed.

"Yes, the very one."

"How nice of you to call. We were all very worried about you, but now that seems to be behind us. When are you flying home?"

"Shortly, I hope. I have a few things to attend to in London, and then I will be ready."

"I'll have you picked up from the airport if you care to give me the details."

"That's very nice of you, thank you. I'll let you have it as soon as I get the details, but that is not why I called."

"I see, what else can I do for you?"

"I'm told you have been trying to contact my fiancé, Ashley Barton but without much success. What's the problem there?"

"The problem is, is ... I don't know quite how to tell you this. We've had the local police send out a constable to his house, but every time he returned a report that no one answered the door. Then, only a couple of days ago, the constable reported a 'FOR SALE' sign tied to the front fence."

"Really! Ashley's selling the house? Can't you track him down by asking the real estate agent selling the house?"

"Yes, we can and that's what we are doing as we speak. If you give me your number, I will call you the moment we find out."

"I don't have a number, as I will be travelling, so can I call you?"

"By all means, please do."

***

"Pepe, what is going on here?" Olaf the cook asked after being herded off in a lounge with all the other staff. "What do the police want from me? I'm just the cook, I've done nothing wrong."

"It's not the police, it's that Minister fellow. He's acting like God asking all sorts of questions."

"If he's not the police, why doesn't Mr Mathew just tell him to piss off."

"Mr Mathew not here."

"Yes, he is, I saw him here just a few hours ago."

"Yeah, sprinting off to the helicopter with Franz already in it, and then buggering off without Franz doing the safety check routine."

"Oh. I take it he's in big trouble."

"No, he flew out of trouble and left us into trouble."

"Bastardo! Now what do we say?"

"You say nothing. You are the cook. You work here five days a week and they fly you home most weekends."

"What about you? What do you say?" Olaf asked.

"Same, nothing, I am the handyman. I fix things, I pick up the crap."

***

Minister Visjak interviewed all the staff members who, with one exception, knew nothing except their jobs.

Mario sang like a nightingale when told that his cooperation would result in receiving privileges. He told of the torture by electricity of unwilling victims to make them more submissive, as well as the force used to hold down those of more athletic build and subject them to being raped. He also included a few guests' names who insisted on a rape scene, even if it was simulated.

Some of the female victims corroborated Mario's contribution and added a little of their own. Others remained mute as if in a trance.

"That about does it," the Minister remarked to the sergeant of the police escort. "As of now, I am cancelling the lease on this piece of real estate and declaring the place closed and off limits. Gather everyone into the helicopters and let Ljubljana Prison know to expect visitors."

"Shall I leave a couple of officers here on guard?" The sergeant asked.

"What's the point? I don't expect thieves to come and ransack the place and besides, how are they going to get here?"

***

There was just enough space to accommodate everyone in the helicopters as they screwed up to the air highway, one after the other, leaving below the old monastery, now just as deserted as it had been for several hundred years.

CH 15. LONDON

As the plane thrust towards Heathrow Airport, Susan reflected on her departure from Vienna.

She recalled checking the contents of the suitcase Victor had brought her, and that surprised her. On top of a few accessories was a warm, knitted, powder blue, business suit as well as a skirt and blouses, underwear and, at the bottom, a small makeup kit in a handbag and two pairs of shoes. There was also one pair of black leather high heels and another pair of comfortable, slip-on walking shoes. She tried on the shoes.

"Perfect," she murmured, "but how on earth did he get my shoe size?" Susan tried on the suit and again, "perfect, like it was tailored for me. I suppose one of the girls in the office must have been my height and build, but how could he measure the shoes?"

***

When Victor arrived to take her to the airport, Susan chose to wear the powder blue suit, not to make a fashion statement but more as a show of appreciation.

"Wow!" was Victor's immediate reaction, "that outfit really suits you. You look terrific. The colour really sets off and compliments your blond hair."

"Thank you, I really appreciate the gesture, but tell me, how did you get my shoe size so perfectly?"

"That was easy. The slippers the hospital gave you had the size embossed on the sole."

Driving to the airport Victor suddenly said, "Oh and one more thing, your passport, have you had a look at it?"

"Yes, I have."

"And?"

"And what?"

"It's not like the everyday Australian passport."

"I wouldn't know, I've never had a passport before."

"It's a diplomatic passport. That means it gets you through all the authorities quickly with no questions asked."

"That was very thoughtful of you."

"It wasn't me; it was the embassy. We thought that if the media get a whiff of your presence, you would be mobbed by them. We don't want you to say anything to the media until this spa business is wrapped up. You will notice too that the passport expires after six months, so you had better not stay in London for too long."

"Don't worry. I don't think I'll be there for more than a week."

"And another thing, I don't think that the $400 we gave you will last long in London. They have places there that charge that much for a cocktail, so you had better sell some of those gems as soon as possible."

"Please don't worry, Victor, I think I can look after myself."

"Of course, you can. Sorry, that was a stupid suggestion."

"Not really. It's nice to know someone cares."

"On that note, would you mind very much keeping in touch? I mean, let me know how you are getting on, that sort of thing. You know, Christmas card, birthday card, any old card."

"That would be nice, I'd like that, Victor."

"Good, when we stop, I'll fish out a business card, so you know where to contact me."

"Thank you, Victor, and thank you for booking me in the hotel in London, that was nice of you."

"Before you thank me again, you had better wait till you see it. It's not The Savoy, but from what I could gather it's clean and reasonable."

"I'm sure it will be fine and besides I'll be there for only a few days."

"Good, and remember, don't get a taxi from the airport. It'll cost you an arm and a leg. Get a tube from the airport to Earl's Court and from there a Taxi to The Scarsdale Hotel. It's not very far from there."

"Don't worry, Victor, I'm sure I'll find it, but by the way, has anybody else been asking about me at the embassy?"

"No, only that one fellow."

"I'm sure it was Mathew."

"That's quite possible. We received a note from the Slovenian government that the spa has been closed down, and a number of people arrested, but the person in charge had managed to escape in a helicopter. Someone named Hudson."

"That's Mathew all right, and he's looking for me."

"Why should he be looking for you? … Oh, I see, sorry, but rest assured, he'll get no information from us. As a matter of fact, if he does show up again, I'll see to it that he's arrested."

***

The airport at Heathrow was much larger than Susan expected. With a diplomatic passport, clearing immigration and customs was the easy part. Once out in the public sector Susan became quite confused. "Which way now?" she wondered, looking round for signage to guide her.

"Can I help you at all, madam?" an airport-uniformed young woman approached her, noticing her confusion.

"I hope so. I'm trying to find my way to the underground, or tube as you call it."

"That's easy, just follow me and I will show you the way."

The rest of her journey went like clockwork. Her escort told her which coloured route to take. Once inside the carriage, she was able to memorise the names of two stations before reaching Earl's Court from the coloured diagram displayed inside the tube.

Once inside her hotel room, Susan did a stock-take of events over the past few weeks. It now seemed incredible to her that she had glided out of the Julien Alps, a range she had never heard of before, from Slovenia, a country she did not know existed until she found herself in it. For months she had been enslaved and raped many times but managed to escape, only to find herself recovering in a hospital in Vienna and treated like a VIP by the Australian Embassy.

The many tearful nights, after her rapist had left, were spent in thinking about what should have been. Married to Ashley, both planning their future, starting a family. Now, this seemed again possible but not a word from Ashley. Surely the Sydney police would have found him by now? The real estate agent selling his house must know where to contact him. Susan decided to ring detective Pike again, but first she needed to access more money. She soon realised that the $400 she received from the Australian embassy was worth about half the amount when exchanged for British pounds.

***

Bent St in Soho lived up to its name, but it didn't take Susan too long to find number 48. She had expected a shop front but discovered a large black door amid row of terraced buildings with the number 48 in large brass digits attached to it. Midways, an intercom buzzer was mounted on the wall. Susan pressed the buzzer button.

"Yes, who is it?" a male voice answered.

"My name is Susan Bauford, and I would like to see Mr Fadil Matar. Miss Patra Kurri sent me."

"Do you have an appointment with Mr Matar?"

"No, I haven't. Miss Kurri said nothing about the need to make one, and I have just arrived in London."

"One moment please."

The moment seemed like an hour as Susan waited for a reply.

Then came a whirring sound from the intercom "Please come in."

Susan pressed on the door, which swung open. On entering, she found herself in an empty wood-panelled hallway with a flight of stairs at the end of it. Two closed doors faced each other on the ground level. One door had a sign printed on the top glass panel.

"F. Matar & Son Lapidary & Jewellery Brokers."

A young man in a dark suit awaited her and without exchanging many words, ushered her into this office.

"Miss Bauford to see you," he announced and left the room.

Fadil remained seated behind his large desk, the surface of which displayed only a desk calendar, two telephones and a blotting pad.

"Please take a seat, Miss Bauford, and tell me how I can help you, or is it Patra I am helping? How is she, by the way?"

"Quite well the last time I saw her, and in answer to your first question, I would have to say probably both of us."

"I see, please continue."

"Patra gave me some precious stones to convert into cash and gave me your address, suggesting I see you and only you."

"That was very loyal of her, and where do you have these precious stones?"

Suddenly a fright entered Susan's mind, 'what if he takes it all and sends me packing?'

Noticing her alarm, Fadil rushed to reassure her.

"I know what you are thinking Miss Bauford, but we are not that kind of establishment. If we were, Patra would never have sent you here."

"No, of course not. I was just being careful."

"And very wise too, but if we are going to do any business, I do have to inspect the merchandise. Now, when and where can I see the jewels?"

"I have it right here in my handbag," Susan replied, prepared to take the risk.

"Good. Let's see what you have?"

Susan reached into her handbag, and, producing the pouch, emptied the contents on the desk.

Fadil selected a few of the stones and quickly studied them. Then, from a drawer in his desk, he took out a magnifying glass mounted on a clamp, as well as a microscope, a desk calculator and a small swinging balance scale with a set of small weights. He picked up each stone and appraised it under the magnifying glass. A few he put under the microscope, but all of them eventually went onto the scale. Finally, Fadil tapped on the calculator.

More than half an hour passed before Fadil had finished his appraisal.

"Some interesting stones you have here, Miss Bauford, especially the emerald and the ruby, but I suppose you know that."

Susan didn't but said nothing.

"From what you have here, I am prepared to offer you ninety thousand pounds for the lot."

"What! Ninety thousand!" Susan exclaimed loudly.

"All right, all right, ninety-five thousand but that is the best I can do." Fadil mistook her exclamation as indignation.

Susan remained silent, mainly as she was still in a state of shock. Patra had said twenty to twenty-five thousand, but this man said ninety-five thousand. The shock was wearing off, but Susan managed to maintain her composure.

"Patra did say to deal with you, Mr Matar, so OK, you have a deal. You did say ninety-five thousand pounds, didn't you?"

"Yes, I did and I'm afraid that stays firm. No further advances."

"No, I'm quite happy with that but how do we handle the payment?"

"I don't have that much cash here. So, it will have to be by cheque, a bank cheque if you like."

"Hmm, I don't have a bank account in London."

"But you do have a bank account, don't you?"

"Yes, but it's in Sydney, Australia."

"What is the name of the bank?"

"The Commonwealth Bank."

"That's good. They have an office here in London."

"Can they do that? I mean take money from me here and credit my account in Australia?"

"I would say so. After all, you are not wanting to take money from them, you are giving them money."

"Fine, it's a deal then, but I have one request."

"Yes."

"Can I possibly have five thousand pounds in cash and the rest by cheque?"

"Five thousand should be no big problem. I'll have my son make all the arrangements. The bank cheque will take the longest, so what say you give me some details now and come back here on ... on Thursday and we'll make the exchange."

**

Susan made her way back to her hotel in a bit of a daze. Only a few weeks ago she was a sex slave in Slovenia, and now she was a potentially wealthy woman in London. She felt a little guilty about that, and vowed that if she ever met Patra again, she would give her half of the sum she'd received for the gems. Better still, Patra could use that money to extradite her daughter from the prostitution industry. That was the one thing Patra wanted. Quite a noble thought but how? "Perhaps I could suggest she buy a small business," Susan thought. "But what kind of business? What does she know?"

**

"Hello, I would like to speak with detective Pike please, I am calling from London ... my name is Susan Bauford, he is expecting a call from me ... thank you."

"Miss Bauford, good of you to call, where are you?"

"I'm in a hotel in London. Have you managed to locate Ashley yet?"

"We have Miss Bauford and ..."

"Wonderful, if I give you my number here can you have him call me as soon as possible. Ask him to reverse charges. I'll fix it up with the hotel management or better still, do you have his phone number? I'll call him right away. Where is he by the way?"

"I'm sorry, but I don't have a number on him just yet. We have only recently located him, but we haven't spoken to him yet. We managed to get his address from the estate agent, but she would not part with his phone number without a legal document compelling her. So far all we got from her is that he is living in Rose Bay."

"What! He's sold his house and bought a house in Rose Bay?"

"Not quite. I, er … don't know quite how to tell you but our information is that he is living in Rose Bay with his wife. It's her house."

"What are you saying?" Susan nearly dropped the phone. "He's married? Married to another woman?"

"I am sorry, but that is the information we have so far … Miss Bauford, are you still there?"

"… Yes, I'm still here … this is quite a shock, you understand … Ashley married …"

"Yes, I'm sorry I had to break this to you, but sooner or later you would have found out. I suppose I'd better let you know too that his wife is quite a bit older that he is, a widow with quite a sizeable fortune."

"The bastard, the bloody bastard. I suppose that's why he married her."

"I can't comment on that, Miss Bauford. We will be looking into the matter further, and as soon as I have anything to tell you I'll let you know. When do you expect you'll be back in Sydney?"

"In a few more days I think, although there seems be little to come back to. Both of my parents are dead, my fiancé has married another woman. I may as well rot here as in Sydney."

"I know you are upset, Miss Bauford, but please don't say that. You are still a young woman with a life in front of you. You can still help us with closing the case of your abduction."

"I don't see how, it's sort of all over now."

"Not quite. There are still a few local villains who had a hand in your abduction. The sooner we get them behind bars the better for all concerned. I wasn't going to say anything but in the light of what has happened, Ashley has been worrying me for some time now. After the abduction he came into a large sum of money."

"Ashley! Why does that worry you? That's unbelievable!"

"Not only that, his behaviour, just simple behaviour."

"In what way?"

"I half expected he'd become a pest. They nearly always do, you know, badgering for information, phone calls, abuse, even threats to take legal action if results are not forthcoming. That type of thing but not one word out of Ashley."

"I know what you mean, but not Ashley. He was never the badgering type. He'd wait silently, certain that if you had some information, you would call him."

"You are probably quite right. It's my policeman's mind. Suspicious of everything."

Susan replaced the telephone handset and walked over to the hotel minibar. Finding a small bottle of brandy, she unscrewed the top and gulped down the contents without bothering to fetch a glass and then threw herself on the bed sobbing.

It seemed like the whole world had ganged up on her, playing with her emotions like a cat does with a mouse. Finally, everything seemed to have worked out for her. She had regained her freedom and en route picked up quite a tidy sum of money. After honouring her promise to Patra, she would be home, ready to resume her life with Ashley. And now, in just a few short hours, the main core of the dream had vapourised.

"Why would Ashley want to hurt me?" She kept on mulling it over and over again.

She walked over to the minibar again, this time selecting a small bottle of scotch. She dispatched it in one gulp and flopped down on the bed once more.

The next thing Susan knew, it was daylight, and her room phone was ringing.

"Hello."

"Hi! I hope I didn't wake you. It's Victor Craddock here, just following up to see if you are OK."

"Oh, hi, yeah I'm OK, I guess, sort of ..."

"Whoa, I sense a problem."

"Well, yes you do, but it's more like a disaster. Problems, one can generally fix."

"Do you want to talk about it?"

The question took Susan by surprise. At first it almost terrified her, but he quickly regained her composure. Why not? It was not as though she had done anything wrong.

***

The taxi pulled over at Charing Cross Road at Cambridge Circus. Susan paid the driver and asked for further instructions of how to get to Gibb St. The driver offered to drive her there, but Susan did not want the driver to see that she was entering a brothel.

"It's right here, Miss. Just walk down this street and the second street crossing it will be Gibb St. I can drive you down there, Miss, no extra charge."

"Thank you, but I'd rather walk, just to stretch my legs a little."

"Righty ho, Miss. Just as you like." The driver slipped the cab into gear and pulled out into the mainstream traffic.

From the outside, one would never guess that behind that ordinary looking door in a street of doors of a row of terraced housing was an established brothel. What was a little unusual was that in the middle of the upper part of the door was a circle of brass numbers, all of them number 7. In the middle of this circle, in larger brass numbers appeared 77. Susan smiled looking at the numbers. It was No 77 Gibb St she was looking for, so she was sure she was at the right address.

Inside No 77 she made her way to what was obviously a reception desk. It was serviced by a handsome young woman sitting behind it perusing a large ledger.

"Can I help you, madam?" The young woman looked up as Susan

approached. "We are actually closed until 4pm."

"I'm sorry, I was not aware of that. I'm here on a private matter, so you may be able to help me."

"How can I do that?"

"I want to have a word with Vicki Hudson. I believe she works here. I have a message for her."

The young woman raised her eyebrows, "I see, you had better come into the office then," she said, closing the ledger and rising from her seat. She led the way to an office.

Once inside the office, Susan was struck by the somewhat gaudy yet expensive décor. Two large, erotic paintings contributed to that. The young woman went behind a big antique-looking desk, and, sitting down, bade Susan do the same.

"Now, if you let me have the message and tell me who it is from, I may be able to help you."

"The message is from her mother who is currently in Slovenia, and I'm afraid the message is confidential, I'm sure you understand."

"Of course, I do, so you had better tell me, as I am Vicki Hudson."

"What? You're Vicki?" Susan exclaimed, somewhat astonished. You never mentioned it before."

"You didn't ask me before. As a matter of fact, you didn't introduce yourself at all, so I don't know who you are."

"You are quite right, I didn't. I'm sorry, I'm Susan Bauford."

"Thank you. Now to be sure we are on the same page, my mother's name is Patra, Patra Kurri, and I know she is in Slovenia, managing a spa."

"We are on the same page, it seems."

"Good! Now what's the message?"

"Your mother is worried about the kind of life you are leading working in a brothel and has authorised me to advance you forty thousand pounds to help you leave and buy some other occupation."

"Wow, mummy is generous. Forty grand, and it's a new ball game."

"It is a lot of money."

"Neither you, nor mummy get it do you? I don't just work here; I'm the manager of the place, and I like what I'm doing. My father is the owner, and he is more than happy with what I'm doing. As for money, I make more than twice that much in a year, compared to what you are offering. Now, can you think of just one good reason why I should leave this?"

"I could think of a dozen, but obviously we would be at odds there. I'm sorry I wasted your time, but I did promise your mother I would speak with you."

"What is it with you two women? First my mother offers me money, and now you turn up offering me more. Did she put you up to this?"

"In a way, yes, but you said she offered you money. When was this?"

"About two days ago."

"She phoned you from Slovenia?"

"No, she was here."

"Here, in London?"

"Yes here, in London, in this very office, sitting in the same chair you're in."

"When did she get to London, do you know?"

"A few days ago. I'm not exactly sure."

"Do you know where she can be reached?"

"Not really, she said she'd call me as soon as she could find a place."

"She must have come here directly from the airport."

"She did or said she did."

"And you didn't offer to put her up, even if temporarily?"

"I did but she refused, she thought Mathew was bound to turn up. Apparently, they have had a falling out or something, and she did not want to see him."

"I can understand that." Susan surmised more to herself, then said, "Look, can I ask for a favour?"

"Go on,"

236

"I'm staying at the Scarsdale Hotel in Earl's Court. If I give you their number, would you pass it on to your mother and ask her to call me?"

"Sure, I'll be glad to, and I'm sorry you had to come out on a wild goose chase."

"As it turns out, I don't think it was."

***

Instead of taking a taxi back to her hotel Susan decided to take the long way, by underground tube. She studied the rail diagram at Cambridge Circus and worked out that if she could get the tube to Piccadilly Circus, the hub of London, have a look around and then get another tube to Earl's Court, she would be treating herself to a bit of recreation, preferable to the solitude of moping in her hotel room.

While she was collecting her room key from reception, the clerk informed her that a visitor had called for her and had decided to wait for her in the beer garden.

Susan ventured to the beer garden, which was almost deserted due to the cold weather except for one table. At that one sat a silhouette in the shape of a woman. Approaching the shape, a little cautiously, she came close enough to be able to exclaim, "Patra, is that you?"

The shape turned round, saying, "It's not the queen so it must be me." Patra stood up to be recognised fully.

Facing each other, the two women stood silently for a few seconds and then opened their arms, embracing in a hug, something that a few months ago would have been deemed impossible.

"How did you find me so quickly?" Susan asked.

"Vicky told me. I must have called her only a few minutes after you left her. She assumed you were going straight back to your hotel, so I thought I'd come down and surprise you. I'm staying at the Clarendon in Kensington South, not very far from here. What took you so long?"

"I decided to do a little tourist rubber necking, but come, let's go inside, it's getting damn cold out here."

"I was surprised to hear that you were still here," Patra observed as they entered the warmth of the hotel. "I thought you'd have been back in Australia long ago."

"I did too, but first I had to spend some hospital time in Austria."

"Are you OK now?"

"Good as gold. I was right. That glider was good for one flight only."

"That's good to hear. Look, I'm getting a little hungry now, what say we have dinner together and talk?"

"That would be nice, and I suppose we do have a lot to talk about, but I have a better idea. Why not order dinner here and have it served in my room? That would give us a lot more privacy," Susan suggested, and Patra agreed.

***

"What's this?" Susan exclaimed as she opened her room door. A large vase of flowers had been placed in the middle of the small table next to the window, their purple wrapper still intact and an Interflora card dangling down one side. Susan picked up and read the card, 'I hope these will lift your spirits as you prepare to travel back to Down-under. Victor.'

Patra watched Susan read the card, "Not bad, not bad at all. Five minutes in London and noticed already," she quipped.

"I wish! It's from the embassy in Vienna wishing me a good journey."

"And when is that likely to be?" Patra asked.

"As soon as I can make a booking on the first plane home. Now, can I order you something to drink?"

"Thank you, a glass of wine would be nice."

"White or red?"

"White thank you."

Susan stuck her head in the minibar. "Oh, look, they have Jacob's

Creek. That's an Aussie wine and very nice. Only the tiny bottles, though, but they will do. We'll get them to send up a bottle with our dinner."

Sipping the beverage, Patra wanted to know everything that happened since Susan took that leap over the garbage wall. Just as she finished, their dinner arrived on a trolley. Consuming that, it was Susan's turn to question Patra.

"It was like in the movies, armed policemen all over the place, helicopters buzzing round, you know. Mathew escaped; you know. One minute he was walking towards us, the next he was in a helicopter with Franz and gone. It all happened so quickly. The Slovenian police arrested a few of the guests and then cleared everyone off the mountain. They held me in Ljubljana prison for nearly two days and kept on questioning me. Then they let me go, as I was merely an employee and there was nothing, they could charge me with."

"Where did you go then? I mean you obviously had no money or very little of it. How did you manage to survive and how did you manage to get to London?"

"You are right, I had no money on me and only the clothes I was wearing, so as soon as I was released, I drew up a formal complaint stating that I was going to sue the police for illegal detention and depriving me of my possessions which were still in the mountain."

"How did that work?"

"Beautifully. They flew me back to the mountain, and I was able to get my possessions plus quite a bit of money as well as the rest of the jewels."

"I didn't know there was cash stashed in the spa?"

"Oh yes, mostly in Mathew's office and some in mine. You forget I was the bookkeeper there and learned quickly about creative accounting. Actually, Mathew introduced me to that. He was making sure that he was getting the lion's share from the profits and not just an equal split with the rest of his partners."

"So, Mathew short-changed his partners, and you short changed Mathew?"

"Correct! What would you do? I agreed to come here and work for a salary, except that I never got paid."

"Didn't you complain?"

"I sure did, and do you know what he said, 'Of course I'm paying you, but you don't need any cash here. Everything you want is here. I'm saving you your money. Each month, I am putting it in a savings fixed deposit for you.'

"Somewhat restrictive, but in a way reasonably fair, wouldn't you agree?"

"Certainly, but the account was in his name and his name only."

"Shit! I should have seen that coming. So, what are your plans for the future now?"

"Plans, I have no plans. Survival is the only one I can think of but what of you? What are your plans?"

"I intend to go home to Australia and open up my own law firm."

"I'm glad to hear it, Susan, and I wish you every success. You not only deserve it, you have earned it."

"Thank you, Patra, and you know, I've just had a great idea."

"What's that?"

"Why don't you come to Australia with me and work with me? I can sponsor you, and you can look forward to some sort of future."

"I … I … er, I don't know what to say. I, your former captor, so to speak. You must be joking?"

"I'm not joking. First of all, you were never my captor. If anything, you were my saviour."

"I don't understand, what do you mean, your saviour?"

"Remember, you caught me building that hang glider. You could have dobbed me in to Mathew, and then where would I be?"

"Oh that. I had my reasons."

"We all have reasons, Patra, but we don't always act on them."

"Yes, and I have a reason why I can't go with you to Australia."

"Do you mind telling me the reason?"

Patra started breathing heavily, her chest heaving.

"I cannot go with you, because sooner or later you would find out and never forgive me for not telling you sooner."

"I don't get it. Telling me what?"

"God, I wish I could keep my mouth shut."

"No no, keep it open. What is it you are not telling me?"

"That your kidnapping was arranged with the knowledge and cooperation of your fiancé, Ashley. There, I have said it."

"Wha … I don't believe it. How is that possible? How do you know this? It's unthinkable. We were getting married that day. He was at the church, waiting for me. Who told you this?"

"Akim."

"Yes, I know Akim had a hand in it, but why should he tell you this?"

"Not just me, he told all of us."

"All of you? What was this? Some ritual?"

"It was after you went over the wall. Mathew was furious and had everybody gathered to find out what they knew. He found out that Akim had taught you to fly with a hang glider and he went for Akim's throat. He wanted to know the whole story, and Akim became weak kneed and could not stop talking."

"About what?"

"About his jealousy of Ashley. Then, digging round Ashley's activities, looking for dirt, he discovered Ashley was in some sort of financial trouble, so he nourished him with a solution. All Ashley had to do was provide a little information and his financial troubles would be over. How else do you think the kidnappers knew exactly when and where the wedding cars would be?"

"There have to be many other ways of getting this sort of information?"

"Of course, there are, but all of them leaving a trail of information which would come out after the news of your abduction became public. This way, only Akim and Ashley knew, and Ashley would be above suspicion because he too would be seen as a victim. The heartbroken groom, left stranded at the altar."

"It's unbelievable but it makes sense. Strange that. I have to hear about it halfway round the world also that Ashley's married another woman."

"A rich widow, I assume."

"How did you know?"

"I didn't, but I know men."

Susan slumped a little in her chair and focused on what would have been her wedding day. Her father had arranged the hiring of the wedding cars, and he discussed the mechanical details with Ashley one evening at dinner at their house. She recalled Ashley suggesting to her father that it might be better to use the quieter back route, as the main roads would be congested with traffic and may cause delays, especially as at that time a lot of Sydney people would be heading to the weekend sporting venues. Her father had immediately agreed, complimenting Ashley for showing such good sense and foresight.

"The bastard!" Susan exclaimed. "The stinking, rotten bastard." She was about to start crying but then braced herself and said, "To think that all the times he was having dinner our place he was scheming to have me kidnapped."

"It's hard, I know," Patra commiserated, "but maybe now you can understand why I couldn't work with you with this knowledge bottled inside me. If I had it my way, I would fly to Australia, seek him out and cut his balls off."

"Patra, thank you. Thank you for telling me. Please don't feel bad about it. I am glad you told me, because I was on the verge of forgiving Ashley. After all, I presumed that he thought me dead, and that left him with the right to pursue his future. From what you have told me, this is exactly what he did, only I had no part in it."

"I am glad to hear you think that way. I can now tell you that I had thoughts of you scratching my eyes out once I opened my mouth."

"Good heavens, no! This changes nothing except for one thing."

"I don't understand?"

"I would like to sponsor you to come to Australia, and we can both track down Ashley. You can cut his balls off, but leave the prick to me and we'll stuff them down his throat until he chokes."

"What a wonderful idea, and after that we can track down Akim and perform the same ritual. Let me think about that. There is really nothing endearing to hold me in London, but I would like to think about it."

The two women drained what was left in the wine bottle, and Susan suggested they get another one.

"Why not?" Patra agreed, "Just so long as you promise me, you'll stuff me in a taxi when we finish it."

The second bottle of wine arrived and after taking the first sip, a flash came to Patra's mind.

"Oh!" she exclaimed, "I almost forgot the real reason for coming here."

"Really?" Susan queried.

"Yes. I told you that Mathew had escaped. Well, he's here now."

"In London?"

"Yes."

"How do you know this?"

"Vicki told me. He's been to see her."

"And? I don't see what that has to do with me."

"He told her how some woman had destroyed his organisation, and that of his partners, and that if it takes him the rest of his life, he will find her and get her."

"How do you mean get her?"

"Well, he's not going to send her roses. He's after blood."

"Mine, presumably?"

"You are not wrong."

"I see. Does he know where I am?"

"No, he doesn't. This was before you came to see her."

"That's not so bad then."

"For the moment, no, but he'll see her again, and she's bound to tell him of your visit."

"Maybe she won't tell him?"

"Probably not at first, but Mathew has a way of wheedling things out of people, so be careful."

"Thank you for telling me. I'll bear that in mind," Susan replied, a little alarmed.

"I'd best be going now; I'll talk to you again tomorrow but please be careful. Mathew can be gentle when he wants to be. He'll purr like a pussy cat, but always remember the cat's got claws."

***

After Patra left, Susan summed up her situation. As long as Mathew didn't know her address, she was safe enough, but what if Vicki discloses her whereabouts? Unlikely, perhaps, but what if she does? She had better find another hotel quickly. First thing in the morning. It was nearing midnight, but the thought of sleep evaded her. She hopped on to her bed and reached for the remote of the television set. Surfing through the various channels for a suitable program, the phone rang.

"Must be Patra," was her first reaction. "She's forgotten something." Susan picked up the phone. "Hello."

"Good evening, Susan, I hope I didn't wake you," a male voice asked.

"Who is this?"

"What! You don't recognise my voice, my dear. You wound me to the core. I'll just have to come around and give you a quick spanking, won't I?"

"Mathew! It's Mathew, isn't it?"

"Well done my dear, it is indeed Mathew."

"What do you want Mathew?"

"Want? Want? I want to congratulate you, my dear. I want to take you out for dinner and talk about old times. I want to congratulate you on the brilliant way you glided out of Shangrila. There is a restaurant called The Sands, not too far from The Scarsdale. Excellent food. Shall I pick you up tomorrow night, say 7.30?"

"Mathew, you keep away from me. I shall call the police. I know Interpol are looking for you."

"That's nice. It's nice to be wanted isn't it? Unfortunately neither the police, nor Interpol know what I look like. Ah well, if you refuse to dine with me, I'll just have to keep an eye on you. London's a big place and full of villains, so you will need someone to keep a lookout for you. Sweet dreams, my dear. I'll check on you sometime tomorrow."

It seemed an idle boast for one man to make but from what Patra had told her, he had many contacts.

If Mathew had wanted to frighten Susan, he succeeded. Susan felt quite a bit weak at the knees, and a ball of anxiety worked up from her stomach to her larynx. She wretched as if to throw up, but nothing came out. She thought of calling the police but on what basis? Initially, they probably would not believe her, and if she revealed the whole story, she would be breaking her undertaking to the Australian High Commission to keep the story under wraps until they were ready to release it.

That night sleep became a stranger. Susan entertained a flock of ideas but when looking at them logically, they collapsed. Dawn was breaking, and the only solution Susan had come up with was that she had to get out of her present hotel. Through the night she had dozed off a couple of times only to wake moments later.

Then, out of the blue, a thought struck her. Why not call the Australian High Commission and ask for help? As soon as the thought struck her, it quickly dissipated. The Commission in London would probably never have heard of her, and by the time they concluded their research, she could be floating down the Thames River, face first.

Maybe not call the embassy in London, then, but perhaps Vienna. Susan fished in her handbag and located Victor's card. It was too early to call Vienna so she worked out at what could be an appropriate time, waited and then rang.

"Victor it's Susan Bauford. I'm glad I caught you."

"I'm glad you rang. I take it you have a problem with the airline?"

"No, nothing like that, a much bigger problem," Susan replied and proceeded to tell Victor the current events.

"I see," Victor surmised what Susan told him. "OK, here's what I want you to do. Don't leave the room, no matter what. Have your breakfast sent up and pack up your things. Remain by your phone for at least one to two hours. I need this time to organise a few things, and I will call you back somewhere in this time space. Have you got that? … Good, I will call you back."

Susan felt a bit better as she put the phone down. She didn't feel like any breakfast, but a cup of tea or coffee seemed to be as good as an aspirin. She had beverage making facilities in her room, and the jug was soon brought to boil. Sipping the tea, Susan mused on just how good it was for her. Then, the phone rang.

"Jesus, Victor, that was quick," she thought as she picked up the handset. "Hello!"

"Good morning, Susan, I hope you slept well?"

"Mathew, what do you want?"

"I want you, Susan. It looks like the start of a beautiful day. What say we take a stroll in Kew Gardens? It's lovely out there. I can pick you up in a couple of hours. We can talk about old times. I can even bring Patra along. Won't that be nice?"

"Mathew, you listen to me and listen well. Leave me alone. You are an ageing pervert and a criminal, and I know what you have in mind."

"Oh, I love it when you talk dirty, but rest assured, not for much longer. You can't stay in the hotel forever. Sooner or later, you must come out, and when you do, I'll be waiting."

"Mathew, why don't you go away and screw yourself?" Susan barked back as she slammed the phone down. She felt a little embarrassed, as she had previously thought she'd never use words like that, but she did, and she felt better.

The two hours had passed, and no word from Victor. She thought of ringing him again but realised there was no point.

Another half an hour went by and still no call. Susan began thinking that something had gone wrong, and maybe she should order a taxi and make a dash for the airport, but she had not booked her flight.

"Maybe if I flash that diplomatic passport, I could cut through the formalities," she thought, and was about to put that plan into action when the phone rang.

"It's Victor, Susan. Sorry I took so long in getting back to you but there was a lot of red tape I had to cut through."

"Oh, please Victor, don't apologise, I'm glad to get any help, no matter how long the wait."

"Good. Now, listen very carefully. In approximately one hour a diplomatic car from our London High Commission will arrive at your hotel. One of our staff, Tom Seedencamp, will come to your room and escort you. He will announce his name before you open the door. The car will take you to Heathrow Airport where we have booked you into a hotel. You will stay there overnight, and tomorrow morning we have booked you on a Qantas flight QF34 direct to Sydney, scheduled to depart at 8.45 am. Have you got that?"

"Yes, thank you, I have. Qantas QF34, 8.45am, but where do I pick up the ticket?

"You don't need a ticket. It's all been done. Simply make your way to the Qantas counter, 1st class, and show them your passport."

"But if I am to stay in my room, how can I pay for my stay at the hotel here? I mean, I can't just rush out without paying."

"That's been taken care of by our High Commission in London. I spoke to the hotel manager before I spoke to you."

"That's very kind of you, Victor, I really appreciate your help."

"All part of the job, my dear, all part of the job.

"I wish you would not have said that."

"Said what?"

"My dear."

"I'm sorry, I intended no offence by that."

"I know you didn't, it's just that someone called me that on the phone an hour ago."

"That was Mathew, I take it. "The man's a psychopath."

"Agreed."

"I will also phone detective Pike in Sydney. He's offered to pick you up from the airport."

"Thank you very much."

"Just one more thing. You can talk to Pike about what happened to you quite openly, but please don't talk to anyone in the media. Not until we get this Slovenian embassy thing settled next month."

"I won't, Victor, I promise."

"Well, that's about it then. Have a good flight back home, and if I may ask again, please stay in touch."

"I will, Victor, I promise, and thank you for the lovely flowers."

"Oh that! They were from all of us at the embassy."

"Like hell they were," Susan said to herself as she put the phone down.

CH 16. RETRIBUTION

Mathew's room in The Duke of York was not plush but adequate and offered all he needed. From his valise he extracted a bottle of cognac which he purchased from the duty-free shop, and searched for a glass. Pouring himself a stiff cognac, he eased himself into an overstuffed armchair, the only one in the room, and relaxed, remembering his lucky escape.

"That was a close call," he thought, sipping the smooth amber liquid. "Who would have thought the chopper would be there with Franz still in it? Lucky for me, the Slovenian police had dropped their guard, feeling confident there was no way for me to escape. And Franz, I never did ask the little bastard what he was doing in there in the first place?"

Mathew refilled his glass, feeling more secure now he let his mind revisit events of the past few days, recalling how the figures on the ground grew smaller as the helicopter propelled skywards. Mathew scanned the ground below just in case the police helicopter was revving up to give chase. Nothing. At least that was a good omen. Now he had time to think.

"So where to now, boss?" Franz asked, "and remember we have to fly at the lowest altitude to avoid radar and some Austrian jet peppering our arses with lead, as we have no flight plan, and we will be considered as illegal and aggressive."

"I already told you, head for Vienna. Look for a quiet road before we hit Vienna. We'll ditch the chopper there and walk to the nearest village. With a bit of luck, we'll get a taxi or hitch a ride to the outskirts of the city, then get another cab into the city."

"Sounds good but why not get the taxi take us right into the city?"

"Don't be an idiot, Franz. The more changes of transport we make, the harder for anyone to track us down."

"I understand that, but what do we do in Vienna? I have no money on me, I can't even pay for a room in a hotel, and I don't know anyone in Vienna."

"Relax, Franz, I have plenty of money and the last thing we need is a hotel room. I have a small warehouse in Vienna. We can stay there for a while, at least till the time we can figure out what to do."

"That's fine, but what happened at the spa? With all those coppers landing, I gather the spa is kaput?"

"It is, but it's too noisy here to go into a lengthy explanation. I'll fill you in when we get to the warehouse. In the meantime, I want you to concentrate in finding us a suitable landing spot."

The two fell silent as Franz guided the helicopter over the mountain tops.

"That's Vienna coming into view now, so when do you want me to start looking?" Franz asked.

"Just a bit closer, then look for a road that's not too busy."

Easier asked than done. Franz circled a few possibilities but for one reason or another, abandoned them. Then hope returned.

"That there would have been a perfect spot if it wasn't for the cows munching on the verge. They should be on the other side of the fence!"

"Bugger the cows, just land," Mathew commanded. "What! Land on top of the cows?"

"Don't worry, they'll take off in a hurry once the rotor and the noise come closer to them."

Mathew was right, the cow did not stick around for long. The helicopter made its approach and performed a gentle landing.

Franz was preparing to leave.

"Where the hell do you think you are going?" Mathew asked urgently.

"Out on the road and see if we can get a lift."

"You just wait here. I guarantee you that the first or second vehicle we'll see will stop to see what a helicopter is doing by the side of the road. We'll tell him the fuel tank must have sprung a leak, and we had only a few minutes of flying time left. Then we will ask if he could possibly give us a lift to the nearest village where we could seek some help."

"That might work," Franz agreed.

An hour went by and then another hour, and although quite a bit of traffic went by, no one stopped. One or two people did wave.

Franz was about to castigate Mathew when a black Mercedes with Bavarian number plates pulled up. The driver, in his late fifties, and a bit short of two-hundred kilos in weight, leaned out the car window, shouted and laughed.

"You boys having a problem? I see your aeroplane has lost its wings."

"Yes, we are," Franz shouted back and ran to the driver's window. "We must have developed a leak in the fuel tank and had to land or fall down."

"What rotten luck. Have you radioed for help?"

"We tried that but it's a little difficult as we don't know exactly where we are. We would be very grateful if you would give us a lift to the nearest village so we can organise some help."

"That would be my pleasure. Please hop in."

"Thank you very much, and my partner as well?"

"Does he not have to stay with the machine?"

"Not really, with no petrol, the machine is not going anywhere."

"Of course, it isn't. How silly of me," the driver replied, and through the car window he waved to Mathew to come along.

It was only a twenty-minute drive to Gerasdorf where the driver dropped off the hitchhikers, saying that from there he was heading north, away from Vienna. Asking one or two passers-by, they soon found a taxi rank and a taxi to take them to Gablitz near Mathew's warehouse, the taxi was directed by Mathew, to stop at a nearby inn.

"Why did you not let him drop us off at the door?" Franz asked.

"Why? Look, you dummy, if worse comes to worst and the taxi driver is questioned, all that he could tell anyone is that he dropped us off at the door of an inn. And now, for the rest of the way we walk."

***

The warehouse was small and old. Mathew used it as a drop-off place for goods which proverbially had fallen off the back of a truck and needed a cooling place. In the middle of the main floor was parked a somewhat battered VW Combi van. Apart from storage area it also contained an office, and a spare room with a potbelly stove in the centre and three camp beds with open racks on two of the walls pretending to be wardrobes without doors. In a corner near the window, a small hand basin was installed below a tap protruding from the wall, aligning with what could be called kitchen cabinets on either side of the basin.

"It's not much to look at, but I call it home." Mathew quipped.

"So, what happens now?" Franz asked.

"First, we light the stove and then find something to eat. For our first night here, I suggest we get some bread rolls and a bit of sausage. A bottle of white Austrian rum won't go astray either on a cold night like tonight. I also think that we should not be seen together until we know what the fallout is from Slovenia. Just a precaution."

"Whatever you say, boss, but you know I have no money. Actually, I have no wallet. I hardly had the time to go back to my room to get it."

"I've told you before, don't worry about it. I have enough to cover both of us. Just before I went down to Ljubljana, I took a wad with me just in case I had to grease a palm or two, but they were too shit scared to take anything. The biggest worry will be you not having your ID papers, but we'll sort something out."

When Mathew returned with a few purchases, Franz had checked the place out and discovered a few bits of cutlery and crockery.

"Sorry about the tablecloth," Franz apologised, "I looked all over but could not find one."

"That's too bad. It looks like we'll have to pretend we're on a camping trip in the woods and make use of what we have got."

Both men got stuck into the bread rolls and Strasbourg sausage, only then realising how hungry they were.

"Now," Franz said, catching Mathew's attention. "What happened at the spa?"

"That bloody Susan. She put the spoke in the wheels."

"What? I thought she was dead. I thought someone had found the body and alerted the authorities?"

"I did as well, but no such luck. She crash-landed in Austria and got roughed up a bit. The first thing she did, when she woke up, was to scream for someone to see her from The Australian Embassy. Susan then refused to speak to anyone until she was advised to do so by some knob from the embassy. When she did, she couldn't stop talking. They took it all down and faxed the details to the Minister of The Interior in Slovenia. He took it to mean that the Slovenian government were involved as partners in the deal. If this was exposed to the media, the government would fall, and he'd be out on his ear. The rest you can surmise yourself."

"This means I'm out of a job," Franz concluded.

"I'm afraid so, old boy. Not only that, but on the run as well."

"Me on the run?" Franz protested. "Why should I be on the run? I'm just the pilot flying a helicopter to and fro, doing as I am told."

"Really, Franz! You surprise me. You've never heard of 'aiding and abetting a felony'? They call it equally assisting a crime, and it carries equally the same penalties."

"I was only flying a helicopter. That's all I've been doing. How does that make me involved in a felony?"

"Oh, come off it Franz, are you going to tell me that you didn't know what the cargo was? It won't wash. By international law it is your duty to know the cargo you are carrying."

Franz didn't need long to think about it. He knew Mathew was right, but he also knew he had other worries.

"That puts me in a difficult position," he told Mathew. "If I have to disappear, I'll need money. Lots of it."

"Won't we all, but what's the alternative?"

"The alternative is that you will have to supply it."

"Me! Why should I supply you with money?"

"Because if you don't, and I get caught, I'll supply the authorities with all the details of your operation at the spa, as well as the names of your partners. God knows, I've flown them around often enough."

"Not good enough, Franz. The authorities already know what went on in the spa."

"That may be so, but they don't know about the surveillance tape I have stashed away of you shooting that Jack Solomon."

"Him again," Mathew sighed. "All right, how much do you want?"

"I think about $150,000 US should cover it."

"What! I don't have that sort of money laying about here."

"Yes, but you have some cash stashed away here, and the rest should be no great problem for you. I know you still have that brothel in London, so that should be easy enough for you."

"OK, you've got me over a barrel. I have some cash here. The rest we'll have to see how to manage it. I don't suppose you'd take a cheque?"

"Yes, sure but on the understanding that, if it bounces, I release the tapes."

"Fair enough. I'll just go to the office and see how much cash I have there. Oh! By the way, have you ever been arrested?"

"No, why do you ask?"

"No real reason," Mathew replied. "You just seem so natural with all this; I was wondering if you have done something like this before."

"I haven't, but the situation you put me in leaves me with little choice," Franz commented as Mathew went to the office.

Before looking for the money, Mathew sat down at the almost antique desk, thinking.

"He has no ID on him, and only I know he is here. The cops saw only a brief image of him from the outside of the chopper window.

They will put two and two together and figure it was me and him in the chopper, but they would not have recognised Franz. The fat German in the Mercedes giving us a lift would know nothing anyway, he was heading back into Germany, so he probably won't even get to hear of anything. Writing him out a cheque could be a problem, but the bank would not recognise him, not the one in London anyway. If the cops ever did get to see the tape, they would also see Franz helping to push out the body. In the small confine of the cabin, the surveillance camera may only show a pistol being pointed but not the full frame of the person pointing it."

Mathew pulled out the second drawer on the right side of the desk. He pulled the drawer right out and reached into the hollow, pulling out a metal box. Sitting on top of a pile of bank notes was a Mauser 9mm handgun. He checked the magazine; it was fully loaded. He took out the money and spread it on top of the desk, leaving the Mauser in the drawer but only half shutting it.

"Franz, come and get it," Mathew yelled out.

Franz entered the office and the first thing he saw was the money spread over the top of the desk. He could not take his eyes of it. It was also the last thing he saw. Mathew took out the pistol and without a word, pulled the trigger three times whilst pointing the gun at Franz's chest.

Fortunately for Mathew, Franz was no heavyweight, making the body easy to manage. A blanket from the camp bed made a good shroud in which to envelop a body, secured by some electrical cord Mathew found in the main storage area. Having made sure the pockets were empty, he rolled Franz's body in the blanket, secured it at both ends and the middle, and dragged it into the Combi van. He drove out of the warehouse heading for the Danube River where he knew a few secluded spots suitable to launch a cadaver. En route, Mathew recapped his situation. The body carried no ID. Fingerprints would not reveal anything, as Franz had never been arrested. The body may never be found, but, if so, the decomposition would be so bad that identification was next to impossible.

Finding a suitable spot, Mathew parked the Combi van as close to the riverbank as he could and got out to see if he could find a few rocks to wrap in with the body so that it would remain under water. He was in luck.

Dragging the body out of the Combi and onto the riverbank, an unwelcome thought struck him. He recalled reading somewhere that a reconstruction of a face could be made just by following the contours of the scull. That could be a problem. Stuffing rocks into the side of the blanket roll, an idea was germinating. Mathew selected the largest rock from the pile he had gathered and brought it down as hard as he could on the head of the corpse under the blanket. He winced at the soft crunching sound but repeated the blows a number of times.

**

Returning to the warehouse, Mathew examined every spot Franz had occupied, looking for anything which could suggest Franz being there. Except for a few smears of blood on the office floor, he found nothing.

"He must have carked it instantly," Mathew thought, "otherwise he would have pumped blood all over the place. A spot of chlorine or bleach should get rid of that. I'll get some tomorrow and make sure there is no blood in the Combi."

The money was still strewn over the top of the desk. Mathew retrieved the metal box but before replacing the money, he took out the last thing still in the bottom of the box: a small booklet with gold printing of a coat of arms and the caption on the cover, 'British Passport.' He smiled and opened the booklet at the page containing his photograph. However, the bearer's name was Mathew Cresswick.

The next day, after cleaning the office and combi, Mathew returned to London, as he felt at risk if he stayed on in Austria. The possibility of Franz's body being found was very remote, but if a heavy rainstorm unleashed itself on Vienna, the water in the Danube would become turbulent and possibly pick up the body, carrying it downstream, then wedging it in the flowing debris where it could be seen by anyone working in the area. From missing persons reports the police could identify him and subsequently connect him with Spa Shangrila.

For that and other reasons, Mathew decided it would be better to stay in a hotel rather than his apartment in London. The Duke of York Hotel had a fancy name but only three stars, yet for Mathew's purposes it fitted the bill, quite central and near his brothel.

***

Qantas flight QF34 approached Sydney airport on schedule. Susan looked through the window at the unfolding harbour below. The Harbour Bridge and the Opera House looked tiny but grew larger as the plane lost altitude in preparation for landing at Mascot Airport.

Once again, her diplomatic passport served her well. She walked out into the Arrivals waiting hall, which was full of people craning their necks trying to recognise their particular welcoming parties. Among them were people holding up placards with the names of passengers they had come to collect written on them.

Walking the incoming passenger aisle, Susan was looking for her name among the placard holders but failed to see it. One placard caught her eye. PIKE was all that was on it. She recognised the name immediately and pushed her luggage trolley towards it, relieved that someone had come to pick her up.

"Detective Pike, I presume, here to pick up Susan Bauford?" She asked politely.

"Oh! Yes. Are you …?"

"Yes, I am."

"Welcome home, Miss Bauford. We do have some photographs of you but did not know if your ordeal had changed your appearance in any way, therefor this, the placard."

"Shouldn't that say, 'Susan Bauford?'

"Ordinarily it would but we weren't sure that one of your captors hadn't organised a greeting party, hence the placard. We thought that since you knew my name, you would figure it out, and, of course, you did."

"Well, that's worked out fine. So now what?"

"Now I drive you home, and you can open the windows and give the place some airing. It probably needs it by now."

"Home ... you know, for weeks on end I thought about home every day. At first, I thought I'd never see it again, but then I changed my tune and became determined I would."

"And that took some doing, by all reports, and not too soon either."

"Really, I don't understand? What do you mean by 'not too soon'?"

"I'll explain that in the car, Miss Bauford. We'd better get out of here."

"Yes, I suppose we'd better, and by the way, please call me Susan."

"Very well, and thank you, Susan. My first name is Edward although I get 'Eddy' every time, but, unfortunately, during any official dealings I have to remain Detective Pike. I hope you understand."

"Perfectly, I have a law degree, so I am well versed in protocol."

As they walked out of the arrivals hall, Susan was surprised to see that Pike's car was parked almost at the door.

"Good heavens!" Susan exclaimed. "How on earth did you manage to park so close?"

"As you can see, it's a police car," Pike was quick to point out.

"One of the perks, I suppose," Susan quipped.

"Not really, I am here on official police business."

"Sorry. I should have known better."

***

The police car left the airport and eased into the everyday Sydney traffic.

"Do you know where to go, or do you want me to give you

directions?" Susan asked.

"Know where to go? Susan, I spent weeks virtually living in your house in Putney. We were waiting for a ransom call or a note or something, but it did not happen."

"Sorry, I've done it again."

"Done what again?"

"I should have known that you've been to the house."

"Aw forget it, but speaking of house, we had quite a bit of trouble with that, the house I mean."

"Really? In what way?"

"When your father died, we were looking for anyone close who could act as an executor of the will we found locked in his desk. To cut a long story short, among some small tokens, he named you as the sole beneficiary. He refused to believe you were dead. The government department dealing with probate issues thought otherwise. They were about to seize the property when we intervened, as the case was not closed, and you were not declared as deceased."

"Thank you for telling me that, Eddy. And I presume you were the party who did the intervening?"

"It was part of my job. Anyway, I did not believe you were dead either, but because the sole beneficiary was presumed kidnapped and murdered, they thought they could dispose of the matter there and then. Anyhow, I declared your father's house a crime scene, so they could not touch it until we said so."

"Thank you."

"I suppose you've made some plans for the future?"

"Indeed, I have," Susan answered.

"Care to share them?"

"Actually, you will most probably be involved."

"Me? ... How do you figure that?"

"I want that bastard Ashley arrested and imprisoned for as many years as the law will allow."

"Whoa there, I know he married someone else, but he must have thought you were dead, so he just got on with his life. There's no law broken there, maybe a bit tacky so soon after your kidnapping, but not illegal."

"Eddy, it has nothing to do with his marrying someone else, believe me. What rages within me is the fact that it was Ashley who arranged my abduction."

"What?" Pike exclaimed as he almost side-swiped another vehicle. "Ashley? How could he have had a hand in it? He was at the church waiting?"

"Yes, but he knew I was not coming."

"Do you have any proof of this?"

"I do, but in our courts, it would be dismissed as hearsay."

"Well, that takes care of that then."

"Not quite. I have at least two witnesses. One willing, and the other one hostile because of his involvement in the abduction. Oh, there is another one, also involved, but he is tricky and cunning like a waterfront rat."

"If what you say is true, and I don't doubt that it is, we can wrap this case up and put the perpetrators behind bars for many years. Why don't you summarise the events starting at the beginning?"

"Glad to," Susan volunteered, "but it might be better if I do it from my place. You can take notes and you don't have to concentrate on the traffic."

"Susan you may notice how well behaved the traffic is."

"Yes, and ...?"

"You're sitting in a marked police car. I have to concentrate, but they have to concentrate even more."

"I never thought of that. Yes of course, I recall now that whenever I'm driving and I spot a police car, my eyes are automatically fixed on the speedo, but I'd rather we talk at home. I'm dying for a cup of tea," Susan said.

"Tea," Pike replied. "Oh, yes, tea, that would be nice." Pike drove on for a few hundred metres and pulled into a petrol station.

"Don't tell me you are out of petrol."

"No, I am not, but you may need a few groceries. They have a mini mart shop in there, so I'll just grab us some tea. I'll only be a couple of minutes." Pike parked the car and entered the mini mart.

A few minutes later, Pike emerged carrying a large plastic bag and placed it on the back seat.

"That's an awful lot of tea you have there," Susan remarked as Pike got back behind the wheel.

"I bought you a few bits and pieces I think you'll need. I don't think your fridge will have anything in it."

"Oh, thank you very much, but I don't want you to pay for it."

"Don't worry about that, I'm not paying for it. Officially you are in police custody, and we can't afford to let you go hungry."

Trying to avoid traffic, Pike turned right at Annandale to join Victoria Road. Susan sat quietly, relishing in seeing all the old landmarks and short cuts she had used to get to her lectures at Sydney University.

"I'm breaking my own rules here, but what can you tell me about Ashley's wife?"

"Not a great deal except that she's a former widow. Her husband was some twelve years older and died in hospital from some sort of cancer, I don't know which."

"How did she come to meet Ashley?"

"Again, I'm not so sure. According to his real estate agent, they met at some cocktail do at the Hilton, not long after you disappeared."

"So, he was really in deep grieving, eh?"

"I can't answer that, but I can tell you she inherited a fortune and a well-established business, which they now run together,"

"Doing what? Do you know?"

"I think they are importing French luxury products and selling them Australia wide, through many retail outlets."

"And the now Mrs Barton, have you met her?"

"No, I haven't. I have spoken to her on the phone but never met her. Incidentally, she's not Mrs Barton, she's Ms LePack. She decided to revert to her maiden name, and Ashley was all right with that. Her first name is Selina, and that is about all I can tell you."

"Has she any children from her previous marriage?"

"I think there is a daughter, I'm not sure. She wasn't really part of our investigation."

The police car stopped at the front gate of Susan's home in Putney. For a while Susan remained in the car and simply looked at the house.

"There were moments I thought I'd never see it again. And now, look … there it is. Even the front lawn's been mowed. Who could have done that?"

"You've got great neighbours, Susan. After your dad died, they formed a roster taking turns to maintain the place for when you came home."

"They were that confident?"

"Looks that way, or maybe they just wanted the street to look good."

Inside the house, the air was a little musty, but a few open doors and windows soon cleared the shutdown smell.

"How do you like your tea, Eddy?" Susan called out from the kitchen.

"Black with two sugars please."

Susan poured the tea and set it down in the living room.

"Now Susan, tell me all that's been happening?"

"At first, I thought the wedding car had been involved in some sort of accident. Then my door was opened, and something was put over my mouth and nose. That's all I know. The next thing I remember was being in some sort of cellar." Susan paused.

"Go on!"

"I felt the jab of a needle and passed out again. When I came to, I was in a large stone walled room, and someone told me I was in the alps in Slovenia. I didn't even know where Slovenia was. It was unbelievable, one minute I'm in a car off to get married, and the next thing I know I was in Slovenia."

"When you did regain consciousness, did you recognise anyone you knew?"

"No, I didn't …"

"Sorry, go on."

Susan obliged. She recalled all the events, almost in chronological order and several cups of tea later, awaited Pike's comments.

"I see now your concern about some of the evidence being tossed out as hearsay," Pike remarked when Susan had finished. "Obviously it would be much easier if we could extradite two of them to stand trial in Australia. Interpol have located Akim, but Mathew has gone to ground with a few other countries anxious to interview him, but that's not going to be easy. How can we prove his complicity? We need Akim to testify. That's our only hope, but how do we extradite him from a hostile Arab country when he must know he faces criminal charges in Australia?"

"I have thought about this quite a lot. From a legal perspective the chances of obtaining a conviction are slim, almost not worth pursuing, but if we can obtain a confession from Ashley, it would change a lot of things."

"Yes, it would, but how are you going to get that? You have a better chance of drawing water from a stone," Pike pointed out.

"There has to be a way, there simply has to."

"The way I see it, it is next to impossible. I cannot see, for the life of me, Ashley fronting up and saying, 'you got me. I did it'."

"Impossible? The people on that mountain top said that about anyone trying to escape. Yet here I am."

"You are indeed Susan. A fine example for the rest of us, but do you have any ideas on how to go about it?"

"At the moment, none, but we do have one thing running in our favour."

"I can't see it but go on."

"Ashley thinks that I'm still in Slovenia or that I'm dead. Either way he feels safe, as I am sure that he agreed to that deal only on the basis that I would never be seen alive in Sydney again. There has been no media release and won't be until after the opening of the Slovenian Embassy in Canberra. He can't have any prior knowledge."

"I'm aware of that, but I don't see how that can help."

"I'm not sure either, but I'm guessing that a sudden, unexpected confrontation with a person he thinks no longer exists may freak him out enough to make utterances which can be considered a confession."

"You know, Susan, that might just work. The problem is how does one orchestrate such a confrontation and back it up with some sort of documentation?"

"There has to be a way."

"I agree with you, but how do we find it?"

"I wish I could answer that but why not think about it? It's like when I was at the spa. I walked past, slept in and fumbled those silk sheets many, many times until it hit me that there was the answer to my escape."

"Yes, I know what you mean. In police work that happens often. You stare at something which is right under your nose, and you don't see it because you are looking over your nose. It's not until you blow your nose that you see it."

"Right! That's exactly what I mean."

"Well, Susan, I've got to go. Thank you very much for the tea and now for the bad news."

"Bad news! What bad news?"

"I have arranged for you to come into the CIB office tomorrow, and I am afraid you'll be in for a grilling."

"What! What sort of a grilling?"

"You will have to repeat all you told me up to now, and it will be recorded and transcribed as an official police file."

"What time, and how do I get there? I don't know where it is."

"Don't worry, I'll send a police car to pick you up. Is ten o'clock all right for you?"

"Ten's fine. It's not like I have a diary full of appointments."

Pike left, leaving Susan alone in the house. She immediately went to her old room to find everything exactly as she had left it. Opening her wardrobe, she found her clothes neatly hanging. On her small desk near her bed stood a framed colour photograph of Ashley. She picked it up to look at it more closely, as she had many times before, only this time she looked at it with loathing instead of admiration.

Every other room in the house received a visit, and in her parent's bedroom Susan felt a shiver run through her body. The house felt cold even though the outside temperature was registering 27 degrees and climbing.

***

At the CIB building Susan was ushered into what looked like a common room were a desk and chair was waiting for her. The desktop was partially covered with recording equipment and two microphones.

Pike welcomed her, and introduced her to Anne Goodall, Phil Morrison and Frank Henderson, the detective team working on her case.

As Susan sat down, the door opened and in walked a stout, middle aged policeman in uniform. He walked over to Susan's desk, and, extending his hand said, "I'm Deputy Commissioner James Stalt. Welcome home, Miss Bauford, it's nice to see you looking so well after your ordeal. You don't mind if I sit in do you?"

Pike dragged a chair over to the desk, switched on the recording equipment and recorded the necessary formalities. Date, time, file name and number, names of all present. Then, turning to the participants, he announced, "I will now ask Miss Bauford to record all the events of her abduction in her own words. For those of you who have questions, please write them down or something and ask when she has completed her statement. Miss Bauford, would you like to commence, starting with the events which took place in the wedding car as you set off for the church to get married."

Susan leaned in a bit closer to her microphone and began her statement.

When she was finished, question time started.

"Miss Bauford, when did you first realise you were kidnapped to be a sex slave? … Miss Bauford, when you first built the hang glider, how sure were you that it would fly? … Miss Bauford, how would you describe your general treatment by the Australian Embassy in Vienna? … Miss Bauford, do you feel there will be attempts to harm you by the criminals looking for revenge? … Miss Bauford…"

Question time over, a tea trolley was wheeled in, and Susan was lauded over her bravery during the whole ordeal.

"Detective Pike," Susan called out, "could I see you for a minute before I go?"

"Sure, come on over to my desk and we can talk."

Seating herself, she began, "When talking about Ashley I had an idea."

"Good, let's hear it."

"Supposing you were to ring Ashley and tell him that you had found some new evidence unearthed at my house. Also tell him that he is probably involved in it and ask him to make an appointment to meet you there so you can properly identify it and comment on it. I will be there, but out of sight until I make an appearance to confront him with what I know about my abduction. That should unnerve him, and he may say something that could be used in evidence, how does that sound?"

"It sounds good but for the fact that we don't have any evidence, and he is bound to ask what the evidence is," Pike replied.

"You tell him it's classified and that depending on what Ashley has to say about it will determine if the house should be turned into a crime scene."

"Could work, but still, he will want to know more about the evidence and the reference to him."

"OK, tell him that a note was found wedged in between the cushions of a lounge chair, addressed to him and signed by Akim. It obviously had slipped out of his back pocket and got wedged into the chair."

"Good so far, but then why your house, why not a police station?"

"Because you also found some interesting photographs in my room, but if the house is declared a crime scene, you cannot remove them."

"No, Susan, it does not work that way. The police can take away and impound what they want from a crime scene."

"Yes, you know that, but Ashley doesn't."

"I don't know, Susan. This is hardly regular police procedure."

"Regular police procedure. Police procedure be damned," Susan almost shouted full of indignation. "I was raped daily for months, and you are worried about police procedure? I get nightmares almost every night. My dream of being a wife and a mother is almost at a zero rating. What decent man would take on a woman whose been fucked by a gallery of international men? And you are worried about police procedure. I thought you were paid to protect my arse instead of police procedure."

"Please, keep your voice down. OK, so it's a little irregular but compared to what you were put through, we can put up with a little irregularity. OK, so let's try it. We'll go with your new evidence suggestion. It has its flaws, but our experience is that the guilty will always re-examine the evidence they gave, but their curiosity is aroused by the suggestion that there is new evidence uncovered. Self-preservation and natural curiosity will often throw caution to the wind. Let's just hope it works."

"Thank you, Detective Pike, this means a lot to me."

"No need, I get paid for that. Now, our driver will drive you home and you will hear from me as soon as I have something to tell you."

***

Three days passed without a word from Pike. Susan was on the verge of thinking Pike had given up on the project when around midday the phone rang.

"Susan? Pike here, I'm happy to tell you that your plan worked. I've had a policewoman talk to Ashley, and he's agreed to come to your house on Friday evening at six o'clock."

"A policewoman? Why a policewoman? Why didn't you call him yourself?"

"Because, if I called him, he might smell a rat. He knows me, but if a female calls him, he would think it's just an office girl given the job of tidying up a file before putting it to bed."

"That makes good sense, I suppose. Thank you for letting me know. I was almost thinking that you had given up on the idea."

"No, I hadn't but first I had to sell it to my superintendent. At first, he thought it was too irregular and too iffy, but I reminded him of what you said."

"Really, what did I say?"

"That you were raped regularly for many months and that he has a daughter just a little younger than you, and you asked him what he would do if she were in your shoes."

"And?"

"He asked me how many men did I think I needed and to make sure that all listening devices were thoroughly tested before we put them into use."

"That's wonderful news."

"It's also news that we have a lot of preparatory work to do."

"Like what?"

"We first have to script it like an act in a play, and then everyone involved has to follow that script to the letter."

"Yes. I agree, most definitely."

"Good. Can I have you picked up in the morning and taken to the station? We can get together with everyone involved and work out a plan."

"Fine, but you don't have to have me picked up. I can drive in myself."

"Don't tell me you bought a car already?"

"No, I didn't. I remembered dad's car and looked in the garage, and there it was. I knew where he kept the keys, so I tried to start it and after a bit of groaning it came to life. I drove it round the block, and it was fine. I like driving"

"That's nice, Susan, but just the same, I'd rather have you picked up. You are still under protective custody, and I don't want to take any chances of anything happening to you."

***

For the second time in her life Susan entered the CIB building. As soon as Pike saw her, he beckoned to her and opened the door for her to a vacant interview room.

"Please sit down, Susan. Overnight, we received an interesting fax from Interpol. They have located Akim."

"Really! Where is he?"

"Right now, they are not quite sure, but they are sure that he's either on his way to Australia or in Australia."

"What? That's unbelievable. I would have thought that after what's happened, this would be the last place in the world he would want to visit."

"So did I, but it seems that there is an international hang-gliding race or competition, or something organised by The Stanwell Park Hang Gliding Club. He is a member, and they sent him an invitation which he accepted."

"Well, I'll be … oops, I nearly said buggered."

"Say it anyway. I did."

"I always thought he was stupid but not that stupid." Susan exclaimed, "Are you sure that the information is correct?"

"Yes, we are. We checked out with the club and there is a competition. We have all the details, and Akim has accepted the invitation. Don't forget, he is the only one, according to your statement, who thinks you are dead. That is why I think he is so brazen in coming here."

"So, how soon can you arrest him?"

"As soon as we can find him. These people often travel using false passports. We have no idea what he looks like, but you do, so guess where the arrest will take place?"

"Yeah, the hard questions first."

"You are quite right, but now we must make a plan to capture another lowlife.

Susan smiled and laughed a little.

"Did I say something funny?" Pike asked.

"No, it's just that the irony just struck me. Here I am. A recent graduate with a law degree, and my first real case is me as the first client, and at 'pro bono' rates."

CH 17. RETRIBUTION II

Pike set out to plan the coming interview with Ashley with great caution. He knew that if Ashley felt a heavy police presence, he would be on his guard and clam up. The total absence of police presence could also seem suspicious. Pike decided to have a marked police car parked inside the driveway.

Two constables were in the cellar with the recording equipment, and direction-finding microphones were carefully disguised and placed throughout the house.

On scripting the coming performance, Susan insisted she confront Ashley first and alone.

"Are you out of your mind?" Pike was shocked. "He sees you first and alone, there's no telling what he'll do."

"He'll be in shock, full of disbelief and questions, and I will have a few questions of my own. I won't be alone. You'll be in another room listening."

"I don't like it, Susan, it's too risky"

"Rubbish, what can he do? There are three policemen in the house, so what's Ashley going to do, shoot me?"

"I suppose you're right. The shock of seeing you first up is bound to have an effect. Let's hope the same goes for his tongue."

***

Shortly before 6 pm, Ashley drove past Susan's house and noted the marked police car parked in the driveway. He looked at all the other parked cars in the area, but none contained any occupants. Puzzled, but satisfied that nothing unexpected was going to happen, he went over his thoughts again.

"There can't be any new evidence. There never was any evidence to start with. There was no link between me and Susan's disappearance." He was sure of that. "They probably are trying to mop up." If the policewoman who called him had not mentioned the word 'Akim', he would have told her to call back later and have a good Christmas in the meantime. Now, he had to know if the police knew anything or not.

Ashley drove around the block again, and having encountered no new developments, parked his car.

***

Susan heard the door chimes peal.

"Come in, the door's open," Susan shouted from the living room. She heard the door shut and continued, "Come right in, I'm in the living room."

Ashley proceeded to the living room and then froze in his tracks. Susan was standing by the fireplace dressed in a white silk suit she had purchased for her graduation.

"Good evening, Ashley. You are right on time. That's very considerate of you."

"Can't be … You're dead …" Ashley stammered, growing weak at the knees. "How come … I don't understand … what are you doing here?"

"Ashley! Shame on you. I live here, don't you remember?"

"Yes, I know that, but how did you get here? I mean … you're not supposed to be here … what do you want?

"I thought that was obvious, I want my cut."

"What cut is this? What are you talking about?"

"The proceeds of my abduction. Akim told me you got $200,000 for me. Split three ways, that's $66,666 you owe me, and I have come to collect."

"You can't be serious?"

"But Ashley darling, I am serious. Akim explained it very well.

I disappear for six months and get shagged a bit and then get my cut from you and yeah, plus a little bit of interest."

"Akim's a liar." Ashley was regaining composure. "He said $200,000 did he? Wherever the hell he came up with that figure, I don't know. All I got was fifty grand, and there was no talk of any split."

"What! Fifty grand, is that all I'm worth?"

"No, of course not. Look, you don't understand. I was in financial trouble, and so was dad. His gambling debt to your father alone was over ten grand."

"I see, so to pay for your father's and your sins, you chose me to sell as a sex slave. Well, just get me my money. I believe your wife seems to have plenty of it. Ask her for it, or we might be able to get a few bob for her on the sex slave market. We've got the contacts."

"And what are you gonna do if I don't?" Ashley asked.

"Not a great deal except let the police have a copy of this conversation."

"And just how are you going to … you bitch! You are wearing a wire, aren't you?" Ashley got closer to Susan and grabbed her, "I'll kill you, you bitch. You are presumed dead, so you may as well be dead." Ashley clasped his hands round Susan's throat and started choking her.

On hearing this, Pike dashed out of an adjoining room.

"Let her go," he shouted as he stormed into the living room.

On seeing Pike, Ashley's grip tightened in anger, as he realised he had been set up.

"Let her go," Pike ordered again, as he closed in on the struggling couple. Failing to achieve anything by physical intervention, Pike drew his service pistol. "I will shoot if you don't!"

Instead of obeying, Ashley tried to position Susan in front of the pistol but somehow managed to get hooked round Pike's ankle, causing the three of them to fall to the floor.

A shot rang out, and Ashley sagged limply to the floor, the front of his trousers covered with blood.

Just then, the two constables who'd been recording in the cellar rushed up the stairs and into the living room, their guns drawn.

"It's all over, boys," Pike told them. "Better call for an ambulance. This one is not going to walk for a while. Did you get that all on tape?"

"Loud and clear."

"Good, we got all that, and now we can add another charge to the list."

"Oh yeah?" the constable quizzed.

"Attempted murder of a person in police protection."

***

The ambulance arrived, escorted by a police car. Two paramedics examined Ashley on the spot before lifting him into the ambulance.

"He'll be OK after surgery. No great damage," one of the paramedics told Pike, "but it looks like his days of siring offspring are over."

"What do you mean by that?" Pike asked.

"It looks like you shot his balls off."

"Oh! Maybe it's just as well. Where he's going, he won't have much use for them for a very long time."

"I suppose not, but every cloud has a silver lining."

"What do you mean by that?" Pike asked.

"I am assuming the prison choir is always looking for a good soprano."

***

"That was terrible," Susan later confessed to Pike, "I did not mean for that to happen."

"What?" Pike asked, "that I shot his balls off?"

"Well, yes."

"Would you rather I let him strangle you?"

274

"Of course not. I don't know, it just seems terrible."

"You are right, it is terrible, but don't you think there is a kind of irony in this or a nemesis perhaps?"

"What do you mean by that?"

"Look at it this way. A man who sells his fiancée into sexual slavery is finally rewarded by termination of his sexual activity on a more permanent basis."

***

With the Ashley matter still in progress, Susan thought of picking up her social life from where she left off.

To her surprise she found some of her earlier friends lacking in sincerity. When she recounted her experiences, a few of them were engrossed with the fact that so many men had had relations with her, never mind the circumstances.

Their attitude made Susan feel almost dirty. She felt that the implication was that she had somehow brought it on herself, and despite her protestations, had rather enjoyed the experience. Susan decided there and then to alter the status of some of her 'friends' to acquaintances.

Two young men she had known earlier assumed that since she had been exposed to much sexual activity, she would be an easy 'roll in the hay'. They tried their luck, but instead of sex, they received a tongue lashing which tore their egos to shreds.

***

It was almost 1.30am when Susan's phone rang, waking her. She had not expected a call, nor did she have any idea who would be ringing her. Her first reaction was to let it ring. It did, but soon rang off. Only moments later, it rang again.

"Someone's awfully keen, or maybe it's the wrong number," Susan thought. "What the hell." she picked up the handset. "Hello."

"Could I please speak to Susan Bauford?" a female voice asked, "I am calling from London, England."

Susan was excited to hear her voice. "Patra! Is that you Patra?"

"Yes, it is, Susan. I hope I didn't wake you. What time is it down there?"

"It's just on 1.30 in the morning."

"I'm sorry, I didn't realise, I mean, I didn't mean to disturb you."

"No, no, you're not disturbing me. It's great to hear from you. How are you?"

"I'm seriously thinking of coming to Australia, that is if your offer still stands."

"Of course, it stands. It's open to whenever you want to use it. This is terrific news. When are you thinking of coming?"

"I got my visitor's visa this afternoon, that's why I am ringing."

"Splendid! Do you have a flight booked?"

"No not yet, I'll take care of that tomorrow."

"Good, let me have the details as soon as you can, and I'll pick you up from the airport."

"That's very kind of you, Susan. I also took the liberty of telling your authorities that you are my contact."

"That is what we talked about. I will also prepare a room for you at my house, so feel free to use my address as your own."

"Thank you, Susan, thank you very much. I'll let you know the details as soon as I have them, and I will see you in a couple of days."

"I look forward to that." Susan replied, ending the conversation.

***

"Eddy Pike here, Susan, I've just had a call from the hang gliders' club. Our friend Mr Akim has arrived in Australia and was seen at the club last night registering to enter the gliding competition."

"Good, I take it you have spies stationed at the club?"

"I'd hardly call them spies. I spoke with the management some time ago and asked them to let me know when he registers."

"I just hope that no one at the club lets on to Akim that the police are looking for him, or he'll run like a scalded cat."

"Don't worry. I warned them that this is official police business. That he is a person of interest, but he has to be kept on ice and not informed of our interest until we are ready to talk to him."

"Interesting isn't it, how things start to fall into place?"

"I'm sorry, I don't quite follow that. We knew that Akim was coming, we just didn't know exactly when."

"Yes, I know but now, in the next few days, Patra will be in Sydney, and she knows Akim very well."

"Patra? She's the woman who helped you escape, isn't she? The one who was in charge of bedding arrangements?"

"Yes, that's the one but you are not going to arrest her for anything are you?" Susan asked anxiously.

"Has she broken any laws in Australia?"

"She isn't even here yet."

"In that case, I can't arrest her for anything, can I?"

"Stop kidding around, Eddy, you know what I mean."

"Yes, I do. We have her mentioned in an Interpol report, and they were happy not to lay any charges, so why should we?"

"Fine, I think that when you do arrest Akim, Patra will be more than willing to provide and support any evidence we have and take the 'say' out of hearsay."

"I agree, and I would like to talk to her but off the record, by that I mean not officially."

"Good, I'll let you know when she gets here."

***

Things must have gone very smoothly for Patra as in only two days after her call to Susan, she rang again to inform her that she would be arriving on Thursday morning on a British Airways flight.

Susan had hardly time to get a room ready for Patra, but she managed and informed Pike as well.

"Would you like me to go with you when you pick her up?" Pike asked on the phone.

"You're not going to arrest her, are you?" Susan asked anxiously.

"Of course not. I simply thought that a marked police car picking her up from the airport would ease a lot of the stress and strain. It's all above board."

"How do you mean, above board?"

"She is a person of interest, a witness in a trial about to be convened, and therefore entitled to some police protection."

That evening, Susan drove down to the hang glider club. She was still a member and entitled to its amenities. Taking great care to avoid running into Akim, she processed her entry in the up-and-coming gala hang-gliding competition.

***

As soon as Patra exited from the customs section into the Arrivals Hall, she eagerly searched to see Susan's face as she walked the gauntlet; the aisle of eager faces seeking recognition from arriving passengers.

Susan, standing just in front of Pike, soon spotted Patra, and joined the gallery of waving arms and hands.

"You made it. Patra," Susan exclaimed, as the two embraced in welcome, "it's good to see you."

"You too, and thank you for coming to collect me," Patra responded. She spotted Pike beside Susan, simply looked at him and said, "Oh!"

Quick to pick up on her oversight, Susan went on, "Patra, this is Eddy Pike, remember, the detective I told you about in London? He's the one assigned to my case to find out where I was."

Patra managed a suspicious smile and held out her hand,

"Nice to meet you, Mr Pike. If you had asked me earlier, I could have told you exactly where she was."

"I should have, shouldn't I, but then I didn't know you, did I?

Welcome to Australia."

Pike had again managed to park almost at the door. Patra looked at the marked police car and stopped, looking up at Susan as in disbelief.

"And I thought we were friends, Susan," Patra exclaimed.

"Of course, we are. What's the matter?"

"That's a police car. Am I under arrest?"

"Of course not. Detective Pike uses it so we don't have to walk too far and don't have to pay for parking."

"That's not quite right, Susan, and you know it. Remember, you are still in police protective custody."

"Does that mean she is under arrest?" Patra asked, somewhat confused.

"No this means that we fear for her safety and have to offer her protection."

During the lengthy drive from the airport to Putney, both women sat in the back of the police car chatting. Pike did not mind at all, as it was at his suggestion.

At Susan's house, Pike helped with the luggage. When asked to stay for coffee he declined.

"You have all the unpacking to do, and I am sure Patra could use a couple of hours sleep to take the edge off the jetlag. I would like to speak with Patra, though, sort of officially, unofficial.

Would it be alright if I stopped by tomorrow, say round about 4pm?"

Patra looked at Pike a little wide eyed,

"Are you asking me or are you asking Susan?"

"Either."

"It doesn't matter," Susan interjected. "Tomorrow's fine."

***

As soon as they settled down and Susan poured some coffee, Patra remarked, "Funny name that, Pike. Sounds like a fish or a long sharp pole."

"Well, it suits him. He is long and lean like a pole, and fishing for information is his business."

"What sort of information does he want to fish from me?" Patra asked. "I have already told Interpol what I know, and they didn't think it was much."

"I think he is more interested in Akim than you."

"Akim! What have I to do with Akim?"

"We know that Akim is in Australia now and has registered to compete in a hang-gliding competition. You and I are the only ones who know what he looks like and can deliver prima facie evidence against him in a court of law."

"So that's why he's being so nice!"

"No, I don't think so. He's just a nice guy, at least I have no reason to think otherwise."

"So, why doesn't he arrest him?"

"Because we don't know where he is, but we will do on the day of the competition."

"So, I take it you and Mr Pike would like me to be there?"

"Yes please, you don't mind, do you?"

"Mind! It will be a pleasure. I still remember what he did to you the first night you arrived. It made me sick, but there was nothing I could do. But you don't need me in court for that, you were present yourself."

"Yes, but as the victim. Whereas you are a witness."

"I suppose that makes sense. I would like to see Akim's face when he sees you. He is the one who told everyone you are dead. He was so sure that that contraption you built would not stay in the air for long and had to crash."

"Odd that you should say that. I too would like to see Akim's face when he confronts me alive. That's why I registered to join that hang glider competition."

"I don't understand. How is joining a race going to achieve this?"

"I won't be racing; I will be harassing Akim in his glider."

"Why?"

"I want him to go through the same feelings of shock and horror he forced upon me when he first walked through that door at the spa."

"What do you expect him to do?"

"I don't quite know, but like most Arabs, he is very superstitious. I'm hoping he sees me as a ghost come back to haunt him. I hope he experiences the same horror and torment as I did when he first walked through my door"

**

"You are kidding! No way," Pike exploded when Susan outlined her intention of meeting Akim in the sky. "Have you lost your senses? Do you realise how dangerous your proposal is?

"There is some element of danger, I agree, but so is driving on the streets of Sydney."

"Hardly the same thing, Susan. No, I can't let you do it. When all the competitors are ready to take off, you point out Akim to me and I will arrest him. However, I will concede one thing. Once I have arrested him, I will turn my back for a minute, and you may kick him in the balls for as long as it takes. How does that proposal sound?"

"You don't understand really, do you, Eddy? A mere kick in the balls will cause some physical discomfort. That to me is neither here nor there. I want him to experience mental anguish, like he's never known before. If it drove him to insanity, I would be satisfied."

"That might happen yet but in one of our prisons."

"Don't be naïve, Eddy, no matter what the sentence he wouldn't serve more than six months. His father's an Emir or Sheik or something and loaded. Money talks."

"Be that as it may, we still have to operate within the law, our law."

"So, what in 'our law' is illegal about flying a hang glider?"

"Nothing, but I think you know what I mean."

"I do Eddy, but I think you have very little idea as regards to what I mean."

"Really, Susan, you are asking more of the police department than it's allowed to give."

"I'm not asking it to do anything. I'm the one that's doing things, hoping just for a little bit of cooperation."

"All right, Susan, I've stuck my neck out before. What's one more time. How do you see this happening?"

"Akim is a Muslim and has been brought up under a mind controlling system. He believes in Satan-angels, torture at the grave, human reincarnation and a lot more. I know, I had to listen to him chanting all this rubbish while he was raping me.

When he sees me in the air, he will think of me as a ghost seeking retribution. How he will react? I don't know, but however that is, I'll be ready for him. Remember, he will be in a state of confusion, but I will be in control."

"Sounds all right in theory, but it has little to do with arresting him. More like a vengeance tactic on your part."

"You are quite right. It is vengeance on my part, but don't you think I'm entitled? Besides, by the time he has landed, I hope he will be so rattled that he'll confess to anything."

"There is that possibility," Pike agreed. "Remote but a possibility. OK, let's give it a shot."

"Just one more thing I think would help."

"And that is?"

"It would be good if Akim knew Patra was here. I mean not verbally, but for him to have a fleeting glimpse. No more, just a glimpse with Patra saying, 'Hello, Akim' and then melting into the crowd. That kind of thing."

"I don't get it! What do you hope to achieve by that?"

"It's the beginning of the unnerving process, don't you see? Seeing Patra, he's reminded of the spa and me. Just seeing Patra will bring up his hackles. 'What is she doing here? What is she up to? What's behind this? And so on. Then, seeing me should convince him that Allah is wreaking some punishment on him."

"I see what you mean. First a warning and then a wham! It could just work. I'll run it past Patra tomorrow evening. I'm taking her out for dinner."

"Wow, that was quick. I hope Mrs Pike won't mind."

"Mrs Pike! There is no Mrs Pike unless you count the Police Department."

"There you go, then, and I always thought you were married with kids."

Pike laughed. "And I always thought I wasn't married, and I know definitely, I have no kids."

***

The green plateau on the clifftops at Stanwell Park was a vivid field of activity. Many colourful gliders nestled on the grass receiving their final touches before the start of the race to Newcastle. A fine Sunday morning was promising a good warm start for the participants.

A police car was present, parked near the hang gliders, but it worried no one. As at most public events, police presence was normal. Its occupants were Pike, Susan, Patra and a young constable.

Pike had organised with the officials for Susan to be among the last to take off. The race was handicapped to take into account individual times, as all the gliders could not take off from the clifftops at once. Akim was relegated to take off five competitors ahead of Susan.

It was Patra who first spotted Akim. It wasn't difficult. Akim's glider had white wings with a silhouette of a black palm tree stencilled on each wing.

She got out of the police car on the blind side and walked up to where Akim was testing the controls.

"Hello, Akim. Good luck," was all she said, and kept walking.

Akim looked up to smile at his well-wisher but then his jaw dropped.

"Patra? ... Can't be!"

By this time Patra was already a few metres away. Akim rose to give chase, and saw Patra enter an outdoors, tin-enclosed ladies toilet, erected specially for the occasion. He decided to wait, but he was not aware that the latrine had an entry at each end. By the time he came to realise it, Patra was safely back in the police car.

"Patra, it was Patra," Akim reassured himself. "She even knew my name. What is she doing here? Something is not right. Why would she seek me out and then carry on without another word? Is this some sort of sign from Allah? Na, it was her all right, in the flesh, but why?"

Susan's turn was coming up. Akim had just taken off, and very soon it would be her turn. She pulled the cover off her glider. It had been put there so that Akim would not recognise it, because it was the glider Akim had given her. Its wings were dark blue with a large white palm silhouetted on each wing.

As Susan took off, she first checked her glider, and, spotting the black palm tree wings, she steered her path to follow it, and, if possible, gain some height over it, thus giving her a better control should the situation warrant it.

It took Susan the best part of half an hour to manipulate her glider into the position she desired. She waited patiently for a favourable wind shift, and when it came, she used all her experience to swoop down and across the path of Akim's glider.

"Damn idiot, what does he think he's trying to do," was the thought that flashed through Akim's mind. "That could have got both of us killed. Who is this goat? I'm going to report him." Akim strained to see if he could recognise the offending hang glider from any markings.

"Blue wings with what looks like … yes it is, a white palm on each wing … Wait a minute, that's Susan's glider. I gave it to her when she first started hang-gliding. "Who could be flying that now?"

Happy with her first sortie, Susan now tried to manipulate her glider to fly parallel with Akim's. It took all the skills she had learned to accomplish this, but she managed to get both gliders on a parallel course, wingtips almost touching.

Susan pushed back the visor of her helmet, revealing her face, leant back as far as she could towards Akim, and yelled as loudly as she could, "Akim, you filthy bastard, this is your last flight … as soon as you land you will be arrested and spend most of the rest of your life in jail and get raped every night by a big guy called Bonk."

Akim didn't quite get all of Susan's dialogue. He simply looked at her, open mouthed.

"Susan!! You are dead. What are you? I mean how are you? … I mean are you a Satan angel sent by Allah?"

Susan manipulated her glider to the other side of Akim's, where the prevailing wind made her voice more audible to Akim.

"You're partner in crime is in jail already, waiting for you. You will have fun, raping each other as well as taking on block 'B'."

"Allah, you have sent me a Satan angel! Why? I have done nothing wrong. First you send Patra, then you send the palm glider and now a Satan angel. Why?"

Susan watched Akim's pathetic behaviour and decided it was enough. She pulled back to disengage the two gliders. To her surprise, Akim's glider rose and then fell. She could see him slumped over the control bar and assumed he still was having his rant with Allah. However, either Allah wasn't listening or maybe he was listening. Akim's glider continued its downward trend before going into a spin and crashing into the side of a mountain.

Instead of being happy and satisfied, Susan was anything else but that. She had long desired punishment for Akim, but now that it was accomplished, she felt no satisfaction.

Nothing could justify the rape she and others had to endure, but death is not a punishment. It is something all of us face; some early, some late. There has not been so much as one escape.

Susan escaped one form of bondage, but perhaps there is another one waiting in the wings.

***

"Hello, Susan, this is Victor calling. Remember me? I'm the embassy chap."

"Victor, how nice to hear from you. What's been happening?"

"Happening is that I have been transferred back to our Sydney office again before my next posting."

"Congratulations are in order, I suppose."

"Not really, commiserations perhaps, but that aside, I would really be pleased if you'd agree to have dinner with me, and we could chat about old times or maybe invent some new times."

"That would be lovely, Victor. When did you have in mind?"

***

Perhaps there is one waiting in the wings. Perhaps not.

Who knows?

About The Author

Following a lifetime of adventure, travel and intrigue, Andrew Kepitis-Andrews finally settled on the north coast of New South Wales, Australia, and opened a gourmet smokehouse.

Always possessing the urge to write but lacking the time that serious writing demands, he retired from commercial food smoking at the age of seventy-four, and had his first book published the same year, 2014.

Andrew says his writing has two simple, sincere and earnest goals: your pleasure in the reading of it and his pleasure in the writing of it.